When We Remembered

When We Remembered

BOOK ONE OF
THE WHITE **TRILOGY**

Jo Anne Myers

Sunstone Books, LLC

Copyright © 2016 Jo Anne Myers
All rights reserved.

ISBN: 0998093904
ISBN 13: 9780998093901

> Dearest Kathy,
> You are the most precious soul who I will never *forget*
> Love,
> Jo Anne

Dedicated to Teachers:

My parents, givers of life and love.
My brother, saver of life and sanity.
And my son, who made life worth living.
I won't forget.

Someone asked, "How much of this story is true?"
I said, "How do we know what is true of any of our stories?"

I do know this:
That which seemed impossible, happened.
That which was likely, never did.

Here's to re-membering!

—Jo Anne Myers

Prologue—The White

ANNA HAD BEEN TO THIS dream before, although she wouldn't remember it upon awakening. Dreams are wispy things, and this one never solidified enough to make it to daylight.

Morning always brought the shadow of feelings left behind by the dream, the same feelings elicited by a brisk walk on an autumn day. Crisp air and brilliant leaves held hope in one hand and loss in the other. The barrenness of winter was a minute away. Throughout a lifetime of dreaming the dream, Anna would awaken with anticipation and despair, never understanding the cause.

But at this moment she was in the dream, and all she could perceive was milky-pale emptiness. In the place she knew only as The White.

The deep of The White pulsed with underlying movement and patches of brighter and darker light. No boundaries, unending space. A doorway to nothing and everything, vibrating at a very high frequency.

She was not Anna in the dream, but a speck of consciousness. And not alone; she sensed the consciousness of others. Like most dreams, it wasn't odd—this bodyless state. Comforting, actually.

When she heard the voice, she recognized it.

"It's time to return to Time." The whispered voice was more like the breath of a lover than a sound. The White sparkled momentarily with…laughter?

The energy settled back, the sudden spikes calming, pausing…

"What's left to learn? What are we doing, or not doing, that sends us back to The White over and over?"

Whispers. Suggestions. Energy danced and then stilled.

"Someone *has* to remember our mission once we leave here and return to Earth. The one who remembers must find and tell the others. Earth is the only place where we continue to learn, but we keep starting over each lifetime. We have to break that cycle. We have to remember while we are *there*."

Sparkles of discussion, then silence.

The twelve beings evaluated themselves in The White, where there are no lies, no stories, and no egos to preserve. Everyone agreed that there were two who had the greatest chance of success. They were chosen to carry out the task of remembering and then to find the others and convince them.

The intention of the twelve created a swell of energy not unlike the rolling waves of the earth's oceans. Bright intensity, then the stillness of The White.

Forgetting had already begun as Anna's sleep-heavy eyes drifted open, soft-gazing at her husband in the darkness.

She wanted to touch him but felt incapable of motion. His gentle snore lulled her back to sleep.

A narrow beam slanted through partially closed curtains, trailing a silver finger of light across Anna and her sleeping husband. In the twilight space between consciousness and not, something glided along the moon's luminous thread.

Symbols.

There was no recognition of the shapes, although she fleetingly captured the meaning. It came from the dream, drawn with intent and sent with urgency by caring hands from The White.

"How many times will you dream the dream before you remember?"

The Earth School: Attempt #999
This Lifetime

CHAPTER 1

∼

THE SAME SATURDAY SHE WAS scheduled to attend a workshop called Death and Dying, the Cosmic Humorist arranged for Anna to be at the bedside of her dying mother. She always was more of an experiential learner. While a roomful of people in Saint Louis listened to the two-hour class about death, Anna was in her Pennsylvania hometown for a few days of on-the-job training.

A month short of her ninetieth birthday, Anna's mother, Margaret, was riding on fumes. Prayers for healing had shifted to prayers for comfort.

Anna sat by the bedside, petting her mother's hair and staring absently out the window. Stark branches of the tangled hedge revealed a bright-crimson cardinal, head turning this way and that. Her eyes softened at the spot of color and life that filled the space. It was late October and the sky was gray, the kind of bone-chilling gray that made Anna glad she had left this town a long time ago.

She had awakened at home in Saint Louis this morning, feeling out of sorts. The leftover feelings from a dream, but without memory of the dream. By midmorning her husband, Dan, had dropped her off at the airport. Then a tortuous two-hour flight, a one-hour drive in a rental car, and here she was in her mom's nursing home in York, obeying her intuition. Although the doctor said she was holding her own, something told Anna that her mom was nearing the end. She'd had enough regrets in life. She wasn't betting against her intuition this time.

Early Monday morning, Anna pulled into the parking spot closest to the entrance of the nursing home. She sat for a few minutes and took a deep breath, trying to shake the sense that she had forgotten something and to steady her nerves.

The start of day three. Waiting, dreading, hoping.

The need for breakfast had warred with a sense of urgency to see her mom. Urgency had won. She opened the front door and walked into the foyer. The floors gleamed, and her sneakers squeaked as she made her way down the hall. If her mother could no longer live in her own home, Anna was glad she was here. The place was clean, the care reasonable, and the nurses and caregivers understood that kindness in an institution was the greatest kindness of all.

Three years ago, when her mother had been admitted, she was fairly mobile and had a quick sense of humor. But time and a series of little strokes had taken their toll.

"And now we're at where we're at. And where we're at is close to the end," Anna murmured as she neared the nursing station.

She didn't know if she could handle the end, or even if her mom was ready. Fortified by a deep breath, she walked into the room, wondering what she would find this morning. Margaret was asleep in bed, dressed in a hospital gown that had ridden up to her hips. The blankets were piled at her feet, and a slight tremor coursed throughout her body.

Anna quickly moved to the bedside, pulled the covers up to her mother's chin, and tucked them around her.

"Mom," she whispered, "how are you feeling today?"

There wasn't any point in shouting. She stood beside the bed, quietly stroking her mother's hair and looking at the aged skin on the frail arms. Paper-thin and torn in some areas, a clear liquid gently seeped through a few of the larger gaps.

Margaret's eyes fluttered open, two brown spots on her wrinkled face. Her mouth tried to form words. No sound emerged, but the sudden light in her eyes reflected happy recognition.

⁓

Back in Saint Louis that same morning, Anna's husband, Dan, sat in his forest-green Subaru staring at the three-story stucco home of his newest client. They could have pushed the paint job back another year or two, but plenty of money and a predisposition for prevention had them calling for the exterior update now. Dan thought it was a waste of their money, but he wasn't one to turn down a check. This had been a mild autumn, and he was fitting as much exterior work into his schedule as possible.

In a silent "cheers!" to the client, he washed away his morning breath with a healthy gulp of vodka. Warmth burned his belly. He took a deep breath as he calculated the minimum number of days Anna would be gone. *Three. No way she'd stay less than three days.* He had dropped her off at the airport a couple of days ago. *Today's Monday. I've got at least until tomorrow.*

But now it was time to get an early start on this house. *One last sip.* He uncapped the bottle again. After taking a long swallow, he carefully replaced the lid, hid it under the seat, and gathered his supplies.

Years of practice had him strolling up the flagstone steps evenly and with confidence. Clients loved him. He was neat, clean, on time, and a careful painter. He walked a fine line between enjoying the warmth of the alcohol and tumbling headfirst into the bottle. Once the line was crossed, there was no easy climb out. He knew it, and he knew how it hurt Anna.

His step faltered a minute, but then he pressed the doorbell of his client's beautiful home and smiled. Show time.

⁓

In an abandoned industrial section of Saint Louis, a stranger to Anna and Dan sat in his Lexus, watching. Eli Sorenson's eyes were drawn to the women, children, and occasional man who formed a loose line that reached halfway down the block. The door of a dilapidated warehouse, the entrance to the food pantry, was their focal point.

If there was a common denominator in this crowd, it might be the look of weariness, even in the eyes of the children. The only discernible emotion was the occasional body language of quick anger and boundary setting that flared if someone tried to cut in line.

Everything here is worn out. The clothing, the people, the place. Eli sat listening to the click of the car's engine cooling and then heard his own deep sigh of discouragement. *Not having enough wears a person out. Not enough stability to even get a toehold on life or food to feel nourished. Not enough "clean." Not enough hope or levity or beauty.*

Their long list of "not enough" hurt him fundamentally. By nature, he was a fix-it guy, and he felt as if this could be fixed if everyone decided it mattered enough to fix. He understood why his wife came every Monday to this decrepit warehouse to distribute food to the souls who stood in line. And felt a wash of shame to acknowledge he couldn't face this kind of problem every week. Rachel was good at contributing her part to the solution. Better a bandage than a bleed-out. He understood where she was coming from, but he was wired differently. If he couldn't fix it, he'd rather not see it. Send money—absolutely. Come here to pitch in? He didn't like thinking about it, but he couldn't do it. His purpose here today was less noble.

Eli was waiting for Rachel to show up at her volunteer work. He realized it was crazy, following his own wife. The reason wasn't the standard one of paranoia or jealousy, but a scientific experiment of sorts. After twenty-five years of marriage, it had dawned on him that he didn't know his wife anymore. Different interests, different paths. As odd as it seemed to Eli himself, he wanted to see his wife the way someone else might see her. Who was she at the food pantry? Chatty and friendly with the customers? Quiet and retiring the way she was at home? Did she recognize the same people each week and acknowledge them? Know their names?

And more than anything else, he wondered why he didn't feel he could ask her.

He had a researcher's mind, so he turned to what he understood: data collection. He began paying more attention to Rachel and her interactions with the world. He noticed whom she was drawn to at the occasional party they attended. The ease with which she chatted with her best friend Ellen on the phone or the quiet conversations she had with their two grown children at the kitchen table. The excursion today was an impulse that had hit him when Rachel was showering to come here. Yeah, maybe he was acting irrational, okay—kind of creepy—but it didn't bother him enough to abandon the plan. *Dammit, I want to know who she is.*

Rachel's parking spot was a block down the street, and Eli caught sight of her walking quickly to the door of the warehouse. She looked younger than her fifty years in a pair of nice jeans, a yellow sweater, and bright-white sneakers. As her path took her past the women and men who waited at the locked door, he heard her calling hello to several people by name. Likewise, they seemed to know her. And if he wasn't misreading the situation, there was genuine fondness in many of their voices. The crowd stirred and came to life. Small groups of people began to chat with one another, and the escalating hum of their voices was punctuated with laughter.

He watched her unlock the door, step back, and hold it open for the duration of the line. Rachel nodded and smiled, joining in their laughter. She took a quick look around to gather up stragglers, stepped inside, and then pulled the door shut behind her.

Eli sat quietly thinking for another moment before he started the car. He was glad he had come here. She was a beacon of light heading toward the door, and he liked seeing the casual camaraderie between Rachel and the folks who waited. Her presence seemed to energize the others, and the weariness had disappeared. True, she had the keys to the food, but it was more. There had been an exchange of affection.

He put the car in gear, checked the traffic, and prepared to merge with the other vehicles heading out of the city. The groan of the warehouse door and a flash of yellow caught his attention, and he paused.

Rachel had stepped back outside and was peering over her shoulder as she held the door open for someone behind her. A tall, nicely dressed man who looked to be in his fifties stepped outside.

Definitely not here to pick up food, Eli noted, surprised at the sharp turn his thoughts had taken. His foot pressed the brake to the floor.

After one last look over his shoulder, the man quietly pulled the door closed behind them. As Eli watched his wife and the man, he couldn't help but notice what an attractive couple they made. Both blond, and the glint of sunlight cast an ethereal glow around them.

What the...

Eli watched as Rachel spoke intently with the guy. The asshole (as Eli had already dubbed him) matched her intensity. They wouldn't have seen him if he were standing next to them, so absorbed were they in the conversation and each other.

He forced himself to stay in the car when he saw Rachel choking up with tears. Throughout their brief talk, the man had gently held Rachel's arm. Now, as she struggled to keep from breaking down, he folded her close in an embrace of comfort.

Eli felt nearly incapacitated by the sucker punch to his gut, but his brain continued to process like an uninvolved observer. *Life changes in a nanosecond. This morning I watched my wife dress for her volunteer work at the food pantry. My life felt like a movie. We go through the motions without passion or joy. I just wanted to feel something again. Dear God, I didn't want to feel empty anymore. I wanted to know who she was. Stare into each other's eyes like living beings instead of cardboard characters. Feel love with her. I thought...I thought I didn't love her anymore.*

The roar in his head drowned rational thought. A tsunami of pain and fear kept Eli in the car while every cell of his being longed to smash the picture in his mind. A handsome blond man holding his wife in the protected bubble of the early day's light, while he watched, insulated in his car. Too far away to own it and too close to escape it. All he could do was drive home and see what would happen.

He knew he wouldn't tell her.

As he carefully followed the speed limit back to the suburbs, Eli's mantra from childhood echoed in his mind. *Put it back in the box. Put it back in the box. Put it back in the box.* Three times was the charm. *Now close the lid.* It was the only way he had known how to survive.

CHAPTER 2

STEPPING FROM THE WARMTH OF the restaurant into the bleak October day, Anna headed to the rental car. It was day four of her vigil, and she decided to take an hour break. As she drove to a store she had heard about from a childhood friend, Anna absorbed the sights of her hometown.

Passing shops and row houses she hadn't thought about for years, Anna remembered riding with her dad in his big Chevy Impala while he ran errands. York was a factory town, and her dad had worked in a lot of them. They only had one car; her mother didn't drive. Her dad did the grocery shopping and drove the family downtown on Saturdays when he wasn't working. She remembered sitting beside her father in that huge car. No seatbelts in those days. Occasionally, her dad had to slam on the brakes, and when he did, his arm would shoot out to stop her from flying through the windshield. She could count on his strong arm to protect her; he never failed in that.

Anna's father had been a humble man, always looking for ways he could be of help. His best friend was another World War II veteran who had been bedridden since after the war. Tom had served in the Pacific and contracted an illness that had paralyzed him. Anna never knew what the illness was, but every week her dad helped Tom with chores, then sat and chatted with him throughout the evening. As she drove through the streets of York, which had become more commercialized over the years, she thought of Tom. She couldn't recall when he had passed away. It felt important now to remember. Was it before or after she left for college? She must not have gone to the funeral, and she wondered why not.

Frustration flared. She was irritated with the inconsistency of her recollection of the past. Some memories were hazy; others were in sharp relief. The pungency of her father's homegrown tomatoes, thick with the smell of sunshine on their rich, red skins, was clear in her mind. To her father's chagrin, Anna never ate the tomatoes. She was a picky eater as a child. But she loved the warm smell of earth and light on those tomatoes, her father's pride and joy. That memory was potent.

Anticipation replaced frustration as she brought her thoughts to the present, searching for the store and a nearby parking space. Although she no longer attended church, Anna had had a deep interest in spiritual and metaphysical issues since she was a child. The store that she sought now catered to those interests.

A metaphysical store in York, Pennsylvania. Who would've believed it? A bell announced her arrival as she stepped through the door. A woman's voice from the back of the store caught her attention. "I'll be there in a minute!"

"Take your time."

She took a deep breath of the faint fragrance of incense and smiled with pleasure at the tasteful arrangement of crystals, drums, books, and other spiritual objects. A large chunk of amethyst caught her eye, its watercolor of indigo light shimmering across the counter.

The sales clerk, a tall woman in her early forties, approached Anna with a smile. To Anna, weary from watching and waiting at her mother's bedside, the lady glowed like a lantern at the end of a long, dark road. The woman's balance and centeredness was appealing.

"Hi, I'm Della. How can I help you?"

Anna smiled. "I think I just need to be here, soaking up all this good energy."

Without really knowing why, except that this woman felt so solid, Anna continued. "I'm here in town because my mom is very sick, and I'm here at your shop because I needed a break."

"Well, in that case, you might enjoy a massage. That's my other job," Della replied, signaling to a young clerk to take care of the store.

Fifteen minutes later, Anna found herself relaxing on a heated massage table. She sighed. The first touch was the best moment, and she knew that an hour of pure heaven was about to unfold.

The magic of Della's fingers eventually took Anna to a semi dream state. She was no longer specifically aware of the Native American flute music in the background, but she felt as if she were in the southwestern desert. Yellow, ochre, sienna, and other colors of the desert entered her body in a flow of energy. She stood on a plateau, eyes softly gazing into the far horizon. Her mother, strong and youthful, was beside her. They stood shoulder to shoulder peering into the future.

"Most of me is ready to go, but a little part wants to hang on. It's hard to leave the story of your own life and wonder what's next," her mother's voice rumbled, no longer the faint, lost sound that Anna had heard at the nursing home.

Anna nodded, at peace with that, her mind momentarily caught up in the story of her own life.

The air crackled with energy and electricity, raising the tiny hairs on Anna's arms.

"I'm not afraid, honey. Kind of eager. There will be a shift, and I'll be on a different frequency. Far away and right beside you. Reminding you to remember."

"Remember you, Mom? My God, you know I'll never forget…"

"I know that, honey." She paused. "Remember that life is a dream, but some dreams are more real than life. Remember the dream that matters."

"What do you mean?" Anna turned to stare, but her mother was gone.

Startled, Anna shifted abruptly out of the meditative state and back to the treatment room, her mind filled with questions. Della had finished the massage and was now using her hand to draw symbols in the air over Anna's body.

"What are you doing?" Anna asked, confused and still partially in the high desert.

"I'm giving you Reiki, a type of energy healing. I do the energy work along with the massage sometimes. It felt like you needed it, and you soaked it right up."

"Feels good," Anna murmured, not really understanding but without a strong need to know. Warmth enveloped her body.

"All done." Della smiled. "Rest for a few minutes. When you're ready, meet me up front in the store. Take your time."

A few minutes later, Anna was up, dressed, and ready to leave. Standing by the checkout counter, she picked up the large rock with spiked amethyst crystals and watched a spray of glowing, deep-purple reflections bounce across the counter.

"I'd like this, too," Anna told Della as a thought came to her.

"Della, do you ever go to nursing homes to do your Reiki? My mom can't have a regular massage; her skin is too fragile. But I think she would like the Reiki."

Della said she did and she would, and they made arrangements for her to come to the nursing home later that night. With a final look around, a sigh of contentment, and a sense of leaning into the will of the divine, Anna left the shop.

She settled into the silver rental car and thought about her husband, then pulled her phone from her purse and dialed. Four rings, no answer. No answer yesterday, either. The hollow anxiety about Dan's drinking, so familiar but still shocking, pulled her down like a stone.

Trying for a breezy tone, Anna chirped, "Hi, Dan. Can you give me a call as soon as you get this? I wanted to check in. Hope everything's okay on your end. I'm mainly hanging out with Mom, but I'll talk to you about that when you call. Love you, and talk to you later." She searched for the button. End call. Then she closed her eyes as the relaxation of the massage disappeared.

She wouldn't see this place again. Which was why Anna now sat in front of her childhood home, slouched in the rental car and trying to be as inconspicuous as possible. She gazed at the walkway that led to the tiny two-bedroom aluminum-sided house and remembered.

Anna and her mom sitting at the kitchen table. Her mom telling her stories, her dad napping in his recliner in the living room.

"When your dad was growing up, his brother was the bad kid. Your uncle drank too much. He even stole from his mother.

He was drunk and drowned in the creek when he was only thirty. Your dad had to be the good boy, to balance out his brother. That's why he's always helping people."

"It isn't because he cares about them?" eight-year-old Anna asked, brow furrowed.

"Of course he cares, but that's the reason. Guilt for having a brother who broke his mother's heart. He had to be the good boy."

When her dad died, strangers streamed to the house in his memory and told his wife and daughter how he had helped them. Years of kindness to others when they were down on their luck. He had known what they needed at that moment, and now they were showing up at the door within days of his death with food and money for his survivors.

On this damp, gray day, the warmth from the heater left the car quickly as Anna sat trying to reconcile the past. Memories, interpretations, and the realities of behavior seemed at odds with one another. *Are the stories we tell about others just a projection of our own personality? Who were these people—my mom and dad—beyond the role of my parents?*

Other memories.

"Here's my definition of hell," her mother would say. "Standing on a wrinkled kitchen rug and doing the dishes with two flies buzzing around my head."

Anna smiled. *That one's probably true.*

Then the image of her mom gazing out the kitchen window, watching the sun rise and quoting Bible verses from memory.

"I will lift up mine eyes unto the hills, from whence cometh my help. My help cometh from the Lord, who made heaven and earth."

Anna particularly liked when her mother got to the dramatic part, which she would quote with gusto. "The sun shall not smite thee by day, nor the moon by night...The Lord shall preserve thy going out and thy coming in from this time forth, and even for evermore."

She had an abrupt reentry to the present moment when the door of her old home swung open with a snap. A young woman peered out in silent warning to the car parked in front of her house.

Turning the key in the ignition, Anna gave a quick "no worries; I'm friendly" wave as she pulled away and headed toward a childhood bright spot.

I knew my dad through the eyes of my mom, and my mom through the stories of her life. But I'm beginning to suspect that I didn't know a damn thing about either of these people who gave me life. My mom was the spinner of the tales and the interpreter of their meaning. How accurate were they? How real?

The impending loss of her mom hit her hard at that moment. Rubbing her eyes with one hand and holding the steering wheel with the other, Anna carefully wound her way along the curvy, dusty road.

She came to a stop at the limestone quarry that had been actively worked when she was a kid. Periodic and regular blasting in the quarry had shaken a lot of neighboring houses during Anna's preschool years. Tiny man-made earthquakes that rattled windows and vases. Controlled chaos, logical, and therefore no cause for alarm.

The things we allow ourselves to get used to, Anna mused.

She parked the rental car near a barbed-wire fence that surrounded the abandoned quarry and slowly got out as she stared through the fence. Total silence—not a birdsong nor the sound of a car beyond the tapping of her engine as it cooled. She pushed the door closed, expecting a sharp slam instead of the muffled thud she heard. The thick silence swallowed everything.

Anna decided not to seek a tiny forbidden entrance that had most assuredly been cut into the fence by kids. Back in her quarry-climbing days, she had never been bold enough to cut the fence, but someone always was. Forty years ago, she had crept through those secret openings many times.

The walls of the quarry were jagged, and the height varied from 150 feet at the south wall to 75 feet closer to where she stood. It was one very big hole, blasted into the side of a hill. She had logged hundreds of hours climbing these chiseled walls. *Dangerous.* Anna wondered if her mom had known. She couldn't imagine that Margaret, world-class worrier, would have let her eight-year-old tomboy play on these cliffs. *Another unsolved mystery.*

It was here that Anna had met her angel for the first time. Bellies pressed to the wall and hands grasping tightly, she and her friend Kevin had shimmied along a south-side ledge. Anna led. Kevin was a year younger, so Anna felt responsible to check things out first. Abruptly the ledge petered out, leaving them with no place to go except back up to safety.

Even today as Anna stood looking at the wall, her throat tightened as she calculated how high she and her friend had been. Maybe a hundred feet or more. *This, I remember.*

Eight-year-old Anna told Kevin to start back to safety. She waited for him to carefully reorient his body for the return trip and then did what she knew she should never do. She glanced over her shoulder, looking down. At that moment she felt herself shift ever so slightly off balance. The slightest beginning of a backward fall with no way to correct it and nothing to hold onto.

Before a sound could tear from her frozen lips, she felt a firm open palm between her shoulder blades, pressing her tiny body tight against the wall. Not Kevin; he was intently working his way to safety. No one was there, only the air and open space of the massive quarry. Even then, Anna had known in her heart and throughout her whole being that she had been saved.

Now she stood, faced pressed against the fence, and remembered that it had been another twenty years before the angel touched her again. *There's no logical reason that I'm alive.* Her eyes darted from the ledge to the bottom of the quarry again and again. *My mom is dying.* Her heart broke inside of her. *And I've done nothing of any importance yet. I had to be saved for a reason. Do I need to know who I am in order to know why I'm here? Or do we just serve and never know what we serve?* The eight-year-old had never made a promise to make her life matter, but it was time to begin.

⁓

Back at the nursing home, Anna sat quietly holding her mom's hand. Despite the wrinkles, torn skin, and faint sour smell, her mom looked young. The skin on her back was soft and delicately tinged pink. Anna smiled at the beautiful juxtaposition of the very elderly and very youthful look of her mother.

She stared into those brown eyes full of trusting innocence. Sadly, that was from the strokes. The worrier in her had been erased by time and age. The restful part of the current Margaret was not who Anna had grown up with. No, that Margaret worried about everything, but especially about Anna's safety. *Was she home for the night? Was she safe?* That was the woman Anna knew, but that woman was gone as the tiny vessels in her brain broke down like the skin on her arms.

"One blessing of age." Anna sighed.

⁓

Later that evening, Della hesitantly entered Margaret's room. Anna smiled with relief as she took her coat and put it over the lone chair. Her mom lay quietly resting. Anna slipped out of the room to ask the staff for privacy for her mom for an hour. They readily agreed. *Thank God.* She had no idea how she would explain what her visitor was going to do.

In the room, Della stood beside the bed and began to draw more of the strange symbols in the air over Anna's sleeping mother.

Is it impolite to watch? Anna wondered, but she didn't want to interrupt to ask. So she gazed down at her mom. She wanted to let her know that she shouldn't hold on for Anna's sake. She couldn't bring herself to say the words out loud, so, from her heart, she urged the words into her mother's heart.

Go, Mom, if you're ready. You are a storyteller, a writer, and the funniest person I know. Thank you for giving me life and love and true acceptance. You weren't perfect, but you used every drop of who you are to learn and grow. All beings enter the earth through the doorway of their mother. I hate that I never gave that chance to someone, but you gave that gift to me. I don't have a clue how to say thank you. And I don't know what will happen next, Mom, but thanks to you, I know this: "The Lord shall preserve thy going out and thy coming in from this time forth, and even for evermore." Wherever you go, you don't travel alone. You go wrapped in my love.

And as she finished silently speaking the gift of release, tears coursed down her mother's face.

She hears me, Anna realized in wonder.

And she watched as her own falling tears made big, wet circles on her mother's institutional-blue hospital gown.

After twenty minutes or so, Della smiled that "lit from within" smile that Anna had seen earlier to signal that the Reiki session was complete. Anna tucked the blanket around her mother and walked out with her new friend.

"This was a beautiful night, Anna. You have a great gift of healing," Della told her as they stepped from the glow of the lobby into the sharp night.

"What do you mean? You did the comfort and healing work."

Della smiled. "Someday you'll know what I mean."

Whether that was true or not, Anna felt warmed by her words and understood by Della in a way that even she couldn't comprehend. All she knew was that one moment she had felt empty, and in the next, she was filled. She had felt the same way earlier when she stood on the desert plateau with her mom. Centered and filled. And dreading going back home to Saint Louis, where she felt so empty.

CHAPTER 3

THREE WEEKS LATER, BACK IN Saint Louis, a bell jingled sharp and sweet as Anna opened the shop door. She stepped hesitantly across the threshold, feeling fragile. She had never been to this metaphysical bookstore, but it still filled her with memories. She'd been scheduled to attend class here the day her gut had screamed to get home and be with her mom. Good thing she had, and now she was back for another class and feeling superstitious. Hopefully, nothing else would go wrong.

She centered herself with a deep breath, and the first thing she noticed was the incredible smell of incense. Not the artificial kind, but something rich and deep. It smelled...well, spiritual, and that incredible scent permeated every book, every crystal, and every sacred object in the store.

Unease gave way to a sense of excitement about the class she was here to attend. Since she hadn't made the class on death and dying, she'd signed up for the Tree of Life in memory of her mom.

She looked around at the crowd gathering for the class. Everyone seemed so normal. She had expected that somehow they would look different, dressed funny or something. But no, they looked like everyone else, and, on top of that, they looked happy.

Based on that alone, people here are a hell of a lot more abnormal than I thought at first glance. She giggled to herself. She had been talking to herself a lot lately. And to her mom. Who sometimes answered.

Since her mom's death two weeks ago, a lot of things made no sense. Anna felt more alive than she had in a long time, but it was as if she were in a strange world. Her senses were heightened, yet she felt like an observer of the life around her, not a part of it. While she normally saw life in kind of a blur, now every leaf, every bird, and every rock stood out vividly. Her dreams were filled with hidden symbols that seemed familiar but which she was unable to interpret. That strange mix of fullness and emptiness.

A world full of significance yet empty of meaning had been the catalyst that had sent her to this store. This metaphysical—whatever that really meant—bookstore. Which smelled really good.

"Hello, honey. Are you here for the class?" A lovely woman with long white hair, jeans, and a pink T-shirt surveyed Anna.

Normally Anna hated to be called honey by strangers, but somehow, this timeless woman could get away with it. Anna saw that right off and wondered what this woman saw about her.

"Yes, the Tree of Life class. Am I at the right place?" she asked hesitantly, knowing full well that she was and wondering why she had brought it up.

"You are exactly at the right place, and at the right time. I'm Hannah, and this is Awakenings. Welcome."

And with that, Hannah rang a small bell and called her students into a back room.

"Okay, everyone, let's get started. We have a lot to learn today."

She spoke with relish, as if learning were the most important thing in the world. Suddenly Anna felt excited to get started.

She settled into one of the twelve squeaky folding chairs that formed a semicircle around Hannah, who in turn stood beside a huge painting. The painting held a game board made up of ten circles or spheres that were connected by pathways. The spheres and paths seemed to be identified by Hebrew letters or words.

Must be the Tree of Life, but it doesn't really look like a tree, Anna thought, and then she looked around at her classmates. Three men and the rest were women. Most looked to be in their thirties or forties. Anna had turned fifty a few months ago. She remembered at the time that her birthday hadn't bothered her nearly as much as turning forty had.

She felt surprisingly comfortable with this group of strangers.

It was clear that many of the people knew one another. The casual, relaxed chatting and cheerful camaraderie of people who gather frequently created the white noise of the room. The atmosphere buzzed with quiet anticipation, and their excitement was catching. Anna felt it too.

Hannah started the class by talking about ancient Jewish mysticism called the Kabbalah and how the word derived from Hebrew and meant "to receive." As in, "to receive the information."

"The seated position is the position of receiving, of learning." Anna listened intently to Hannah.

As she heard those words, something shifted inside her. While she was still aware of her surroundings and the class, time froze. Anna felt her heart beat slow and deepen, seeming to synchronize with a larger beating heart.

Bold words, *You are about to receive,* filled her mind. She didn't hear them aloud or imagine hearing them. It was as if the words were inserted into her mind. It didn't frighten her. Every emotion and thought was on hold.

As she was suddenly released from this strangely empty state of mind, yet filled with the knowingness that something very potent was about to occur, a ten-year-old memory surfaced from the early days of her marriage to Dan.

In this memory, Anna was lying on the couch feeling numb from learning that Dan, an alcoholic in recovery, had been drinking. Anna saying words that sounded as if they were coming from a long way off. "Well, I know one thing. I'm never getting married again!"

Dan, standing above her, looking down, his mouth forming words that came out like a cartoon character's word bubble. "What do you mean, *again?*"

The bubble floating hollowly upward to the ceiling, hitting and popping, a silent broken balloon. And then the words became dust and fell upon Anna and Dan.

Frozen, the world tilted on its axis like a malfunctioning carnival ride until it jerked back onto its tracks. Numbness gone, Anna keened. Dan crumpled to his knees in slow motion, filled with shame for the rut of addition he felt powerless to leave. The memory had ended.

The out-of-body feeling was similar. But the deep knowingness was completely different.

It might have been a second, or a minute. Anna had no way of noting how much time had passed while time stood still for her. As she mentally rejoined the class, she felt a wave of interest coming from someone in the classroom, and it surrounded her. She looked around and met the warm brown eyes of one of the men.

His hair was dark but streaked with silver. Although he was tall and slender like her husband, there was a solidness about him that Dan lacked. She felt his presence and most assuredly his interest. It was palpable, as if he had tossed her a ball and now it was her turn.

His eyes looked inward, his face expressionless. When he realized that she was looking back at him, his face changed into a welcoming smile, and he gave her the slightest nod.

Irrationally she wondered if he had seen the memory with Dan. Instead of feeling embarrassed, she experienced something she had rarely felt in her life. She felt understood.

CHAPTER 4

NANCY FROWNED AND SIGHED. SHE and Anna were at their Saturday morning meet-up spot, eating scrambled eggs and hash browns and discussing world affairs. Their personal world affairs.

"I think it was awful that Dan didn't go with you to the funeral," Nancy said, studying Anna. Short and compact, Anna had her mother's brown eyes, but her hair had begun turning gray early. A legacy from her dad. Silver strands wove through the light brown, and Anna hadn't gotten around to figuring out whether to dye it or not. A long overdue decision, but worrying about how she looked wasn't part of Anna's nature.

Nancy, on the other hand, was tall, curvy and exuberant. She was a natural redhead, always knew what she wanted, and went after it without a second thought. Anna decided that she might want to come back as Nancy in her next life and smiled at the thought.

"Why is that funny?" Nancy asked, exasperated. "He's a jerk, not to speak too harshly of your husband..." Her voice trailed off as she realized she might have gone too far.

"Dan thinks funerals are depressing, and he was busy. I don't even care, but what I do wonder is why he's acting so irritable lately. He's hostile. I told him what we were having for dinner.

He griped about the food and stalked out of the house. Then he came home so late I was already in bed."

Nancy raised an eyebrow. Anna wished she could do that without looking strange. With Nancy it meant, "Oh really?" and "Tell me more" in one elegant gesture. Anna didn't have elegant gestures, although she had been told that her smile lit up a room. Whenever she checked her smile in the mirror, she never saw it.

"He's acting like he did when he had that relapse last year, but I don't think he could be drinking. I think I would know. I'm always on the lookout…" Anna frowned.

Nancy stared at Anna, remaining silent.

"He fricking better not be," Anna said with passion in her voice.

"I don't know how many of his relapses I have left in me, but it *is* a finite number," Anna murmured. Nancy hummed a nonintelligible word in commiseration, keeping her thoughts to herself.

Change of subject.

"How are you doing without your mom?" Nancy asked quietly.

"I keep thinking I need to call her. She was declining for so long that I feel like I'm already on chapter eighty-two in the long Book of Mourning. But it felt very spiritual, Nancy. She was ready to go, and I could tell she was going. And you know I had the lady from that store come in and do that Reiki thing. It made me feel better. And my mom keeps talking to me," Anna said sheepishly.

Nancy didn't share Anna's interest in spiritual or mystical topics. However, she didn't mind listening when Anna felt the need to talk about this stuff with someone. "Talks to you now?"

Anna nodded.

"How?" Nancy was attentive but confused. Her parents were both alive and well, and no one close had ever died.

"Okay, this falls into the category of weird, but I hear her voice and guidance in my mind," Anna said bravely, but she was still looking carefully at Nancy for a reaction.

"Like what?"

"I've had this weird dream since I was a kid. All I can remember are voices, but I can't understand what they're saying. Also a feeling of vastness and standing in white fog. Since my mom passed away, I've been dreaming it every night. If that isn't strange enough, I hear her voice in my head as I'm waking up."

"What's she saying?" Nancy asked.

Anna hesitated. "She tells me to follow the dream."

"What does it mean?"

"Not a clue, except she told me something in a meditation, too, about dreams. About dreams being more real than real life. I can't remember her exact words, but I think it's connected."

"Maybe it's the way you're staying connected to your mom, keeping her close."

"Maybe. Also, you know how I'm going to that class at the Awakenings store?"

A nod.

"Something strange happened while I was there. I saw this man who looked interesting. After class, I heard him talking with someone else about the Reiki stuff. He said he teaches it. I felt like my mom was telling me to find out more."

Raised eyebrow. "Married?"

"You overestimate my powers of observation. I didn't look at his hand."

"Cute?"

"It wasn't like that, but he is nice looking. Something about him just feels…good." Anna looked down, a little embarrassed. "I felt like I wanted to keep talking to him all night. He smelled good. I felt...like I was closer to God when I was with him. That everything was possible. I don't know how to explain it. Do you think I'm a weirdo?"

"I think you're a weirdo for staying with Dan, not for talking to a nice man and feeling good," Nancy said in her direct way, but with a mischievous smile on her face.

"Nancy, Dan is broken inside. I feel like I help to fill in his broken spots. I have enough strength to spare. But what I can't handle is being lied to. If he's going to drink, I want the opportunity to make an informed decision about whether to stay with him. I don't like to be fooled. I saw enough of that growing up."

Anna didn't need to explain. The great benefit of longtime friends. Nancy knew her past, and she knew Nancy's. A lot of conversation in shorthand. But there was one thing Anna hadn't told her friend, and she felt it was time.

"Speaking of things that happened while I was growing up... do you remember me telling you that my mom's brother, my uncle, was kind of inappropriate with me when I was a kid?"

"Uh huh." Eyebrows firmly under control.

"Well, when my dad died, my uncle got even weirder. This was thirty years ago. We had the funeral at my parents' church, and a reception there after the burial. My uncle kept following me around."

Anna held very still, her voice numb and monotone.

"He kept asking me for sex, telling me what he was going to do to me and stuff...graphic stuff."

Nancy's face was an overlay of horror and compassion. "He did that at your dad's funeral?"

Anna nodded. "Nancy, I was surrounded by nearly everyone I knew, but all I could think was, 'God, please don't let anyone hear him. They'll think it's my fault.' I felt so alone and ashamed."

"How old were you, Anna?"

"Twenty years old. Not a kid anymore. I could have turned around and told him to go fuck himself. But I kept trying to walk away from him. I was old enough to deck him then. I didn't. He was already in my head from before. I already felt...damaged. He died a few years later, but I didn't go to the funeral. 'I was busy, and funerals are depressing,'" she said flippantly, making air quotes.

Despite the attempt at humor, a tear rolled down Anna's cheek, and she tilted her head down so her bangs hid her face. They were at McDonald's, for goodness' sake. They *knew* people here.

Nancy slid a napkin across the table and rested it under Anna's hand. A minute passed.

"Anyway, when I went to my mom's funeral, it was the same church and many of the same people. I was eating the obligatory tuna fish sandwich at the reception afterward, and I thought, *Well, at least I can eat my sandwich in peace. The old bastard's dead!*"

She looked up at Nancy's shocked face and immediately dissolved into giggles. They both laughed, albeit Anna a bit hysterically. Even after they got it out of their systems, one or the other would start again until it was time to head home.

Anna gave Nancy an extra-long hug as they said good-bye. "You crack me up. Your face when I said that!"

Both were grinning as they drove to their respective homes.

CHAPTER 5

FROM THE FIRST MINUTE OF the next Tree of Life class, Anna was enthralled with the information, but she wondered if she was drowning at the end of two hours. The Tree of Life was ancient knowledge and a type of roadmap for the spiritual journey. God was at the top of the "tree," we humans at the bottom. It looked like a board game more than a tree, with stopping points and lessons to learn. This map was simple, yet it seemed to hold every basic spiritual truth in its structure. There were Hebrew words, angels and archangels, and different colors, and every part of it held a special meaning.

She wasn't sure how she felt about it all, but it definitely stirred something inside her, like a half-remembered dream or the feeling of déjà vu.

At the end of class, Anna wandered around the bookstore where the class had been held. She needed a few minutes to herself before she went home to have dinner with Dan.

The man from the previous week caught her eye and walked over to chat. Anna felt nervous; he seemed so centered and solid. She, on the other hand, felt like a wreck.

"Hi, I'm Eli Sorenson," he said, holding out his hand. "Hannah is quite a teacher. How do you like the class?"

Anna was short, five two, and she had to tilt her head back to look into his golden-brown eyes. He was probably six two, around Dan's height, lean yet solid. She took his hand briefly and then smiled, pleased that he had introduced himself.

"Hi, I'm Anna Woodland. It's mind boggling. I'm still trying to sort everything out. It's so different from other things I've studied."

"Definitely can't expect to learn it in a few classes." He smiled gently. "Scholars study it for a lifetime."

Anna suddenly felt touched that he seemed in tune to her confusion and apprehension.

"What about you...are you enjoying it?"

"Very much! In fact, this is my second time through this series of classes. There's a lot to absorb, but I think it is one of the most important classes they offer at Awakenings."

Anna liked the extremely earnest look on his face. Normally she had a hard time committing faces and names to memory. She tended to go through life in a state of oblivion, the world a blur unless something caught her eye. When that happened, she was able to laser focus her attention. Eli was the object of her laser focus at this moment.

His hair had been dark brown but was lightening from the silver strands clustered at the temples. It was not quite shaggy, but it would be soon without a haircut. His brown eyes were electric and radiated intelligence.

His hair, eyes, skin, and build worked well together; he looked complete. Anna blushed, the deep one that was way too revealing when she realized she had been staring and missed her cue to speak. "Well, I'd like to hear more about that, but I, uh, need to meet up with my husband soon. We're going out to dinner."

She purposefully added the part about Dan in case Eli thought she was "inappropriately interested" due to her staring. It wasn't that kind of interest. He just looked so familiar to her.

She blushed even more when he smiled in an understanding way that indicated *I know why you mentioned your husband, and don't worry about it.* Anna briefly wondered if he could read minds. The jury was still out for her on whether that was possible, but at this moment, she prayed it wasn't.

"Well, Anna, let's talk more next week. My wife is picking me up, too. She dropped me off here today and went shopping."

Anna smiled, feeling relieved. Note to self: tell Nancy.

"That's good. Oh, I meant to ask you something. I heard you talking about Reiki last week and wondered if you could tell me a little more about that next week, too," she said hesitantly.

"Absolutely. One of my favorite topics," he replied warmly.

"Good—well, until then." She smiled and turned toward the door.

Anna had a big grin on her face as she walked to her car. She glanced back in time to see Eli jump into the passenger side of a Lexus. He must have seen her look back because his arm rose in a quick good-bye. She could see only the dark silhouettes of Eli and his wife as they drove away. Anna found herself wondering about the wife of a man like Eli.

That question unanswered, her thoughts turned back to her own spouse. She had been feeling unsettled the last several weeks. Naturally the emptiness in her heart regarding her mom's death was ever present. Standing closely beside the emptiness was a sense that her mom was still with her, much like the way she had felt during the massage with Della.

But this unsettled feeling was something else. It gnawed in her belly like an ulcer. And even though she didn't want to think about it, the ache was the fear that Dan was drinking again. The idea drained her of every emotion, leaving a numbness that was worse than pain.

Is he? Isn't he? What if I ask him and he says no—will I believe him? Or if he says yes, can I stand it?

Dan's relapses usually had the element of bad timing. One occurred after she'd had a scare with cervical cancer a few years ago. Another, years before that, when her job caused her to travel a lot. It all felt off somehow. *Would he put me through that pain again? Especially after my mom...how could he?*

It fits the pattern, she thought with resignation and bitterness.

It fricking fits. Should I bring it up at dinner in public, or at home in private?

She knew she'd ask him the minute she saw him. When it came to being the fool once again, strategy wasn't her forte. Trust *had* been her forte, before the relapses.

CHAPTER 6

"What?" Rachel asked, sounding almost irritated.

Eli had a smile on his face as he folded his lean frame into the car, but he was startled at his wife's tone. He tried for equanimity.

"This class is great. Well worth hearing again."

"Who were you talking to when I pulled up?" she asked casually, although they both knew better.

"A woman from the class. Anna's her name."

"Her second time, too?"

He glanced at Rachel. He couldn't believe she was going where he thought she was going, not after what he had seen a few weeks ago.

"No, first for her. I just met her. She looked a little lost."

And then, a bit too quickly, he asked, "So where are we going to dinner?" He knew he should have let her play it out a little longer and change the subject in her own time. He was so far out of his league right now. He didn't have a clue what he was supposed to say. He knew the script three weeks ago, but that was before everything had changed. Before he saw her with the man at the food pantry.

He went with the script he knew. Stuffing the image of his wife with another man into one of the carefully constructed compartments in his mind, Eli said, "Rachel, I know it's hard when ninety percent of the people who are interested in the same stuff that I am are women and that we have this long-standing 'elephant in the room' thing between us. But you have to know I would never hurt you or cheat. You know it, right? It's been twenty-five years, and I have never, ever cheated on you. When will you trust me?"

He was exhausted and anxious, and the words came out more exasperated than he intended. A hard thought crossed his mind. *You don't even want me, but you sure don't want anyone else taking a shot at it.*

Suppressing the sudden pain, he shifted in his seat to face her more fully and continued. "Look, I'm sorry I snapped. But think about it. I married you. You were the girl of my dreams. I felt like the luckiest guy in the world that day."

Rachel had had a rough first marriage with an untrustworthy guy. Eli vowed to her and to himself that he would never become that guy. He never had. He and Rachel owned a technology business. They had worked and sweated side by side for a long time. It was only recently that their son and daughter had taken over the business. Rachel still did the books, and Eli had oversight responsibilities, but they were able to back out of the day-to-day work. It gave him more time to pursue classes, read, and take hikes. Rachel spent a lot of time shopping and volunteering at the food pantry.

Eli allowed himself a feeling of relief for reassuring his wife, even as he tamped down his own anger. There was no passion in the anger, just the sludge of unresolved and misunderstood history. A tiny thread that had invisibly choked their relationship since the beginning. It didn't get worse or better. It had settled in for the long haul. Until three weeks ago, when anger and fear had flared from the sight of the blond man at the food pantry.

I can't believe I'm reassuring my cheating wife that I'm not cheating on her. I have to be the most screwed-up person in the world...

He *did* feel connected to many of the women at the store. They shared a lot of common spiritual interests that he and Rachel didn't share. But prior to the blond man, he thought he and Rachel shared something else—two kids, a business, and twenty-five years. He had spent a lot of years wishing she could feel secure. But a cheating father and a cheating first husband had taken something from Rachel that he could never give back, despite his best efforts. It often left him feeling lost, and sometimes tired.

And it was for nothing.

I'm not perfect, but God knows being unfaithful is not one of my vices crossed Eli's mind. Then another thought crept right behind it, causing him to tense and glance at Rachel's profile. *She doesn't know me well enough to trust me, and I don't know her at all. Two cardboard cutouts held together by a leftover intention.*

Oh, fuck. Where did that come from? Stuff that thought back in the box and tape it shut.

~

As Rachel drove, she thought about a secret she was keeping from Eli. *He's so damn perfect; he probably never has cheated. Which means I'm so screwed up I can't even see the truth when it's right in front of me. One thing I do know. He wouldn't do what I'm doing now.* The fear tightened her throat. *Soon. We've got to fix it soon before we lose everything.*

CHAPTER 7

"CAN I GO FIRST TONIGHT?" Anna asked. She had somehow managed not to attack Dan with her suspicions that he was drinking again. But it was time to empty the jug, pour out her thoughts and feelings, because she couldn't hold them back any longer. They had been practicing a communication technique for the last few weeks that their marriage counselor had suggested, and she planned to use that technique tonight.

"Sure."

Although they lay side by side in their darkened bedroom, Anna couldn't see him clearly. The curtains were drawn, and only a sliver of light from the street filtered through a gap in the drapes.

"I'm feeling worried because it seems like you might be drinking again."

She heard a sharp intake of breath, but, in keeping with the rules of the therapy, he didn't respond until Anna was done talking.

"I feel like you're always trying to pick a fight. I mean, *frequently* pick a fight." She was trying to honor the rules of the technique, too, by not using words like "always."

"Then you stomp out the door, acting mad, and I can't figure out what happened. It reminds me of the other times when you started drinking. I feel like I have to walk on eggshells. And I hate that. And I'm scared that you are making a fool out of me again. And mad that you might drink when I have so much to deal with now. So, I guess it is your turn." Anna lay frozen, holding her breath.

"Since you are the judge and jury, it sounds like you've already decided I'm drinking. I don't know what I can say that would make you believe that I'm not."

Anna lay beside him, frustrated about the rules that didn't allow her to respond immediately. "I didn't judge; I asked you the question!" she wanted to scream. "And your response isn't making me feel any better!" But she bit her lip and tried to listen.

Dan continued. "I've been worried about you because of your mom, and I don't know how to express that. I get frustrated. I'm sorry if I'm making it worse. I don't like that everything I do is perceived as if I'm drinking. How would you like that if it were you?" Dan's body was tense beside her; she couldn't see his expression as they lay in the dark. Waves of anger rolled from him.

Dan's use of the word "perceived" triggered a recollection of something her teacher had said in the Tree of Life class. About how the things we perceive, the things we think are real, are just an illusion. About stepping outside of our own perceptions.

It's my perception *that Dan is drinking,* Anna thought. *Why do I care if he is fooling me or not? Is it the "human part of me" that doesn't want to feel like a fool?* Anna found her attention wandering and brought it back to Dan.

"Your turn, I guess, assuming you still want to play this game," Dan muttered.

From topics she was learning in class, Anna had been working on understanding more about her personality self, her very human side. She had been trying to act more like her "Higher Self," her soul, the part that saw the bigger picture.

But those thoughts washed away in an instant on the heels of Dan's statement.

"It's not a game, Dan. It's our *marriage.* You think I can let the past go like it never happened? Am I supposed to forget that you have relapses that put me and other people, not to mention our marriage, at risk? You drive drunk. You drive with me in the car drunk so that I don't suspect you've been drinking. You go to work and mess up because you've been sneaking alcohol. Am I supposed to forget that you did that?" Anna shouted.

"And when you do that, you act like you're acting now. Mean, pick fights, walk out, come home late. I can't stand not knowing! Just tell me the truth!"

Her rage swept her beyond words. She felt mean-spirited, and her anger was so hot she wanted to be meaner. She wanted to hurt him.

"Anna, I'm not drinking," Dan said quietly. "I'm not. I wouldn't do that to you again. I wouldn't. I'm sorry that the history is there and you can't forget it. I won't drink again. I promise."

And with that, her anger deflated as quickly as the rage had flared. The space her anger had held now filled with tears.

"Oh God, Dan." A strangled cry from within made her words nearly unintelligible. "I can't stand it. I can't stand not knowing, and I want it to never be true again. I don't want to trust and to be let down again. I'm sorry that I said those things. The anger… I think it's gone, but it's just gone underground. It grabs me, and I want to hurt you. I'm so sorry."

"No, Anna, you're right. I could easily be drinking and doing what you said. You're right to worry, to be scared for us. I get scared for us. I wrestle with this thing. It doesn't go away," Dan said, looking into the pale blur of Anna's face in the darkness of their room. "You can't hate me any more than I hate myself," he murmured.

"I don't hate you. I love you, which is why the pain is so sharp when you act differently. It feels like there's a secret. And I don't seem to notice it for a while. It dawns on me that I'm walking on eggshells. Then it dawns on me more that this is how it goes when you've been drinking. And I get furious at myself that it takes me so long to realize it. We're way into the cycle before it reaches my conscious mind. It makes me hate myself." She tried to see his expression in the darkness.

"What a pair we are, both of us hating ourselves," Dan said quietly. "I won't do that to you again. I promise."

They held each other and lay in silence for a minute.

"What are you thinking about?" Anna asked.

"Ugly thoughts. I was thinking about when my brother and I lived with Mom and her boyfriend. When I was little, Reggie would go out and get stinking drunk. He'd come home after the bars closed and pull us out of bed and berate us. My mom would stand there looking miserable but afraid to say anything in case he'd get worse. He'd beat Ron something terrible, until my brother couldn't take it and ran away from home," Dan said, lost in the memory.

"I used to tell myself that I would never be a stinking drunk like Reggie, never hurt innocent people. But I am, and I have," he said, the shame heavy in his voice.

"You never acted like that, Dan, and you never would. You aren't that person, whether you've been drinking or not," she quickly reassured him. "Please don't add that burden to yourself."

"You're a good person, Anna. No one should ever hurt you, least of all me. You know, this home we have here—this is the only place where I've ever felt safe. I can't let it go. I'm so selfish, Anna. Having this safety is more important to me than letting you live in peace without me," Dan said, his voice breaking.

"I don't want to live without you, Dan. I never have." Anna found his forehead in the dark with her lips, kissed his eyebrows, and moved down to his closed eyelids. "It's okay. We're in this together." She waited a moment. "You could show me how sorry you are for making me worry," she whispered against his eyelids.

Her breath tickled his face, and he nuzzled hers to relieve it.

"I want to, honey, I really do. But tomorrow is an early morning, and I'm tired. Can I take a rain check for tomorrow night?"

"Of course," she replied, masking her disappointment. He didn't need that additional pressure. "Tomorrow night. Goodnight, sweetheart. I'm glad we talked, and I'm sorry I yelled."

He kissed her soundly on the cheek and whispered, "It's okay; I deserved it. Now let's get some sleep."

In a more formal voice, Dan announced, "And this concludes our jug emptying for another night."

Anna giggled, turned over, snuggled her backside against Dan, and fell asleep feeling better than she had in weeks.

Dan lay there remembering. As a kid growing up in Texas, he had liked exploring the countryside. He felt whole being outside, sleeping outdoors under the big sky. But he eventually had to go home. He left home permanently the day he picked up a shotgun and pointed it at Reggie, intending to make the world a better place. Somehow he laid the gun down without using it, fixed his eyes on the man he hated, and backed out of the house. Once he got to the main road, he faced forward and never returned.

He'd gone on to make something of himself. He had his own business. He could work seven days a week if he chose to; he was that much in demand. Except lately. He had lost one lucrative paint job before he even started. The homeowners had smelled alcohol on his breath. *As if I can't paint with a drink or two in me.* Then he'd been asked to leave two of the last three jobs before they were completed. *Idiots.*

Thanks to the last several screw-ups, he hadn't gotten paid. He obviously couldn't tell Anna. *She'd freak.* Dan had started dipping into their savings to pay the bills. He broke into a sweat thinking about it. If Anna looked into that account, she'd find they were down by over fifteen thousand dollars. *Why are things so screwed up?*

He started thinking about the Marston job and slowly calmed himself. The Marstons were rich. The *really* rich kind of rich. They wanted him to paint the whole interior of the house, and he had put a price tag on the proposal that would pay back the savings account and a lot more. He would see them tomorrow and find out if it was a go.

He hadn't wanted to become an alcoholic or to lie to Anna and the others who had come before her. As he drifted to sleep, he resolved that he would make good on his promise and become that person who didn't drink. Tomorrow.

CHAPTER 8

"Dan, I'm gonna take three hundred dollars out of savings today to make my car payment this month. My check from the publishing company isn't here yet, but I'll replace the money when it comes. I just wanted you to know in case you wondered when the statement comes in," Anna said.

"Why don't I just give you the money? I'm getting paid this afternoon from my last job. That way we won't get in the habit of hitting the savings account," Dan said, staring at the mail in his hands. He laid the letters back down, glanced at Anna, and walked toward the front door.

"Are you sure?"

"Absolutely. Not a problem."

"I'll pay you back as soon as that darn check gets here."

"You don't need to do that. It's okay. I'm going over to see the Marstons. If I get that job, three hundred dollars will be no big deal." Dan reached for the door without looking back.

"Dan? You okay?"

"I'm great. Just planning my strategy for the meeting with Marston. I'd better get going so I'm not late. That definitely wouldn't make the right impression."

"Okay. Good luck, honey! Let me know how it goes!"

Anna gazed at the door as Dan pulled it shut behind him. *Mom, what is going on?*

The only answer was the ticking of the living room clock and Anna's sigh.

⁓

Shit, now I have to stop at the bank, too. Nothing's simple. As blasé as Dan wanted to be about the close call with Anna and the savings account, he felt shaken. *I gotta get this stuff out of my head. Do the meeting with the Marstons, get the job, do the job, replace the money back into the account. Oh, yeah. And don't drink.*

Putting the morning's events out of his head, Dan rang the bell at the Marston home. In a neighborhood of impressive homes, this one stood out as the crown jewel. *If I do this job and they recommend me to their neighbors, this could be a real turning point for the business. I could hire employees and start making some serious money.*

He heard the unlocking of latches just before the door opened. A lovely woman whose age Dan judged to be about forty looked at him inquiringly, a mischievous smile on her face.

"Well, hi! I'm Dan, the painter that your husband called. Is he in?"

⁓

A nerve-wracking forty-five minutes later, Dan was out the door with a start date for the entire interior painting of the house. Mr. Marston looked to be about twenty years older than his wife, but it was obvious he kept in shape. He was clearly a tough businessman, but despite that, he agreed to Dan's price for the job.

Walking to the car, Dan replayed some of the conversation in his mind. *I checked your references, and I have to say I'm impressed. Everyone said you're one of the best.* Said it would take longer because you work alone, but it'd be worth it. That felt really good to hear. *Yours was one of the highest bids, but Lu and I want this job to be done right.* For once he hadn't underbid the job.

Marston seemed like a decent guy despite being rich, powerful, and smart plus having a trophy wife. But there was something that seemed off. *The eyes. His eyes are the kind that sees everything, but there's a lost look there. Sadness. And Mrs. Marston—Lu—nice lady, but also kind of sad. Interesting.*

Wonder if there's a happy couple on the planet?

Dan reflected on his life with Anna. It wasn't bad, but he had to keep so many secrets. Fucking alcohol. And Anna was getting suspicious. *Why can't I drink like normal people? Stop at two?* It was a question he had asked himself a million times, and he never came up with the answer. *Well, today is the day to stop for now. No screw-ups on this job, and I'm skating too close to the edge with the savings account, I've got to make this right.*

There was an inch of alcohol left in the vodka bottle tucked under his car seat. *Last sip before I stop for good.*

CHAPTER 9

ANNA AND ELI GRAVITATED TOWARD each other after the third Tree of Life class. The bookstore was bustling after class had let out.

He's so easy to talk to. Anna smiled warmly.

"Eli, what's the big picture of the Tree of Life? I feel like I understand the individual things we're learning, but I can't put the whole picture together." She felt comfortable enough to admit she didn't understand, and the feeling surprised Anna.

Eli smiled back, happy to be helpful. He was both an avid student and a natural-born teacher, and this subject was near and dear to his heart.

"Think of the Tree of Life as a roadmap. And while it looks a lot more like a game of hopscotch because of the ten spheres placed on it than it does an actual tree, it's a system that was created a long time ago to show how God created the world, how to master the lessons we need to learn on this Earth, and how to eventually reunite with God."

"At the top of the tree, we start out as being one with God, but closer to the roots of the tree, where we humans exist, we feel more like very separate beings. We have our separate personalities, our idiosyncrasies, our wants and desires—our ego self.

Nevertheless, we long to return to feeling connected with one another and being one with God again," Eli explained.

"It sounds like our life lesson here on Earth is to 'rise above' our personality, our ego, and the feeling of separation?" Anna said, a bit more confident.

"Exactly. And just like in a board game, the goal is to work our way up the Tree, to learn our lessons, and to resonate more at those higher levels. Many of those lessons are about having balance in everything we do."

"It's pretty incredible," Anna said, reflecting on Eli's words.

"Well, keep in mind this is just my own limited interpretation. One human's lens," Eli said, smiling.

"I had no idea when I took this class that it was a doorway to a whole different way of seeing the world," she said.

Eli continued. "The more we expand the ways we perceive, the easier it is to lose our personality self that makes us feel so separate. We gain perspective from our higher self. I think of the higher self as our soul. It vibrates at a different frequency, but it is connected to our personality self on earth. It's the part of us that sees the bigger picture, the higher meaning to what happens to us.

"So that's my story, and I'm sticking to it!" Eli said, finishing on a lighter note in case Anna was finding this boring or too far out for her taste.

He had encountered a lot of skepticism in his life, and he had learned to keep his thoughts to himself. But for whatever reason, he felt safe enough to give his thoughts on the topic to this sad-eyed but sparkling woman. He wondered what her story was and hoped she would tell him one day.

Anna smiled, nodded, and then said, "Eli, can I switch the conversation for a minute?"

"Of course."

"Last week you mentioned a type of energetic healing called Reiki. My mom passed away a month ago, and she had Reiki while...while she was sick. I'd like to learn more about it, how to do it. I heard you say that you teach it. Do you think that you could teach me? I mean, would you mind?" Anna asked shyly.

Eli smiled a gentle smile, remembering his own teacher who had brought him the Reiki. "A lot of people have helped me along this path. I would be honored to introduce you to Reiki."

And with that, they made a plan to meet later that week.

CHAPTER 10

ANNA SETTLED DOWN FOR AN hour of serious editing on a new article she had been asked to make "more readable." Mind wandering, she sighed. She had woken up this morning feeling out of sorts. A fragment of The Dream, as she had begun to call it, had left her feeling hollow. Since her mother had died, the dream had robbed her of sound sleep nearly every night, and she strived to remember the content. Nothing.

Dan had already left for the day. He had an indoor painting job near home this week. Around nine in the morning, the phone rang, and she saw from the caller ID it was Dan.

"Hi, honey. What's up?"

It was unusual for him to call while he was at work.

"I was wondering if you wanted to go hiking tomorrow. The weather is supposed to be good, almost like spring. After that, it's back to winter, and then I'll be busy for several weeks at the Marstons'. Any interest?"

Dan was the person in their family who thought of interesting things to do. Anna was always happy to go along with plans to hike, visit the art museum, see a concert, go to a movie, or any number of things Dan thought of, but she wasn't the initiator of these adventures. This added a nice balance to her somewhat sedentary life.

"That sounds great! I've been wanting to get outside for a long walk," Anna said happily. "I can't believe we're going to have such a nice day, and it's almost Christmas. The weather really is messed up, but for the good this time!"

Dan promised to be home early. They made plans to go out to dinner that evening and get an early start tomorrow morning. As Anna hung up the phone, she sighed a deep breath of contentment. Bleak feelings from the dream were forgotten.

It seemed as if things were getting better. Childish or not, she quickly crossed her fingers as a thought flitted through her mind: *Don't jinx this.*

Dan didn't like chain restaurants, preferring to direct his money to family or individually owned places. His standards for the food were also high. Although he had not been formally trained as a chef, his mother had taught him all she knew. Plus, he had spent his early years working in the restaurant at a ski resort. He did most of the cooking at home, an aspect of their marriage that Anna was extremely grateful for. Cooking was not her strength.

Tonight they decided to stay close to home in their Saint Louis suburb town of Kirkwood and go to one of the local Italian restaurants. Jim, the owner of the restaurant, knew them well and handed a menu to Anna and then to Dan.

"Anna, I already know what you want, but Dan, do you need a minute to decide?" Jim asked, smiling at Anna so she would know he was kidding her, but gently.

Anna rolled her eyes. Yes, she was predictable. Dan was the more adventurous one and tended to try something different each time.

Jim didn't bother to ask if they wanted wine with dinner. He knew that neither of them drank.

"You know, Jim, I'll have what Anna's having, the eggplant Parmesan. I had a bite of hers last time, and it was delicious."

"Okay. Your bread will be out in a minute. Dan, do you want your eggplant prepared like Anna likes it?"

"'Whatever's fine with me—cook's choice," Dan said before taking a sip of water the busboy had placed in front of him.

Jim returned to the kitchen, and Anna and Dan looked around to see if anyone they knew was dining here tonight. Another couple caught their eye. Dan was active in Alcoholics Anonymous and had a lot of friends, not to mention customers, from his AA group. One of Dan's friends from AA was sitting with his wife by the window.

"Hey, Anna, I'm going to say hi to Ed. Be back in a minute."

Dan pushed his chair back and stood. Anna watched his lean, attractive body as he strolled over to Ed and Donna's table. Dan was a little over six two, and, although wiry, he was stronger than he looked. He hauled twenty- to forty-foot ladders around as part of his profession, and they were quite heavy. That tended to strengthen his upper body, but the length of his arms was what he valued most as a painter. A wide "wingspan" meant he could paint a wider area and therefore move the ladder less often.

She took another admiring peek at her husband and then waved to Ed and Donna when they noticed her looking their way.

Anna waited and wondered what they were discussing as the muted sounds of ice cubes tinkling, the hum of voices, and the occasional bark of laugher provided background noise.

Dan came back in a few minutes.

"Well, that was a fortunate encounter. Ed's parents need their house painted, and they asked Ed for my number. He was going to call me tomorrow."

Anna decided not to ask why Dan hadn't seen Ed at their AA meeting last night, so she nodded her agreement that it was fortunate to see them here.

Keeping the topic positive, Anna asked, "Where do you want to go hiking tomorrow?"

"Hmm...do you feel like a long or short one? That will help determine the best spot," Dan said.

"A long walk would be nice. It's going to be a beautiful day, and we should take advantage of it," Anna said. "We haven't been on a walk for so long, I can't even remember where we went the last time." She frowned, trying to remember.

"I know. Well, this is a great little break in the winter weather. I agree. Let's take our time and really enjoy it." Dan smiled and seemed more relaxed than he had in months. They chatted about their friends and caught up with each other. With work, Anna's classes, Dan's meetings, and a host of other activities, it had been a while since they had sat and talked.

"So what's the class like at Awakenings?" he asked.

Anna's trust level constricted. Dan wasn't known for being tolerant of her interest in metaphysical matters. But she asked him gamely, "Are you familiar with the Kabbalah and the Tree of Life?"

"Isn't the Kabbalah connected with Jewish mysticism?" he said.

Anna was always impressed with the range of topics Dan knew something about. He was very gifted intellectually, but the monkey on his back of addiction had gotten in his way during the school years. He had never gone on to college, but he had educated himself. He was curious and loved to learn but had no degree to show for it. Addiction was a hard taskmaster.

"Yes, it's pretty interesting." Anna hesitated, not sure how much he would want to hear.

"Tell me about it."

Anna figured he was more interested on an intellectual level than on a spiritual one, but that was fine with her. She began to explain it very much the way Eli had explained it to her, with additional information. The class had come to make more sense with each additional week.

"At the very bottom of the tree is what we think of as our world, which is called Malkuth. It's not literally the planet Earth. You could think of Malkuth as the stage where we act in the 'play of life.' We bring the drama, the interactions with our physical world and with other people."

She looked into Dan's eyes to see if he was still interested. He appeared to be listening and processing what she was saying. She smiled because it was fun to have this kind of conversation with her husband.

Anna continued. "It's here that we are most separate from God, yet this is where we learn most of our lessons. Here is where we learn to understand the nature of illusion. If we choose to use the Tree of Life as a roadmap, the map helps us to become our highest and best self. We can use the roadmap to learn balance and how to integrate important spiritual lessons into our everyday life. We can use it to return to the state of oneness with God, a state of divine love. We get to 'practice' at different frequencies here on Malkuth."

Dan stopped her. "You lost me. What do you mean by frequencies?"

"I think of it as the level we're vibrating at. Let's say, for example, when I'm all caught up in my negative personality self—being 'me' with all my little wants and desires, stomping my foot and throwing a fit—then I'm vibrating at a lower frequency." Anna tried her best to explain a concept that she sensed inside but hadn't actually verbalized to anyone before.

She continued. "Contrast that to the part of myself who wants to be of service to other people, or the person who lets petty things go and doesn't get all wrapped up in them, who sees the bigger picture. Then I'm vibrating at a different frequency, a higher vibration."

"Interesting."

"Do you really think so?" Anna asked hopefully. "You're not humoring me, are you?" she asked a little self-consciously, since this was new territory for her.

Dan looked at her for a minute and then said, "I think it's actually a bunch of crap. I think the Jewish scholars of the Kabbalah would be horrified it was being taught in a metaphysical bookstore."

A thousand thoughts and impressions flooded her. *Why did I bother? Why try?* Then, suddenly, her perspective shifted. At that moment she felt she was looking down from a great height at the two of them gathered around the table, eating a meal.

As she peered down, she became an observer of two people vibrating at different levels. One was no better than the other, just different. And not even worlds apart, but separate places regarding this topic. Neither one was right or wrong, better or worse. Simply two sets of experiences and learnings—two people who had come together for discussion.

Anna felt a great sense of peace. She reached over, took Dan's hand in her own, and said, "It was fun to share this with you, even if you have a different thought about it. Thank you."

Dan held Anna's hand within his two hands, leaned over, and kissed her cheek. "I'm sorry, sweetheart. I wanted to see at what frequency *you* were vibrating. You were awesome."

It took Anna a minute to realize what Dan was saying. She stared at him, mouth hanging open, while he had a bemused expression on his face.

"You're serious," Anna stated firmly.

"Uh huh."

"I think we'd better pay Jim and get home. Because I am going to pay you back tonight. And then we'll see at what frequency *you* vibrate," Anna whispered to Dan.

"Promises, promises," Dan said, pulling bills out of his wallet.

As they drove through the night to their home, Anna kept replaying the exchange between them at the restaurant and smiled.

She was learning. But more importantly, she was putting the pieces together and applying it to her life.

CHAPTER 11

"It's still a little chilly," Anna remarked as she and Dan walked the trail at the Nature Conservatory, "but I'm glad we got an early start."

"Yeah, I thought coming here might be better than a long drive to one of the state parks."

The Nature Conservation Center was a few miles down the road from their house. When morning came, neither had felt like a whole-day hike, and they opted for a walk. It was steep in places, but the trail was paved.

A small critter rustled the leaves beside the path in search of food. Anna stopped and peered down, forcing her eyes to seek a form that didn't fit the pattern of the leaves.

"Squirrel," Dan whispered, pointing a few feet away. He paused. "Whoa, Anna. Look farther into the woods and don't move."

Dan's eyes were much better than hers, but she stood still and finally found the doe that he had seen. The deer stood watching them on quiet alert, poised to leap away if needed.

Anna sighed, smiling. *Beautiful.* She reached for Dan's hand, and they stood together, fingers laced, watching as the doe relaxed and resumed foraging for food. In unison and without discussion, they turned and applied themselves to the trail, which had suddenly become steeper.

"What do you think life would be like if we didn't die?" Dan asked out of the blue.

Anna looked sideways at his profile for a second and then began to think. "Well, there would be a lot less fear!" she joked.

"Yeah, and no one would have to work because we wouldn't need shelter or food," he added. "We need that so we don't freeze to death or starve!"

"I'm not giving up food. No way!"

"I'm not giving up exercise." Dan smiled.

"I might give that up." She laughed. "Although I *am* loving this walk."

"Yep. This is definitely good," he said and gently squeezed her hand, which was enveloped by his larger one.

Anna gave him a sweet smile. For a moment she felt like a child walking with her dad, safe and protected. He released her hand and laid his arm across her shoulders, pulling her close. She felt his warm breath and then the pressure of his lips on her head.

"Definitely good," he repeated.

～

"I think I'm gonna see a person at the Awakenings store who can read people's past lives."

They were heading up the sidewalk to their front door after a quick lunch at McDonald's, and Anna was feeling relaxed and happy from their walk and shared morning.

"You mean reincarnation?"

She nodded.

"How's that work, and how can you tell if the reader is real or full of shit? It's not like they can prove it, right?"

"Good point, but I still wanna go," Anna said, thrusting her hip into Dan's thigh, knocking him off the sidewalk.

He grabbed her around the waist, pushing her forward. "I think you were a trained assassin in a past life." He laughed, pushing her up the steps.

"I think you were the guy I was after, but you escaped and ran off to Tibet. I had to go find you, which I did, and we fell in love, so I couldn't kill you."

"Were you a guy?" Dan asked suspiciously.

"Yep, and I was so good in bed that you couldn't resist. You renounced your family and became gay; I was that good." She nodded her head in satisfaction.

"Damn! And you only remembered a fraction of that hot sex! Let's go back to *that* life!"

"Now I'm gonna hurt you. You're gonna pay for that!"

"Just don't kill me," Dan mumbled as Anna stood on tiptoes and covered his mouth with her own. She then pushed him through the front door, closing and locking it behind her.

Her warm breath tickled his lips as she kissed him and whispered, "I'm gonna kill you with kindness." He groaned and pulled her tight against him. "Maybe I do believe in past lives," he muttered, and then he pushed her backward onto the couch. "If I'm not careful, you might convert me," he said, unzipping her coat.

"I'm not sure if I'm *that* good" was the last thing Anna said before she unzipped his jacket and pulled him down to her. "But I do feel inspired to try."

An hour later, Anna realized with a start that she hadn't thought about Eli all day. And a second shock when she noticed how often she *did* think about him.

"More walks, more practicing with my husband. Definitely," she concluded.

⁓

Tired from their walk, Anna thought she'd sleep like a baby that night. She needed a good night's sleep. The dreams at night had been getting more insistent, and Anna felt as if she were sleepwalking through each day.

She and Dan settled into their bed, and, within minutes, both were fast asleep. Around three in the morning, Anna's dream awakened Dan. She was mumbling something about having to remember. He was reaching over to awaken her when she sat up, still asleep, eyes peering into her dream world.

Dan jerked back, startled by a clear voice saying firmly, "Find them." It had come from Anna.

He reached with more urgency to awaken her. Resting his hand gently on her shoulder, he had just begun to quietly say her name when the whole room was enveloped in milky whiteness.

He snatched his hand away from her and peered around. The whiteness was gone, and he was back in their bedroom. Dan realized that some time must have passed because Anna was lying down, peacefully asleep.

Did I just dream Anna's dream?

As he lay there in the early hours of the morning, he decided he was having some kind of withdrawal symptoms. He hadn't been drinking for a few days. That had to be it. *I'm not getting involved in that crazy stuff of Anna's. I'm just not.*

He repeated that to himself until his alarm rang at 5:30 a.m. He also decided he was keeping this shit to himself.

CHAPTER 12

ANNA AND ELI MET AT Cheryl's house, which was equidistant to their two homes. Cheryl was a good friend of Eli's from Awakenings. They had known each other for a long time and did Reiki work together. The three of them settled comfortably into the chairs in Cheryl's living room.

Anna felt relieved that she'd finally had a good night's sleep. She wanted to feel refreshed on this special evening.

She had just met Cheryl that evening but liked her already and loved the atmosphere of her home. Eli had taught Reiki to Cheryl last year. "Taught" was somewhat of a misnomer.

"If you watch one person give Reiki to another person," Eli explained, "it might look like they are healing the person through a 'laying on of hands.' The Reiki practitioner can learn how to place the hands, where to place them, and that sort of thing, but that alone is not enough to do Reiki."

He continued. "Reiki is a form of energetic healing where the practitioner is like a lightning rod for the Ki, or life force, to flow through to the person who is being healed. It isn't directed by the skill of the practitioner or anything that they have learned; it is directed by God, or Rei, the Higher Intelligence. Our job is to 'stand back and let it happen!'"

Anna reflected a moment. "Eli, when the woman did Reiki on me and my mom, she drew symbols in the air over our bodies. What was she doing?"

"The symbols have particular meanings, and they help to amp up the healing. There are different symbols for healing a person's physical body vs. healing their emotional, mental, or spiritual body. I will teach you each symbol. Drawing those symbols is like saying, 'Heal this part!'

"It is also important to know that Reiki isn't a religion. It's a form of energetic healing that draws from a Universal Source, God. Regardless of what someone's personal religious beliefs are, they can do Reiki." Eli looked carefully into Anna's face to check if she understood.

"Are you ready, Anna?" he asked gently.

She nodded slowly. "Yes," she said simply.

The space had been arranged with a straight-back chair in the middle of the living room, facing east. Anna moved to that chair.

Items representing the elements of air, water, fire, and earth had been placed strategically around the room to create the sacred space. Tendrils of smoke unfurled from the burning incense and drifted toward the water-filled urn. A soft halo of light ringed the flame of a tall, white candle. A hand-thrown clay pot brought balance to the ancient tradition of aligning the four elements with the four directions.

Cheryl sat on a couch, spine straight, facing Anna. She would also contribute focus, intention, and energy to this ritual, but Eli would carry out the initiation.

All of this was very new to Anna, but it felt sacred. She could almost see Dan rolling his eyes at the thought.

Eli stood several feet in front of Anna's seated form. He centered himself and then silently called in celestial help. This help came in the form of his spiritual Guides and Teachers, angels and archangels, and his and Anna's higher selves, the best of each of them. They seemed to gather in the room. He then called on Archangel Raphael, the particular angel of healing. As he felt the presence of these beings, Eli circled around behind Anna and tapped her shoulder gently to let her know he was beginning the initiation.

Anna put her hands together in the position of prayer and closed her eyes. She felt a powerful presence in the room, and the floor seemed to bend with the weight of those who gathered. She felt Eli walk around to her right side. She entered a meditative state almost immediately as he drew the special Reiki symbols over the top of her head. He then circled beside and in front of her, cupping her hands in his and visualizing the Reiki symbols entering her hands.

This process went on for several minutes, and Anna lost track of time. She found herself in a dream state as a story played out in her mind. But not really in her mind, because it wasn't clear like a thought. This story felt like a memory.

She sensed she was an elderly man near death. Although Anna was not currently a Catholic, she saw that a young brother had been called to give the last rites. Anna felt the emotions of the elderly man, and she sensed a deep love for this young brother. She sensed more and realized "she" was the abbot of a monastery, and this man was one of the brothers. Her love for him was of a spiritual nature, and it felt as big as the sky.

As Eli continued to slowly walk around Anna, at times kneeling by her side and taking her hands in his, she realized that he was the young monk. As in dreams, nothing seemed odd about what was occurring. There were no thoughts, only feelings of gratitude and love. And then, as Anna drew a deep sigh, the dream and the initiation were complete.

Anna sat, blinking her way back to the real world. Eli stood in front of her until he saw she was with them again. He then walked toward her and bowed. "Anna, congratulations. The world has a new healer." He smiled and then grasped her hands.

"Feel how warm your hands are? That is the Reiki," he explained to her.

Anna rose and sat next to Cheryl on the couch. Do you mind telling me what you experienced, Anna?" Cheryl asked quietly.

Still feeling a little dazed, Anna nodded and then asked, "Eli, do you ever feel like you have lived in a monastery, like in a past life?"

Cheryl and Eli exchanged a glance before Eli explained, "It's odd that you ask. Cheryl and I were talking about that the other day. I was telling her I felt like I had lived many lifetimes in spiritual communities of all types, but especially in Catholic monasteries. Why?" Eli asked.

Anna explained the vision that she had had. The three of them discussed it briefly before they called it a night. Eli needed to get home to his wife, and Cheryl had work to complete before she could go to sleep.

They took a little more time to make sure that Anna and Eli were in a fully aware state before driving, and then hugs were exchanged.

"Thank you, Cheryl, for the use of your beautiful home," Anna said. "Eli, I don't even know how to thank you for this evening."

Eli handed Anna a certificate that honored her Reiki I initiation.

"You'll get one of these with each of your three initiations," Eli said. "Thank me by using what you've learned to be of service to others. That's the best thanks. Goodnight, Anna. It was a pleasure." Eli's smile was gentle, but Anna could feel a sense of power radiating from him.

Anna's mind was flooded with thoughts about the evening as she drove home. It was an amazing feeling to spend time with like-minded people. *My very own spiritual community*, she thought, her face wreathed in a smile.

She had always felt so alone. She was an only child; her parents married late in life, and her mom was nearly forty when Anna was born. Always different. Feeling things others didn't notice, wondering what was real and what was her imagination. And now this. Time spent with these people filled her in ways she had never been filled before. Her heart swelled with gratitude.

Anna felt a soft pressure at the crown of her head.

"Mom?" No answer, but the memory of her mother pulling the covers up to her chin each night and placing a kiss on her head was clear in her mind.

"Thank you, Mom."

Congratulations, sweetheart echoed through her mind.

By the time Anna got home, Dan had already gone to bed. While it was still fresh in her mind, she decided to e-mail Eli a note of thanks. She knew he was an early riser from something he had said that evening, and she wondered when he would see her e-mail.

Subject: And thank you again
I wanted to write a personal thank you for your kind and gentle spirit during the Reiki initiation. You have a lot of power that you made present, but you let me take that in at my own time/ability/frequency. You are a true Teacher.

What did you experience during the initiation, if you don't mind my asking? We didn't get a chance to talk about that.

It was amazing to feel the Reiki coming down and "settling" in my body. I felt like I was changing at the cellular level. I didn't want to move and lose a drop of it!
Anna

CHAPTER 13

FIVE IN THE MORNING ARRIVED way too soon for Eli. He had felt so charged from the Reiki initiation that he couldn't get to sleep until nearly one o'clock. Last night he had experienced more peace than he had in weeks. He ended up sleeping in the spare bedroom so he wouldn't disturb Rachel. As he shut off the alarm, he realized he could have stayed in bed. That was the beauty of turning over the business to his son and daughter. It was sheer force of habit that had him up at the usual time, checking his e-mail.

Eli turned on the computer while he made hot tea. Minutes later, mug in hand, he opened the e-mail. He was surprised to see the first one was from Anna. It brought a smile to his face as he read and reread her words. He collected his thoughts about the experience last night and began to write.

Re: And thank you again
Thank you so much. It was a very special initiation on many levels. When calling in the Guides, I "saw" them assemble around us. When I moved behind you, I paused to let the energy settle. Now we could get to work!

When an initiation is done, I get into a similar state as you, but there is a twist. The person performing the initiation has to be partially in waking consciousness to keep track of the steps and what needs to be visualized.

Each Reiki symbol was visualized individually and placed multiple times into the crown of your head and your hands. Each time a symbol was placed, I could feel a "quantum" of energy going with it.

As I placed the symbols into your hands, I was acutely aware of the heat in your palms and mine. They seemed to merge.

Archangel Raphael was speaking clearly and saying, "Integration." That was meant for you. He said that at several points. Clearly, you were doing that on a very fundamental level.

It was very powerful indeed.

Your question for me about the monastic life told me you had tapped into my energy "signature" and picked up a past life we might have shared. How cool is that!

E

Eli smiled as he hit the Send button.

A minute later across town, Anna felt moved to check her e-mail. Despite the late night, she had awakened early and couldn't get back to sleep. Throughout the night she tried to lie very still, afraid of disturbing Dan. Luckily he slept deeply and was still in bed when she rose. As she made her morning tea, she turned on the computer.

Anna felt a quick tremor of excitement when she opened the inbox. Eli's response!

She quickly settled in front of the monitor and read his reply several times. *That is so lovely.* She wondered if it was too soon to respond, but she had additional impressions during the night she felt moved to relate. She decided to wait until later in the day to reply, not wanting to overwhelm Eli with a barrage of e-mails.

Anna worked until 3:00 p.m., and then she decided she had waited long enough and wrote her note. She felt almost in a light trance and wondered if that was an aftereffect of the initiation.

Re: Re: And thank you again
Eli,
There is really a lot here to meditate on. Thank you for sharing your experience of the initiation in detail. It's so helpful, and beautiful to hear. I want to understand more about integration and the layers of meaning in relation to the Reiki, maybe in relation to other aspects of my life.

Every time you knelt beside me, I very much felt the sense of a spiritual community in your energy.

Today as I reflected on the image I had of you administering last rites, here's more of what I felt. You were a young monk or brother; I was the abbot or whatever the director of the monastery is called. I tried never to have favorites, but you had such a shining Christ light and gentleness of spirit that I had a strong interest in your development and soul's journey. I loved you as if you were my son, and I asked for you when I was failing.

Today I realized I had waited all these years (centuries maybe) to tell you how grateful I am that you were there when I passed on.

Positive frequencies of emotions travel so long throughout time, and it feels very right when they find their intended recipient. Thank you for being there.

A

Anna frowned at what she had written. It seemed too personal to tell him all of that; plus, she wondered what Dan would think if he saw what she had written. She sighed and rested her finger on the Delete button.

Reread it. The image of the young brother had been so clear in her mind. She could still look at her hands and see the gnarled and wrinkled old-man hands transposed over her own. Where does a story like that come from? Sighing, she clicked the mouse. Sent.

CHAPTER 14

It was getting close to lunchtime, and Dan decided to take a break. It was day two of the Marston job, and he was pleased with how it was going. He decided to grab lunch and rest in his car for a few minutes. Poking his head into the kitchen to let Mrs. Marston know he was stepping out, he saw her relaxing at the kitchen table. A bottle of bourbon and two glasses sat in front of her.

She glanced up at Dan. "Drink?"

Dan froze. "Uh, sorry. It's a little too early in the day for me."

"Liar." She smiled as she said it.

He stood still for a moment and then hesitantly headed in her direction.

He pulled out a chair, sat down, and, with a measured look, said, "Mrs. Marston, what makes you think that?"

"Maybe it takes one to know one. And call me Lu."

Dan sat stiffly, wondering what to do next. Lu poured the drink and slowly slid the glass across the table, stopping in front of him. Equally slowly, she pulled her hand back to her own drink.

"It's okay. I won't tell my husband if you won't."

"It's usually not a good idea to drink on the job. You're not worried I'll mess up?"

"I know you won't mess up. I think you can handle quite a few drinks before you mess up a paint job. You've been at this a few years."

"Painting or drinking?" Dan asked as he tilted the glass to his lips.

"Both, I guess." She took a deep sigh.

"Yeah," he said after a long swallow. Dan put the drink down, and, with his eyes still on the glass, he nodded. "I reckon you're right."

He raised his head and gazed into her eyes. "What about you?"

"Never did much painting." She smiled wryly. "But the drinking...well, I've been doing that since I was fifteen."

Dan leaned back in the chair, feeling more comfortable. "We've got a few minutes before I need to get back, Lu. Tell me about it. No judgment here. Was fifteen when you first got drunk, or when you started drinking every day?"

"You know, no one's ever asked me that." Lu was either staring absently at the refrigerator or carefully away from Dan, and he wasn't sure which. "Both, over the course of that year. It was a bad one." She stopped.

They sat quietly together.

"You can tell me, if you want to."

She looked at him for a few moments. "It's a shit story, Dan. Okay to call you Dan?"

He nodded and smiled briefly. "They're all shit stories. Tell you what, Lu. I'll tell you mine if you tell me yours," he said lightly, and then he sat very still, hoping she would know it was safe.

After what seemed a very long time, Lu picked up her glass. She stared at it with love and disgust before she took another drink. He knew that look.

Then she said, "Okay…"

CHAPTER 15

ANNA HADN'T HEARD FROM ELI since her last e-mail, but he came up to her before the Tree of Life class. She had been feeling self-conscious about what she had written and hoped it wouldn't interfere with their Reiki work.

"Hey," Eli said with a big grin on his face. "How is the integration work going?"

She felt herself relax. "It's weird. I think it's brought up a lot of childhood issues. The stuff that surfaced seemed to format itself differently in my brain, or how I saw it was different. It was like I was in the observer mode rather than in the thick of the memory. The things that happened were a part of me but didn't define me." Anna's voice faltered. "Does that make any sense?"

Eli leaned against one of the glass cases in the store and gathered his thoughts for a moment. "It sounds like you're saying there were things that happened in your life that were important, but they didn't feel like a part of you. They weren't 'you,' yet they defined you in some way that felt negative. And now all of those pieces are fitting more comfortably inside you. You're integrating them. By accepting them, you aren't at their mercy. You don't need to feel defined by them. You're accommodating your light and your shadow," Eli said. "Is that kind of what you mean?"

Anna stared. "That's exactly what I mean but better said. Okay, I have to ask you…can you read my mind? I'm serious."

Eli chuckled. "I don't think I can read your mind, but if I ever do, it's our secret!" He laughed and then became more solemn. "I've had to do quite a bit of work on myself. It isn't easy."

"You have light and shadows in you, too?" Anna was honestly curious. He definitely seemed "integrated." Or maybe she would use the word "whole."

"Oh yeah! Everyone does, Anna. That struggle is at the heart of the spiritual journey. Acceptance of all those pieces of the self, but, even more importantly, learning from them. Taking the negative things from the past and using them for your own growth and development."

He shrugged. "Pain without learning something important is just…well, just *pain*! But learning—that's what you and I and others on the spiritual path are looking for. And everything, good *or* bad, can teach us something!"

"I'm sorry to go on about this." Eli straightened and said somewhat apologetically, "I don't get much of a chance to talk about it except with Cheryl and some of the others here at the store, but it is a passion of mine."

"It's fun for me, too." Anna nodded. "I've been interested in this kind of thing for a long time—since I was a kid, but not consistently. For years at a stretch, I would put one foot in front of the other and focus on work or family issues. It's only recently that I've found my way back to the spiritual path on a more full-time basis."

As Hannah rang the bell to call everyone to class, Eli asked suddenly, "Would you want to grab some dinner after class today? My wife is going out with her friend tonight, so I'm flying solo. Unless you need to get home…"

"That would be nice," Anna said enthusiastically, albeit with a twinge of guilt. "I'll call my husband to let him know. He had plans with one of his friends, too, so that will work out great!"

Two hours later, Anna and Eli were seated at a Chinese buffet near the store. They had filled their plates and were settling into their chairs. The first few minutes were spent discussing how good the food was, interspersed with silence as they ate and thought about the class.

Anna had the odd realization that she hadn't eaten a meal with a man other than Dan in years. She looked up from her plate and observed Eli more carefully. He was a nice-looking man, his hair curling near the collar of a high-quality cotton shirt.

Between the first round of food and the next, Eli asked, "What's your life like, Anna? What do you do for a living? I know you're married; do you have kids?"

Anna smiled. "I've been married to Dan for fifteen years. This is my second marriage. No kids. I kind of missed the childbearing years; I was thirty-six when we got married. The first time, I was only eighteen when I was married, but that ended before we had kids. You?"

"Rachel and I have been married for twenty-five years. We have two great kids, Tim and Chris. Tim's our son, and he's twenty-four. Chris is our daughter, and she's twenty-two—just graduated from college. Rachel and I started a technology business about twenty years ago. It grew enough over time that she and I are both semiretired. Our kids grew up in the business and like it, thank God, so they are doing the day-to-day running of the business now. Which leaves me time to go to Awakenings, take classes, and basically have fun! I'm very grateful," Eli said.

He poured himself another cup of tea, looked inquiringly at Anna, and then poured a cup for her at her nod and smile.

"Wow! That's the way to do it." Anna fell quiet for a moment. She had made the quick comparison in her mind that reinforced she'd done it wrong. The failed first marriage; recuperating from that during the years she would have been having babies. Dan, the toll his drinking had taken, and even now having worries about whether he was still drinking. The sudden hollow feeling.

Eli saw it reflected in her eyes without her saying a word. He gently stirred the sugar in his teacup while the spoon chimed against the ceramic. He had an odd desire to tell her about following his wife, seeing her with the man, running a hundred scenarios through his mind that fit more with the Rachel he thought he knew.

It wasn't going to happen. He looked down at his plate to hide the flash of shame. Anna deserved better from him, but he wasn't going to show the tender spot that had been hurting so badly these last few weeks. And he wasn't going to risk losing the respect he had seen in her eyes. So he told the story that was true in its own way, but not the bare-bones truth that he was grappling with now. He gave her the processed version from the past. More than that was too much to risk.

"Anna, it wasn't always a pretty picture. This marriage is the second one for both me and Rachel. Hers was horrific; mine merely unwise, empty. I think I married for the wrong reasons the first time around. My first wife was a young guy's idea of perfection, which meant that the package was pretty and I didn't think much about what was inside. I was a driven, want-to-make-something-of-myself kind of guy. I left her alone too much, didn't share enough with her, and she got sick of it. She found someone else—kind of wish she had waited until we were divorced!" He shrugged in a self-deprecating way.

"But I went on to find Rachel, who was the girl of my dreams. Although she had been badly hurt by her first marriage, that shared experience brought us closer together. But Rachel has staying power, like I do, and she joined me in building a business rather than fight it. We made it happen together, which brought us together even more." He paused and then asked, "What kind of work do you do?"

"I'm a freelance editor, which is nice because it gives me a lot of flexibility. If I need to do something during the day, like take a class, I can work later at night," Anna replied.

"What about Dan, if I'm not being too nosy?" Eli smiled, trying to get back to solid ground.

"Dan has his own business, too. He's a painter—houses, not pictures. He's very good at what he does and stays busy nearly every day. We do okay, but no retirement plans in the immediate future, although that sounds heavenly," Anna said with only the barest trace of envy.

Her words triggered a touch of defensiveness in Eli. A lot of his friends kidded him about living the life of leisure and being semiretired at age fifty-five. So his words were a bit more brittle than he wanted them to be when he replied, "We worked like dogs for a lot of years, put off vacations, put off fun, mortgaged our house a couple of times in preparation for this day. It wasn't an easy road."

Anna felt chastised. "I'm sorry. I know it couldn't have been easy."

Now it was Eli's turn to feel regretful about his reaction. "Anna, I'm sorry. I didn't mean to sound defensive. Rachel and I both have family members who forget the hard years and end up making us feel guilty about how things are now. And, if the truth be told, I feel kind of guilty myself about having leisure time now, too. After all, a lot of people work really, really hard and can't retire when they're seventy! I'm sorry. That was my stuff," he said ruefully.

As Anna stirred the sugar in her own tea, she watched Eli in near amazement. Images of Dan's defensiveness and her own defensiveness flew rapidly through her mind. How did this guy get it all together?

"That's okay. Here's a totally tangential thought. When I took my Reiki certificate home after the initiation, I noticed that your full name is Elijah. It sounds very biblical. Is your family religious? I mean, a particular religion…"

"My parents are both gone. They weren't particularly religious, but my dad liked stories of all kinds, including stories from the Bible, and he liked the name. I have a brother, David, who lives back east. It's just the two of us now. Do you know about the prophet Elijah?" Eli asked, not wanting to assume Anna didn't know her Bible.

"I know he's from the Old Testament," Anna said, trying to remember what she had learned as a child in Sunday school.

"That's right. He was an Old Testament prophet and he killed a bunch of people in the name of God, which I could do without. He was one of two mortals from the Bible who ascended into Heaven alive rather than dying and going about things in the normal way," he said, his voice slightly mocking. "Enoch was the other. The killing aside, it's kind of cool because I am very interested in Ascension work."

Anna didn't know what that was exactly, but she thought it was time to get home. It was starting to get late, and she wondered if Dan was back from dinner with his sponsor. She did have one last thing that she wanted to ask Eli.

"I'd like to know what Ascension work is, but let's save that for another day. I'm having fun, but I'd better get moving or Dan will wonder where I am. I couldn't reach him when I tried calling earlier," Anna replied. She hesitated. "Can I ask you a question?"

"Sure," Eli said, looking intently into Anna's eyes.

"For about the last six months, I've been feeling that I would like to work with someone, a teacher, on spiritual issues. Would you… would you have any interest in working together like that? I mean, it's okay if you don't want to; I don't want to put you in an awkward situation. You don't have to answer now. Maybe think about it…" Anna trailed off.

She had been rambling to cover up her discomfort in asking for his help. She had learned early on that "help" rarely came from other people. It was usually better to do it yourself than to rely on others and be disappointed. But something inside of her thought this guy might be trustworthy. She had been thinking about it since she felt the floor buckle when Eli did the initiation. He held a lot of power.

Eli stared at her for a long moment while Anna sat frozen, waiting. "Anna, I am humbled to be asked, and I would be honored to share what I know with you. I have to warn you: I'm no guru. But a lot of people have helped me on this spiritual journey, and working together will honor their kindness. I would like to work with you. Very much."

"Thank you," she said simply. She felt more lighthearted than she had in years.

With that, they paid for their meals and got into their respective cars. Eli rolled down his window and called out to Anna.

"Let's both think about what that will look like and talk more about it next week. And feel free to e-mail me."

Her eyes crinkled to tiny slits from the grin on her face. She agreed and pulled out of the parking lot.

Eli sat in the car, thinking for a moment before he headed home. While he had given short-term classes and done some spiritual work with friends such as Cheryl, he had never taken on a longer-term student. He liked her. Anna. He realized with a start that he hadn't considered Rachel. What would she think about it? He wouldn't keep it a secret. Neither did he want to rock the boat of their marriage any more than it already was.

He felt troubled and angry. *I want my old life back.*

Eli sighed. Rachel was supportive of his spiritual endeavors but definitely not interested in pursuing them. She had been raised in a fundamentalist household that was a bad mixture of religion, judgment, and deceit. It had soured her on everything spiritual, and Eli knew she would have to find her own path. He couldn't force it. He understood her reaction, but sometimes he longed for a partner to share the spiritual journey.

Rachel had been his partner in every other way. He mentally berated himself. What they shared should be enough, was enough. But if he were honest with himself, he knew that he had an empty space in his heart. That emptiness had prompted his search to know his wife again. And look where that had gotten him. And continuing down that path of self-honesty, he knew the emptiness would make him vulnerable if he worked with Anna.

He wished he had the courage to ask Rachel what was going on. Despite seeing her embrace another man, part of his intuition said there was something else going on. More going on than a simple affair.

Did he want to try to save his marriage or let it go?

Another feeling rolled across him like clouds blocking the sun. *Am I good enough to do this? Do I know enough? I have so much work of my own that I haven't faced.* He wondered if he was a fraud. And took a cleansing breath as he glanced back at the restaurant where he and Anna had eaten.

He would have to be very, very careful. But for this moment in time, he allowed himself to feel a great joy in working with another soul and prayed that he could be of service to her without destroying something precious to him.

~

Dan wasn't home when Anna walked into the house that evening. She tried calling him again, but it went straight to voice mail. She decided to put it out of her mind. She wanted to enjoy thinking about her conversation with Eli without the heaviness of life interfering.

During the ride home, she had found herself chatting with Eli as if he were beside her in the car. She felt his presence acutely. Anna wondered if Eli was doing the same thing, continuing their conversation in his mind. The connection felt comforting; she felt touched that he wanted to work with her, and a lump formed in her throat.

Dan sometimes called Anna his prison guard. Anna didn't want that role; she wanted a partner. As time had gone on, she had become lonely. There was an emptiness that came from having to protect herself from Dan's addiction. She realized that if she wasn't careful, she could begin to depend upon someone like Eli.

Be honest, Anna. Not someone like Eli, but Eli himself.

Finding herself wanting to continue the connection and despite her concern about becoming dependent, she settled in front of the computer.

Just a quick note.

Subject: Working Together
I didn't realize how much I wanted you to say yes about working together until I found myself tearing up on the way home.

These simple words on a page can't communicate enough, but it's kind of like this:

When I was a kid, my mom and I would take long walks. Sometimes on our evening walks, the setting sun would be partially hidden by a cloud, but the rays would stream around it, outlining the cloud in shimmering gold, pink, and light blue.

We would stand still in awe. And my mom would say, "Anna, that's what hope looks like."

—Anna

As Anna clicked the Send button, Dan walked in the front door.

"Are you still working?" he said, a bit too loudly. "I thought you'd be in bed by now."

"I'm almost done. How was dinner and your meeting?"

Dan went to Alcoholics Anonymous several times a week and often had dinner with his sponsor.

"It was fine. Everyone said to say hi," Dan replied, heading toward the bedroom. "You going to bed now?"

A second before she replied, Anna saw that Eli had already responded to her e-mail. "I'll be there in a few minutes."

"Okay. I'm going to turn out the light and hit the sack. I'm exhausted."

"Okay," Anna murmured, her attention already on Eli's message.

Re: Working Together
You have a way with words, Anna. That was beautiful. But remember, as I said before, I'm no guru. Just a guy on the spiritual path who has had the chance to study some things.

Oh, I wanted to tell you that I met with Hannah a month ago to seek her advice about something. She told me I should prepare myself for teaching others, that it was time.

Your Guides and Teachers must have been having lunch with my Guides and Teachers!
Eli

Anna smiled as she wrote one last note to Eli before shutting down the computer.

Re: Re: Working Together
I didn't pick you for what you know (although my Guides and Teachers said that you know everything that you need to know, at least as far as my stuff is concerned), but for who you are.

A wise man who loves his family and friends. Balanced. Whole.

You honor the promises you make to Spirit. Show integrity on a lot of levels.

"They" picked you, actually. When our Guides were lunching and plotting, they probably had big smiles on their faces.
Anna

As Anna quietly brushed her teeth and got ready for bed, she decided she would talk to Dan some other time about working with Eli. She wanted to figure out how to word it. It didn't escape her notice that neither their home nor their marriage was big enough to hold two people with secrets.

CHAPTER 16

THE NEXT MORNING ANNA SAT on her favorite chair, feet resting on the sill of the dining room window. Light glinted from the early morning dew and ice on the bare branches. Their glimmer reminded her of the mystical side of the mundane world.

> Normal. Magical.
> Ordinary. Sublime.

She stifled a yawn. If these dreams didn't stop soon, she was going to spend most of her daytime hours walking around in a dream!
Sighed.
With soft eyes she stared outside again, collecting her thoughts. Anna had just finished a long conversation with Eli in her head, but she finally wrote:

> Subject: Brave New World
> Hi, Eli.
> I have a question, and I need a little help. Things are accelerating so quickly with changes of consciousness and such. I don't want to be afraid of it because I don't want to slow anything down.

Eli, when you have made a jump from one way of being in life to another way—a higher way—is there anything you do specifically to integrate the new way of being?
Signed,
Freaking out in Saint Louis

Later that night, Eli's e-mail showed up. Anna opened it eagerly to see what he had to say.

Re: Brave New World
Hello You,
Integration can be a bear.
When I make a shift in consciousness, I use this process. I think of my old way of thinking about something, or my old behavior, and compare it to my new one or the one I want to have.
This becomes a recalibration point.
The next step is to integrate this new perspective into my subconscious through checking my thoughts and being mindful. Prayer is one key for me. I give thanks and list out what I'm grateful for. This is still more reinforcement.
Then comes the big test.
For me, it happens in my dream work, which I have practiced diligently for years. I sleep for one-third of my life; I might as well use it for something useful. :-) We need to discuss this at length, but in short, here is what I'm doing.

To check to see if my new insights are integrated into my subconscious (the big actor in my dreams), I "ask" for a dream that will test whether I've grown and reached a higher state of consciousness. Or not.

If I dream in accordance with the values of my new self, the integration into my subconscious was successful.

If not, I make note of it and stress that aspect in my waking thoughts, affirmations, behavior, and prayers. The cycle continues until progress is made. Then, when the time is right, a new integrated level of consciousness graciously presents itself, and I give thanks and work on the next.

I'm sending you Reiki. When others assist me, it really helps! You've tapped into a deep and profound area, one that would do us a lot of good to talk through.

Eli

Anna read and reread Eli's note. It was mind boggling. Who could control what he or she was dreaming? Yes, she definitely wanted to talk about this way of doing things. Was there some way she could learn this and figure out what her dream meant? Or at least remember more of it?

She could hardly wait until the next class.

Until then, she would sit at the computer to edit the book she had been assigned the previous day. For the next four hours, she pored over her work and then decided it was time to stop for a while. Her eyes were gritty from lack of sleep and staring at the computer, and she was afraid she would miss something important in her editing.

Drained from the detailed work, Anna decided to do something she rarely did. She walked into the bedroom to take an afternoon nap. Before crawling onto her side of the bed, Anna pulled the curtains shut. It was as dark as night in the room now.

It felt cozy snuggling into the flannel sheets and pulling the comforter up to her chin at this stolen moment in time. Normally she didn't want to miss a minute of daytime waking life, but right now she could barely keep her eyes open. It seemed like a good idea to catch up on sleep before doing any more editing. Dan was working, and she had the house to herself. Then she remembered something as she was falling asleep.

A friend had given her a clear quartz crystal a week or so ago, and Anna had started sleeping with it by her bedside. The crystal felt very powerful and seemed to radiate healing energy. For some reason, she thought that it might stop the dreams and help her feel a little less stressed at night. She decided to put the crystal under her pillow while she took her nap.

So, reaching over to her nightstand, Anna grabbed the crystal. It felt warm in her hand. She tucked it under the pillow and fell asleep almost immediately.

An insistent light glowed through Anna's closed eyelids, and she struggled to open them. So very tired.

Three beings stood by her bedside. She should have been afraid, but she was curious and excited as exhaustion drained away. Three balls of light, cylindrical and elongated, gazed at her peacefully, their forms blurred and indefinite. Light streamed forth in every direction. While she could see individual beings, they also merged in a golden ball of light. Licking flames of blue, pink, and yellow stretched upward, disappeared, and reappeared to reach upward again. Their energy lit the room in a comforting yet exhilarating glow, and Anna knew they were there to heal her and bring knowledge.

You are about to receive... echoed in her mind. She realized that these were angels, her celestial Guides and Teachers.

Without words they instructed her to take the clear quartz from under her pillow, hold it, and then tap the crown of her head with the crystal. She did as they instructed.

"You are opening the door." As she tapped on her crown, there was a small explosion of energy and a flash of golden color.

They urged her to tap the crystal at her brow and her throat, with the same resulting explosion of light and energy. Then her heart, followed by a golden-sand explosion of color once again. Her belly, same thing. A total of seven points were tapped along the front of her body.

Without sound, Anna received their messages. "You will need to do more work on your heart, to detoxify the shame your heart carries. We want you to feel the lightness and the light."

They continued. "When you see the ant carrying the bit of food, you do not question 'What did he do? What is his secret shame?' You only see the ant carrying the food. The same is true with us. The cause of your shame has as little meaning to us as what the ant has experienced has to you. We only care that you are blocked, that there is an obstacle to remove, that you are in pain. But what happened has no real meaning. It carries no charge of good or bad. It just happened."

Anna had a very strong urge to put the crystal in her left hand and do more work on her heart. She began tapping. They nodded their approval. "Work with your heart, and it will become translucent." A memory of sunlight streaming through the stained-glass windows of her hometown church flashed through her mind. Translucence.

"It doesn't matter why the bad stuff happened. Transmute it and let it go. You will be a clear transmission of the energy.

Remember the Magician, the Snake, the Healer. Release all toxins. The cells need to release old patterns and belief systems. Let the light settle into you."

So very often Anna felt she carried the weight of the world within her own body, the weight of other people's woes. She thought of this when they said, "You are the Magician's wand, not a receptacle. Let the pain flow through you, including the pain of your uncle, your mother, your father, your husband. Theirs is not your pain. You were the keeper of their pain, but that is no longer useful. Be the Wand, a clear channel. Your body has to catch up with the work we did. Let it detox. After that, you will *Remember.*"

Anna slept for two hours. When she awakened, the vision was still clear in her mind, unlike her reoccurring dream, which disappeared quickly. She switched on the bedside light and picked up the pen and tablet that lay on her nightstand.

Remember every word, she told herself as she scribbled her experience into the notebook. The last sentence she wrote was "Ask Eli about the Magician's Wand and the Snake. What does it mean?"

CHAPTER 17

Re: A Visit from Them
Anna,
You are going through rapid and fundamental changes, and a visitation of this nature shows it. We have much to discuss after our class on Saturday. Until then, see if you can find a Native American interpretation of the Snake. It is very common in most Native American traditions to relate to the essence of different animals, birds, insects, etc. and draw that essence within ourselves to gain greater personal power, strength, and understanding. I think you will find the Snake to be a very important piece of your puzzle.

There is great symbolism associated with the Magician and his Wand from the tarot cards and from the Tree of Life. I will bring some of that information with me on Saturday, but check out the Magician's wand if you can before then. His wand is shaped the same on both ends. This is so the divine current can flow through it, not be held in it—just as the current should flow through you, not be held within you.

Oh, and remind me that we need to have a conversation about recapitulation.

Dorothy, I don't think we're in Kansas anymore.

Eli

~

Re: Re: A Visit from Them
Eli,
Thank you for telling me about the Magician. That description of the Wand is exactly what they were talking about—don't be a vessel (don't hold the pain of others within me), but let it flow through. I need to keep remembering the Wand. It is the same principle as Reiki—let it flow through us, like the divine current.

Here is what I found out about the snake. It's about taking something bad and transmuting or changing it into something good. Taking the poison of what happens to us and using it to become whole. There's a lot of creativity associated with the snake.

Not only aren't we in Kansas, we might never remember how to get back again!

Anna

ANNA SAT AT HER COMPUTER and thought about the interconnectedness of all of these things. Part of her wondered if she had dreamed the visit from her Guides and Teachers. It was hard to know what was "real" in the intangible world. She decided she would travel this mystical path until she had a reason not to. Until then, magic sounded pretty good to her.

This line of thinking led to Eli. Something odd was going on between them. She could feel his presence, and it seemed as if she could tell when he was awake or asleep. Each morning when she awoke, he was immediately in her thoughts. She talked to him throughout the day and evening as if he had taken up residence in her mind. He was the silent observer of her every thought and action. His e-mails were pleasant and insightful, but she couldn't imagine he thought about her every waking and sleeping hour. Her mind said she was crazy; her heart gave a different story.

It didn't feel like a crush or an infatuation, she mused, but it had to be. Why would she think about him that much if it weren't? He seemed very happily married. Of course, outside observers might think that Anna was happily married, too.

She stopped. Where did that come from? She was happy, wasn't she? Dan was a great guy. The worry about his drinking took its toll, but he was the ideal partner without that.

Where did that come from?

Frowning, Anna remembered a story a friend had told her. This friend also thought she was happily married, but her husband had ended up cheating on her. In despair, the woman went to see her priest and asked whether she should stay in the marriage or not. The priest told her to imagine a nice bowl of chocolate pudding and think about how good it would taste. Then he told her to imagine that someone put a tiny drop of poop in that chocolate pudding. Would she still want to eat it? Trust was like that. The loss of a little bit took its toll.

The woman ended up leaving her husband. Two percent poop was too much for her. Anna wondered if two percent alcohol and the sneaking around that came with it was too much for her, too.

She tried to convince herself that this running conversation with Eli was actually enhancing her marriage, not detracting from it. She and Dan had begun connecting more and having interesting conversations. Dan was sharing what had happened during his day, his thoughts and ideas, and continued to ask questions about the classes that Anna was taking at Awakenings. It felt as if things were going better than they ever had.

But Eli. She could tell him anything. She thought she could even tell him about the running conversations they had in her head without freaking him out. And there was one thing she did want to tell him that she hadn't told anyone: what had happened with her uncle. One day, when it was the right time.

CHAPTER 18

"So WHAT FREQUENCY DO WE vibrate at?" Lu asked, half seriously.

Dan looked at her across the table. "I can't believe you asked me that. Not you, too!"

He was quiet for a moment. "I don't know what frequency, but I do know this whole thing is so weird. I feel like I can tell you anything. We've known each other for what…three weeks? Maybe that's what Anna's talking about when she says that people vibrate at different frequencies. I'm totally in love with Anna, Lu, but neither of us can really talk about what's on our minds. I filter it, and I think she does, too. I don't do that with you. There's no editing between what I think and what I say to you. I don't try to make anything sound better. Hell, I don't try to make myself sound better."

It was lunchtime, and they had both finished their first drink. As Lu poured their second, she said, "What's also weird is that most people would think we're having an affair. But what we have together is better than an affair. For one thing, there's no guilt!"

Dan started coughing as he choked on his drink. "That's what I'm talking about! We can say anything to each other! And you're right. This is the best friendship I've had since I was ten years old." He raised his glass in a silent toast.

"Speaking of frequencies, the other thing Anna was talking about from her Tree of Life class has to do with connection. She thinks a big part of life here on earth is learning about how to return to God, where there is no separateness, no aloneness, no loneliness. Everyone is part of God." Dan was quiet for a moment, and Lu waited to hear the point he was trying to make. "Maybe when we resonate closely with someone, like you and I do, when we're on the same frequency with someone, it's a little piece of heaven on earth. Maybe that's the closest we can get to feeling one with another person on earth."

"That's deep," Lu replied. "I feel that way about you, too. Where does Anna get this stuff? It's weird, yet it kind of makes sense. But, you know, I wouldn't have had a clue what she's talking about if I hadn't met you and felt this way with you."

Dan nodded. He understood.

"I love my husband. He's a good guy, and he really loves me. People think I'm with him because of the money, since he's older than me. It's not the money, Dan; it's the safety. I feel like bad stuff won't happen if he's here. He keeps the bogeyman away," she said, trying to lighten things up. "But, whatever 'frequency' really means…I'm not on the same one with him. I love him, we make love, and it's good. We go places together. Sit and eat breakfast and dinner together. I couldn't stand it if something happened to him. We occupy the same space, but we're in different places. If that makes sense."

"Total sense. I know exactly what you mean."

They sat in companionable silence, each lost in his or her own thoughts.

After a while, Dan sighed. "Well, Lu. I'd better get back to work. I'd much rather sit here and talk to you, but I'm already behind schedule, so I'd better get at it."

"Wish I could help you, but I think Rich would notice a difference," Lu joked.

Dan laughed and then stood and strolled to the sink. He carefully washed his glass, dried it, and put it in the cupboard.

"Someone trained you very well," Lu said, smiling.

"I trained myself. And it's more about being a 'good alcoholic' than it is about cleaning up after myself," he said wryly. "Leave no evidence." He rested his hand on her shoulder for a moment.

Lu reached up and patted his hand. "I know. But thanks for thinking about it."

He nodded, glad she couldn't see the stark sadness in his eyes as he headed back to work. Later, when Dan looked back on things, he realized it was at that moment that something changed for him.

CHAPTER 19

∼

CLASS HAD GONE VERY WELL. While the Tree of Life material was complex, Anna was starting to put it together and understand more. She was really looking forward to the after-class dinner with Eli to discuss her visitation or dream. There was so much to learn. Talking about it was exhilarating. Eli felt like an electrical outlet, and their words were the cord that plugged into the outlet. From that connection came illumination.

"Want to leave your car here? Let's drive together to the restaurant, and then I'll drive you back afterward. Is that okay?" Eli suggested as he opened the door for Anna.

"That sounds good." She smiled and settled into the passenger seat of his car.

At the Chinese buffet, they carefully ladled the first round of food onto gleaming white plates. The waitress had directed them toward a window seat, where their coats were neatly hung on the chairs next to them. Anna was so looking forward to this get-together. Eli's eyes were smiling as he settled into his chair.

"I think you had a true visitation from your Guides and Teachers," Eli said immediately. "What a great gift."

Anna nodded, eyes shining.

Eli stopped for a moment and stared at Anna. He hadn't realized how pretty she was. It was the smile. Anna was around his age—early fifties, he assumed. He hadn't paid much attention to her looks, and she tended to downplay whatever attributes she had. Her standard "uniform" was blue jeans and a navy T-shirt. Sneakers. Brown coat with a faux fur collar. Her light-brown hair had silver highlights. Glasses.

Just your average middle-aged woman. But at this moment, she looked lovely. There was a glow inside her; a lamp from within had been lit since he had seen her last week. He wondered if it was the healing her Celestial Guides had brought to her and concluded it had to be.

He took a deep breath and asked, "What was your takeaway from their visit?"

"I think they were healing things that had happened to me a long time ago, detoxing the ugly stuff. I wonder if our experiences, good and bad, leave an energy trace or something in our bodies. I think they did the healing so I could be clearer, better able to hear and interpret their messages. Does that sound weird?" Anna asked hesitantly.

He smiled. "What can be weirder than the path we travel, experiencing the mystical undercurrents in our everyday lives? You never need to worry about weird with me, okay? In our world, not thinking about the underlying meanings, the divine messages—well, *that's* weird!"

Anna smiled and thought for a moment before she continued. "Eli, what did you want to tell me about recapitulation? I looked it up, and the definition is 'to summarize,' but what does it mean in the context of the visitation?"

"Think about it this way. Our goal on Earth is to see beyond the illusion, beyond our limited perception, beyond what happens in our everyday world. If we truly 'see,' we can truly know life beyond how we are socialized to perceive it. On one level, what if we could see each other as energy?" Eli said.

"If we see the whole world as energy, we can see the energy signatures of each person, animal, plant, and so on. What you explained about experiences leaving a trace in our body, I absolutely believe that. It's beautiful that they are clearing much of that from you and are continuing to work with you on your heart."

"Yes." Anna's voice caught a moment.

Eli gazed at the waitress pouring water at the next table and couldn't seem to look away. He paused for a second and then said softly, "Your heart feels like an ocean of tears to me."

Where did that come from? He made himself stop. *Too dangerous,* he realized when he saw the startled look in Anna's eyes.

After a mental shake, he continued with his original train of thought. "'Seeing' allows us to determine the essence of everything. It is the first step toward a new way of thinking about our experiences on earth and looking past the illusion of the stories we've told ourselves.

"One particular spiritual tradition defines recapitulation as looking at every aspect of one's life, first in summary form, and then moment by moment. The goal is not to beat yourself up, but to understand your life. And then to change what is unbalanced or doesn't serve you." Eli gazed out the window for a moment, thinking or perhaps remembering. He didn't share what was on his mind but continued with his train of thought.

"Recapitulation is an important part of ridding ourselves of the filters we've developed over our lives. Our experiences affect our way of perceiving. What happens if we remove those filters? We learn to see very clearly. Maybe even see that we are not separate beings at all.

"Some therapists call those filters 'schemas.' Schemas are belief systems we form early in our lives. They are our interpretation of the things that happened to us and the things we did. We begin to make our interpretation of life events become our reality. We go through life acting 'as if' that is truth."

He took a deep breath and exhaled. Anna felt his breath gently brush her fingers. It made her feel…aware. She brought her mind back to the conversation as Eli told a story.

"Let's take an example that happened to my son when he was four years old. Rachel and I were busy in the house, and Tim was running around. He climbed on a cabinet, and it fell over, pinning him beneath it. We both rushed to lift the furniture, pulled him out, and smothered him with hugs and kisses because we were so grateful he was okay.

"Now, as he looks back and remembers the cabinet falling on him, whether consciously or subconsciously, he could remember the incident in very different ways. Twenty years later he could be telling his therapist that no one was ever there for him. In fact, his parents were so negligent that he was nearly killed when a cabinet fell on him!

"Or he could go through his life feeling like there will always be love and support when he's having a difficult time. He can remember the hugs we gave him rather than our absence. Either schema will influence his whole lifetime and define him, if he lets it. Recapitulation is looking back over those defining moments and clearly seeing the stories it forms in our minds. And deciding we no longer have to believe them if our personal illusions no longer serve us."

"Well," Anna said, "I guess it's recapitulation time. How do I go about that?"

"Brave girl. Therapists, ministers, best friends, books, classes, workshops, audio tapes, to name a few, I guess," Eli said.

"What about spiritual teachers?" she asked, looking at Eli.

"Anna, I have to warn you, I'm no—"

Anna cut him off. "Guru?" she supplied.

Eli grinned. "No guru." He sobered. "And no therapist. Do you think it's more of a therapist kind of thing?"

"I've seen a therapist, and it helps. I would like to see what we can do together, if you feel comfortable enough doing that. I think my stuff is 'soul sickness,'" she said, making air quotes.

Eli leaned back in his chair. Logic wrestled with a desire to help.

"Here's what I feel I can do without overstepping my abilities or training. I can be a listening presence for you. I can't give advice or even offer much about my thoughts. I can be a presence for you as you capture the learning from what happened. I know from the conversations we've had already that you can do that. Once you have found the true meaning beyond the illusion, I might be able to reflect on that with you. How does that sound?"

"Your presence would be a great gift. Thank you." Anna smiled and nodded her appreciation. "When can we start?" she said, and then hastily added, "Not to be pushy!"

It wasn't until Eli took a deep cleansing breath that he realized he'd been holding it. He felt instantly relaxed and mostly comfortable with the outcome. It worried him that he had never done this type of activity with his own teacher and mentor. He still wasn't sure if he was wandering into the wrong territory, but he decided to trust his gut and see where this led.

"Anna, I should be getting back home now. Rachel and I are going out later, but Rachel is spending the day with a friend of hers on Tuesday. Would you want to get together for lunch and talk then?"

They agreed on the time and place, and Eli dropped Anna off at her car in the parking lot at Awakenings. As she walked away, she suddenly remembered that Eli worked through dreams at night.

"Wait, Eli!" she cried out.

He stopped.

"Next week, can you also tell me how to do the dream work? I'll tell you more about it later, but I have a dream that's driving me crazy, and I would like to understand what's going on."

"Absolutely," he said as he smiled and buckled up his seatbelt.

As Eli drove home, he wondered what he would tell Rachel. Some other woman wants to tell me about her life? Dangerous territory all around. He prayed for wisdom, insight, and the gift of discernment. And tried not to be intensely curious about what she would tell him.

CHAPTER 20

Subject: Recapitulation—My first marriage and a dream
Hi Eli,

I thought it might be easier if I e-mailed you the background of what I want to talk about on Tuesday, and then I can discuss it when we see each other. Thank you again for doing this.

A lot of things happened before my first marriage, but I'd like to start the recapitulation there. I never really understood why I couldn't stay married to my first husband, who was a wonderful guy. I believe it influenced how long I waited before I married Dan and why I chose Dan, but I never really understood what happened. So let's start there.

This is really a long description of a dream I had when I was twenty-two years old, but the story starts a few years earlier.

I graduated from high school, and everyone expected I would go off to college. I was dating Gabe, my neighbor up the street. We lived in a blue-collar neighborhood. My dad was an unskilled laborer who worked in factories and warehouses. Gabe's dad was a laborer at a cookie factory, where he worked most of his life. Almost everyone I knew worked in a factory.

Gabe's mom was very intelligent, and she had higher dreams for Gabe, who was extremely gifted. He applied to Princeton University and got a full scholarship. By the time I graduated from high school, he was finishing his sophomore year at Princeton.

I loved learning, but I didn't like going to school, so I was trying to decide whether I should go to college or take time off. All of my teachers said, "Don't waste your mind. Go to college." For some reason, I was resistant. Gabe and I talked about it, and he asked me to move to Princeton and live with him and sit in on classes there to see if I liked college. I couldn't take them for credit, but I could still keep learning. And we loved each other, so I said yes.

It was a rough summer. No one liked the idea of the two of us living together. I hadn't even turned eighteen yet—"living in sin, wasting your mind; get married like a decent girl." Lots of opinions and emotion.

The day before we were scheduled to leave for Princeton, the pastor of my parents' church finally heard about the ruckus. He came over to our house and for the next four hours told me I was going straight to hell. I said I didn't think it was a sin, but if it was and I was going to hell, then so be it.

My dad was sitting with us in the living room, white faced and nervous. He didn't like what the minister was saying, but the blue-collar tradition is to "listen to those who know better." My mom couldn't take it after the second hour and went into the kitchen to wring her hands and pray.

When We Remembered

By the end of hour four, my mom stood up, came into the living room, and told the minister it was time to go; he had done his best, but go. Now.

After he left, my dad stood and put his arms around me. He looked into my eyes and said quietly, "Anna, I don't care what the minister says. You're still my little girl." And then he broke down and cried. And with that, my dad accomplished what four hours of interrogation, months of conversations with disappointed teachers, raging ministers, and threats of hell could not. I got married a few months later.

And turned a beautiful, loving relationship into a prison. This prison was in my mind. I wasn't ready. Gabe was, and is, a good and wonderful person. He didn't do anything wrong. I wasn't wired for it, I guess. I didn't want to hurt him by leaving the marriage, and I couldn't stand to stay. I cried for four years.

Then I had a dream. Gabe and my parents' dog were standing in the backyard of my parents' home. I was standing outside the fence watching them. A beautiful butterfly came by. It was large, and the wings were blue and indigo and violet. I held up my finger, and the butterfly landed on it and waved its beautiful wings at me. The colors were rich and shimmering.

Then the butterfly flew into the yard. The dog jumped up and caught it and began ripping it apart. I kept screaming and begging Gabe, "Save it, save it." He stood still, and then he looked at me and said, "I'm sorry, I couldn't. The dog ate its eyes out."

Not long after that dream, Gabe found me crying. He said he loved me, he wanted it to work, and he kept hoping it would. But it had been four years, and I was no happier, and he worried for my life.

So he let me go. I moved out the next day and began a new journey into some of the happiest years of my life. The guilt about hurting Gabe stayed with me for many years. I think it was why I didn't remarry for a long time. I never wanted to hurt someone that much again, and I never wanted to risk feeling trapped.

I know that marriage is an incredible journey with another soul. Just not then, and the "then" turned out to influence the "thens that came after."

Ten years to the day we had married, Gabe and I ended up in our hometown at the same time, visiting our parents for the Christmas holidays. He was remarried to a great woman, and I was remarried to my own soul. He asked if he could come to my house and visit with me and my parents, so of course I said yes.

He brought a present. It was jewelry, a pin—a beautiful butterfly with blue and violet wings. I still have it and keep it on my altar.

Sometimes the highest love lets go for the sake and the soul of the beloved.

That was my dream.

Anna

CHAPTER 21

Eli wondered if it was possible to have a heart attack from the thought of telling Rachel about his work with Anna. He could feel the anxiety in his chest, and he was actually perspiring.
Pitiful.

And amazing. This might be an indicator that I'm doing something wrong. Or thinking something wrong. Or that Rachel is too jealous. Or that I should have told Rachel sooner. Or that I'm traveling into the wrong territory. In any case, I need to come clean.

He grimaced. *Shit. And fuck.*

He kept going back and forth in his thoughts. He had wanted to teach someone who was interested in the spiritual path, and he felt as if he had been handed the perfect student. Anna was intensely interested, she invested the time, and she was constructively introspective. *Nothing wrong there.*

Next, he should have cleared it with Rachel before he agreed to work with Anna. Which made him feel a little bit resentful, but he understood that if the situation were reversed, he would have wanted to know. Because now it felt as if he had a secret, and he didn't want to have one. *Okay, that's one thing I did wrong,* he realized.

Next, was his thinking about Anna wrong? It was strange. He thought about her a lot, couldn't wait to tell her things or hear from her. Felt her with him throughout the day and noticed the companionship was nice.

It's the conversations I have with her in my mind.

Okay, that can't be good, but I don't think about sex with her... although he did think that it would be fun to go on a hike with her. Rachel used to like hiking when they were younger, but she hadn't enjoyed it for a long time. Why did he think about hiking with Anna? *What the hell is wrong with me?*

When Eli and Rachel used to go hiking, it was a great time to enjoy nature, be with each other, and talk together. Nature was the closest she came to be interested in the divine, so it was a nice way to meet some of his need to talk and connect on a deeper level.

And then he had an epiphany. He couldn't believe he hadn't let himself see it before. He was lonely. He was lonely most of all for his wife. Not exactly the woman that Rachel had become, but the woman she had been in the early years, before the business became successful.

During the years they struggled, he and Rachel had worked side by side. When the kids arrived, they set up toys at work and worked the same way with the kids. Eli realized things were starting to change when they began to make serious money, about ten years ago.

Rachel began to spend less time with Eli and more time shopping. Her closets were overflowing with really nice, quite expensive outfits. These days she dressed like a million bucks and made sure her hair, nails, and toes were perfect. And it was around this time that Rachel quit hiking. He remembered she thought it made her too sweaty.

And it was a couple of years later that making love became too sweaty, too. She loved him; he loved her. They held hands and were affectionate with each other. But he couldn't remember when they had made love last. Six months ago? A year?

Eli remembered the incredible passion they had shared. Then, eventually, they got into a rut about making love. And then, sadly, they got into a different rut—the one where they had stopped making love. With a rush of emotion, he realized this put him at an even greater risk with Anna. Not from sexual desire, but from emptiness.

No wonder I don't know who the hell my wife is. Why I'm so pitiful that I follow her around to find out who I'm married to. I need to work on my marriage. But first I have to get over this hurdle of telling Rachel about teaching Anna...shit. And then I have to ask her who the man at the food pantry is. And why he held her when she cried.

~

And so it was with dread that Eli sat down with Rachel after dinner and told her that he wanted to chat about something. Rachel looked worried and asked, hesitantly and a bit defensively, "What's it about?"

"Rachel, you are always incredibly supportive of my spiritual work and have been for a long time. You don't fuss when I take classes at Awakenings even though it means I'm gone more often. I know it isn't easy, having friends there, but I try really hard to keep you informed of what I'm doing and who I'm seeing so you don't have greater cause to worry," said Eli, leading up to the real topic.

"Okay..." Rachel said, now looking confused.

"One of the things I've been wanting to do is to take on a spiritual student. I loved working with my own mentor, and I've always wanted to pay back that favor."

"Did you find someone?" she asked, looking relieved.

That's odd. But he decided not to think about that right now.

"I did. Someone asked me, and I said yes, but I realized I should have asked you first. Not because it will take that much time away from us. I can fit meetings in when you're with friends. But because it's a woman. I guess I would have preferred working with a man so it wouldn't cause any trouble between us, but it didn't turn out that way. I will let you know whenever I'm meeting with her and introduce you, if you would like. She is married also, if that helps at all." Eli was starting to ramble and forced himself to stop talking.

"A woman?" she said, looking glazed. "Who?"

"The woman you asked about from the Tree of Life class, and who I told you about when I did the Reiki initiation a few weeks ago at Cheryl's house. Anna."

"Why you, Eli? What does she want from you? I might trust you, but I don't know her or know if I can trust her. Why would she ask a man to be her teacher? That's just asking for trouble."

She stared at Eli and waited a moment before she asked, "Have you already said yes?"

"I'm sorry that I didn't discuss it with you first, Rachel. I did tell her yes." Eli looked miserable. "Would you like to get together for dinner with her and her husband so we can both get to know them better?"

Rachel looked at him. "You'd be okay with that?"

"Of course, honey. It might make it easier all around," he said, a wave of hope washing through him.

"Look, I'm glad you told me. I wish I'd had some input, but I think it would help to get to know her and her husband..." Rachel's voice trailed off.

"I arranged to have a meeting with her at lunch on Tuesday. Since you were going to drive to the winery with Jeanne on Tuesday anyway, I thought it would be a good day for me to meet with her. That way it won't interfere with our time together. But how about I see if she and her husband can have dinner with us on Saturday after class?" Eli asked.

"Okay. For the record, I don't like it or think it's a good idea to work with a woman. There's a reason ministers and priests have affairs with parishioners. It's got to be..." Rachel struggled to find the right word. "Intimate," she concluded.

"True, but not intimate like you and I are intimate." Eli smiled gently at Rachel. "And speaking of intimate, I don't think I've been wining and dining you enough lately. I've missed you." Eli looked almost embarrassed. "You know, in that intimate way. I think we need to go on a date," he said, looking at Rachel to gauge her reaction.

Body relaxed, she looked at him archly and said, "Well, ask me out and see what happens."

"How about Friday night, just you and me?" To which Rachel readily agreed.

The whole thing had gone much better than Eli had thought, although he wasn't naïve enough to believe this would be the end of the discussion with Rachel.

~

"Frank?" Rachel said quietly into her cell phone.

"Rachel, is that you? Is everything okay?" His voice was deep with concern.

"I hate to ask you something on such short notice, but is there any chance I could come to your office tomorrow? Things are happening at home that I don't understand. If I don't get this mess straightened out, we're going to lose everything," she whispered.

"Come at nine. I'll make time for you, Rachel. You know that. But has Eli found out?"

"For now we're okay." Her voice caught, but the next words poured out with no forethought. "God, I'm scared!"

Frank spoke reassuringly. "Come in, and we'll figure out how to handle it immediately."

"I hate involving you in this," Rachel said with regret.

"You're worth it. We'll figure it out together. Goodnight, and try to get some sleep."

After murmuring good-bye, she slowly ended the call. *He's going to leave me.*

꘏

That night as Eli got ready for bed, he remembered Anna asking him how he integrated new ways of thinking and the response he had given her. He decided tonight might be a good time to do "new thought" integration and dream work.

As he prayed, he asked God to give him a test in his dreams to make sure he wasn't thinking incorrectly about Anna. The dream was the test. If he passed, he was home free. If he didn't, he needed to work more on his marriage.

His prayer was followed by another realization. Regardless of how the dream turned out, he still needed to do more work on his marriage. Anna had already gotten the chance to be his teacher. She had taught him that he was lonelier than he had realized and more vulnerable than he had thought. He needed to reconnect with Rachel. For their sake, and for the sake of the others who depended on him.

CHAPTER 22

"I'm sorry I'm late," Eli said to Anna on Tuesday as he moved quickly toward the table where she was already seated. His hair was ruffled from the wind and his brisk pace. She noticed that he had gotten a haircut recently.

"You look nice," Eli said. In addition to her usual attire of jeans and sneakers, Anna was wearing a simple light-blue blouse that contrasted nicely with her skin and hair. He realized he had never seen her in anything other than her dark-blue T-shirts.

"I felt festive," Anna said, joking while she also blushed. She knew she wasn't a fashion plate, but she did occasionally wish she had a little more interest in clothing. Nancy had recently dragged her, kicking and screaming, shopping for clothing.

Her husband had noticed her outfit this morning and had also complimented her. Two compliments for a simple blouse was reinforcement that she had been letting herself get too much in a rut with her appearance. Anna sighed. It might be another six months before she could face shopping again.

They looked at the menu and gave their choices when the waitress came for the order.

"Okay, that's done," Eli said. "I read your e-mail. It was very helpful having the background."

Anna lit up with a smile. "And there's more!" she exclaimed. "What else happened?" Eli asked. Things were moving very fast.

Anna said excitedly, "Something amazing happened this morning." She slowed down. "First of all, that day I wrote you about my dream and my marriage, I cried for hours afterward." Eli leaned back in his chair.

She worried he didn't feel equipped to handle too much emotion and tears, but Anna continued. "I'm not sure what it was all about, but some of it was a loss of innocence, and grief, and a little bit of, what's wrong with me?" Anna said ruefully.

Eli leaned forward again, resting his arms on the table as he nodded compassionately.

She continued. "But that amount of tears about the past made me realize it must still be affecting me, and therefore I needed to explore it and get to the root issue. I've thought about it for years, but I decided to call Gabe and ask him what he remembered about our marriage and the breakup."

She went on to explain. "Gabe and I still chat every couple of years, but we haven't talked about our marriage for a long time. When I asked him if he would mind talking about what happened in our marriage, he first said, 'Look, everything worked out okay. Don't spend time in the past; look to the future.'"

Eli nodded. He understood the need for recapitulation, but he personally didn't like dwelling on the past either.

"I told him I felt this part of the past was affecting my future and asked if he would help me remember some stuff. Then he said something that had *never* entered my mind. He said it was his fault. I never thought of the failure of our marriage as being his fault. I thought it was my mine because I somehow couldn't handle marriage. He told me he didn't think he had treated me as an equal," Anna said, eyebrows raised.

"When I asked for clarification, he said it was because he couldn't handle my emotions or the way I saw things from a psychological or spiritual standpoint, and he reminded me that he wasn't very nice about it."

Anna continued to relay what Gabe had told her. "He said there was nothing for me to feel guilty about. I hadn't hurt him on purpose. I had only needed to find myself.

"Eli, he said something in a voice so sweet, it made me cry. He said, 'It wasn't a crime, Anna. You have a right to be happy, don't you?'" Anna teared up, remembering how Gabe had granted her the ability to forgive herself. Eli refrained from reaching across the table to touch her hand. He instinctively knew she had to unfold the story without his interference, even his well-meant interference.

"When I started crying all over again, Gabe pretended to be mad at me and growled on the phone, and then he told me again to let the past be gone." She smiled in happiness and relief at how Gabe had turned around the conversation as well as her beliefs about the past.

"I decided to tell him about the dream of the butterfly and reminded him how he had given me a butterfly pin on our would-be tenth anniversary. Now comes the most important part.

"Gabe said to me, 'Anna, I think that was a coincidence. There's a jewelry store near my house, and I like butterflies.'" She paused and stared at Eli. He stared back, his eyes nearly as wide open as hers.

"And for the first time, I 'remembered' why I had to leave—no magic was ever allowed. Logic was important. And he was two years older than me, incredibly brilliant, and so he must be right. But I still needed magic," Anna said. Her smile was big, and her eyes were filled with peace.

Eli thought she was done, but she had more to add.

"And guess what happened. I had a change of consciousness. It's not that I couldn't do marriage. I can't do a life without magic. It's the same reason I can't work for certain companies, why I pick the friends I do, why I love Awakenings."

Anna was almost finished, but she added, "I'm so grateful that Gabe filled in the parts I couldn't or wouldn't allow myself to remember. I can literally feel the healing of my emotional, mental, and spiritual self from my conversation. I mean *literally*. I've wrestled with this for years."

Eli and Anna stared at each other. Eli reached across the table now and covered her hand with his. He said only one word. "Beautiful."

His heart swelled with pride on her behalf. She had been so brave to dig until she found the gem at the core of the boulder.

They realized simultaneously that neither had taken a bite of food. Both reached for their forks and applied themselves diligently to their meals for a few minutes. They would occasionally look at each other with a smile and nod in appreciation for the day, the food, the conversation, and Anna's new state of mind.

After the plates had been removed by the waitress, Eli said to Anna, "I have something I want to show you."

He laid a tarot card on the table facing Anna. It was the card of the Magician, raising his wand to the heavens. The magician stood in a garden, wearing a white tunic and a red cloak. There was a table in front of him, and a sword and other objects lay on the table.

"Anna, what you are learning about your life is pure magic, and you are the Magician," Eli said with a huge grin on his face.

He continued. "Let's think about the Tree of Life for a minute and its metaphorical meaning. The top of the tree represents the infinite source of the divine. The energetic tsunami of the divine pours 'down'. At this level there is no form or physical world, and there is no duality or separateness. There is only energy and the oneness of all. Remember this part from the class?" Eli asked.

"Uh-huh," Anna murmured, focused on what he was saying.

"Good. Now let's move to the Magician. On the Tree of Life, the Magician resides right before God's creation takes physical form. The Magician is a manifester, a creator, and an alchemist. He is the conductor of the divine current. He takes 'potential' or potential energy and directs and harnesses it." Eli smiled at Anna, whose brow was wrinkled in concentration.

"I brought the tarot card along so I could show you what I am describing. It's easier if you can see it rather than just hear it. Tarot cards in general got a bad rap along the way because people think of them as fortune-telling cards. Let's think about them as Jungian psychology in a deck of cards! A roadmap to understanding our humanity, and it is rich in symbols. So it's worth knowing. I want to show you the symbolism of the Magician, since you are the Magician." Eli took a deep breath.

"Look at the card. The Magician stands in a garden. His right hand holds the wand, which points to Heaven, and the finger of his left hand points toward earth. He has created a beautiful space—the garden. This represents the things we can manifest." Anna nodded her understanding.

Eli focused on the card in front of them and said, "As I mentioned in my e-mail, his upraised wand is the same at both ends, showing that the current flows through it from God without being changed or diminished. The Magician has raised himself to a level of clear intent. He created the garden, and his whole reality, through his intention. Just as God created everything through his intention." Eli stopped for a moment.

Anna replied, "I had no idea all of that was present in this one picture." She took a sip of water as she concentrated on and assimilated the information.

"Incredible, isn't it? And even more amazing is that every one of the tarot cards holds an equal amount of symbolism. Take it a step further—every religion and spiritual practice in the world has its own special symbols and hidden meanings. Each religion, each path, in its own way, is trying to explain, What is God? How did we get here? How are we supposed to act on this earth? and How can we get back to God?"

They looked at each other, mirrored expressions of awe.

"The Tree of Life is *one* of those roadmaps, isn't it?" Anna speculated.

"Yes, a very useful one because it can be interpreted in so many ways," he replied, nodding.

Eli placed the Magician card off to the side. "I want to explain something that I think is important. It has to do with frequencies. Every sacred system we know about, as well as every healing system, uses a hierarchy or steps or levels of some sort. In the Christian faith, angels are on the hierarchy above humans. They vibrate at a different frequency. They are 'more divine'—closer to God, so to speak. We humans try to raise our frequency through prayer and ritual so we can be in contact with the angels. Being in contact raises our frequency even more.

"With me so far?" he asked in a gentle voice.

Anna nodded. She didn't want to make a sound, wanted him to continue.

He smiled and went on. "The same idea of frequencies is present in the Tree of Life. Each higher step up the tree represents some aspect or attribute of God. Every level is equally important, but the frequency is finer the higher up the tree we go. It becomes closer to the pure essence of God," Eli said.

"Our goal is to 'connect' at each step, to learn its frequency *and its lesson*. When we integrate that into our being, when we 'become that vibration temporarily,' we increase our own frequency. We do those kinds of practices to build up our 'soul muscle,'" he said, laughing quietly.

"What I really mean to say is what we do here on earth builds up the home we are creating elsewhere. That home is the evolution of our soul we are investing in.

"Anna, our life is about doing what's hard now so we can learn what we came to earth to learn and then go home. That's our job," Eli said, staring at Anna meaningfully.

"Okay..." Anna said slowly. It felt as if he was giving her a secret message, but she didn't understand the secret. She waited for Eli to say more about what he meant.

Instead he said, "Getting back to you as the Magician, let's remove time. Time is a construct used on earth to understand and experience cause and effect. Cause and effect is the same as karma.

"So if we remove time, you'll see that you have already reached the top of the Tree of Life—you have already ascended, you are already the Magician, vibrating at that frequency.

"What you are doing now is 're-membering your self.' I mean that as two words—your *self*. You are healing your *self*, putting your 'self' or 'selves' back together. You are re-*membering* who you really are. You said it yourself when we started lunch. I'm paraphrasing, but it was something like, 'I can *literally* feel my emotional, mental, and spiritual bodies healing,'" Eli said.

With golden-brown eyes bright, Eli said, "Of course you can't live without magic in your life, Anna. You are already the Magician, and magic is your creative power."

She stared at him and then at the table. Her eyes pooled with tears, and she bit her lip to keep them from spilling over.

A man who had known her for not quite two months saw in her what no one had noticed in her previous fifty years. And held up the mirror so she could see it too.

At that moment, Anna prayed. She prayed that even if someday she lost her memory as her mother had, she would never, ever forget this moment. That she would never forget that she, like everyone else, came from the sacred. And, in some timeless way, she had already made it home, even now as she continued to search.

Eli gave Anna a moment to collect herself and then suggested it was time to leave. "I think we've given each other enough to think about today," he said.

As he stepped off the curb into the parking lot, Eli stopped and turned to Anna. "Oh, I almost forgot something. This Saturday after class, instead of you and me having dinner, do you mind bringing Dan along, and I'll bring Rachel so everyone can get to know each other? I told Rachel about our work together, and she thought that it would be nice to get together. I know it's our work time, but it would just be this once." Eli waited, holding his breath.

"Oh, that's a good idea. Let me ask Dan if he can come. I assume it's okay, but sometimes he gets together with people on Saturdays around that time. But I think he would like to meet you and Rachel, too. I'll e-mail you as soon as I know," Anna said, smiling.

She moved toward him and held out her arms. "Eli. Thank you," she said, enfolding him in a hug. "Thank you so much."

He held her and for a moment leaned forward, nuzzling his chin against the crown of her head. It was an oddly comforting gesture.

"See you Saturday," he said before letting her go. He watched to make sure she got safely into her car and on the road before he pulled out of the parking lot.

As he drove home, he prayed to do the best for Anna, for Rachel, and for himself. Anna was learning so much, so quickly. Their conversations kept him on his toes and reinforced lessons that he needed to learn, too. Watching her grow helped him grow. And the companionship helped him to re-member also.

He hadn't passed the dream test about Anna. There was still work to be done, but conversations such as the one today were an inspiration, not a temptation.

"Focus, Eli, and stay in the right frequency," he told himself aloud. The good to be achieved was worth the risk. He prayed that he was right.

Anna felt as if she were flying home; she was so keyed up from her conversation with Eli. He had opened a door she had sensed was there but could never seem to access. Over time, she had quit trying. Until now.

She thought it would be useless to work in this frame of mind, but she did sit down to look at e-mails. Two were about work, and one was from Gabe. She had written a thank-you e-mail after their call that morning, and he was responding. She eagerly opened it to see if he had further insights.

> Re: Thank you
> Anna,
> I'm happy I could help. It's always a revelation to find out how different people's recollections of shared experiences are and how many are remembered vividly by one person who was there and forgotten entirely by another. The human mind/brain is not a video camera. The untrustworthiness of memory is one reason I don't dwell on the past. I may not even recall events correctly, and the significance of them changes over time anyway.
> On the subject of respect, a permanent problem with us as a couple was my attitude about anything spiritual or psychological. I was more hostile toward religion than I am now.
> You could probably hear in my voice my surprise that you placed any significance in your butterfly dream. To me, dreams are essentially meaningless, and I can't remember any of them right now.
> So interests and subjects of importance to you would always have been objects of derision for me. That had to be pretty corrosive. I'm not saying I was a bad guy (maybe an asshole), but we both knew there was a part of your life I could never share—and didn't want to.
> Love, Gabe

Anna closed the e-mail and sat quietly thinking for a while. Gabe was right; it had all turned out for the best. Gabe was married to a great woman now and had two wonderful daughters. It had broken Anna's heart to hurt him by wanting to get out of the marriage, and she had never given herself the forgiveness that Gabe had granted a long time ago. He had set her physically free years ago, but today she allowed herself to be emotionally free.

After Gabe, she had waited a long time to get involved with someone special. There had been plenty of encounters but no real relationships. Even with Dan, she always felt she loved him more than he loved her. It was safer that way. She never wanted to hurt another person the way she had Gabe.

And the one niggling thought she had but didn't want to look at was whether she had continued to punish herself by living without magic in her second marriage. She decided to wrestle with other recapitulation issues before she tackled that one.

She had to figure out how to tell Dan about Eli. She had put off telling him, but now she had to. Dinner on Saturday. What was Rachel like? Well, there was one mystery that was going to be solved soon.

CHAPTER 23

Saturday was overcast in the morning, but the sky had brightened by class time. The temperature had reverted to winter weather once again. Rachel dropped Eli off at Awakenings and and then drove back to pick him up for dinner. Anna had driven separately, and Dan was going to meet her at the restaurant. They had chosen the Chinese buffet based on convenience and accommodation of the various taste needs and desires. Plans and schedules in the mundane world had been worked out; every one of the cast of characters felt nervous and out of sorts.

Class was over, and it was show time.

Anna peeked into the Lexus when Rachel stopped in front of the store to get Eli. She waved to Rachel, who smiled and waved back.

Anna heard Rachel tell Eli to save the introductions for the restaurant.

"I'm blocking cars here." Impatience tinged her voice.

Eli looked at the car behind them and then rolled down the window. "Anna, we'll see you at the restaurant in a minute, okay?" He spoke over the noise of the traffic nearby.

"Great! See you then!" Anna shouted back, nearly at her own car by that time.

Eli sighed as he rolled up the window.

"What?" Rachel asked. Eli looked over at her quizzically. You sighed," she explained.

"I'm good. Just hoping this will be comfortable. It feels a little forced, but I think it'll be fine once everyone is there and we start talking," he said.

Rachel nodded. The only sign of tension was a tightening of her mouth. After twenty-five years together, Eli recognized the nuances of her expressions. He realized she had taken his comment as a criticism of her and reached across the seat and laid his hand on her thigh.

"This is a good idea. It'll work out," Eli said, following the script. That was the other thing that twenty-five years of marriage had taught him.

He didn't notice Rachel rolling her eyes. She knew the script as well as he did.

Then silence for the remaining five-minute drive to the restaurant.

~

When Rachel and Eli walked into the restaurant, he immediately saw a tall, slender man with light-brown hair standing self-consciously by the door.

"Dan?" Eli asked hesitantly.

"Hi. Eli?" the man asked in a stronger voice than Eli would have expected from his first impression.

"Hi, Dan. Anna is behind us and should be here in a minute. This is Rachel, my wife." Dan reached out to shake Eli's and then Rachel's hand. Anna stepped through the door at that moment, and a gust of cold air swept through the entrance.

"Well, winter is definitely back," Anna said, shivering.

The three of them turned to her and smiled, and Dan quickly reached to help her with her coat.

Coats were laid on a nearby chair as the waitress seated them in a booth near the window. Eli and Rachel sat side by side, with Anna across from Eli.

"Well, shall we get our food first?" Rachel suggested, and they all rose to make their way to the buffet.

Back at the table, conversation was slow. Dan made a valiant attempt to keep it flowing. "Anna says you own your own business," he said, looking at Rachel.

"Yes, we help other businesses with their technology and telecommunications needs. Eli and I are mostly retired, and our two children are running the show now. We've been very fortunate," Rachel replied, her voice proud. Dan refrained from asking more.

While Eli often had a similar response to that question, he flushed with embarrassment now, looking down to cover his discomfort.

Dan tried again. Looking at his wife's teacher, which had been a shock in itself, he asked, "So Eli. Anna says you take a lot of classes at Awakenings. What kinds of things are you interested in?"

Rachel answered first. "It's probably easier to list what he hasn't taken. It seems like he's had them all and is working on round two!" She said it pleasantly, and there didn't seem to be an undertone.

Anna watched Eli's wife with curiosity. She was tall, a good six inches taller than she was, and slender. Rachel's hair was blond and highlighted, and it softly framed her face. The brown wool slacks that Anna had noticed earlier fit Rachel well and emphasized the length of her legs. A tan silk blouse and soft brown sweater put the outfit together nicely, and her brown boots were stylish.

A depressing thought went through Anna's mind. Looking at the perfection of Rachel, she began to discount her intuition that she and Eli had a special connection. She must have been overthinking there was some mystical reason they had met. After all, Eli sat there smiling with his lovely wife. They had worked to build a successful business together. It looked as if his hand was resting gently on her leg under the table. Suddenly she felt let down, and she tried to focus more on the conversation. She wished she hadn't felt obligated to meet Rachel.

Probably better this way. Better to nip the infatuation thing right in the bud. Anna looked more closely at Eli. A thought suddenly came to her. Had he done this so she wouldn't get too attached to him? That thought made her angry at him, until she got a grip and realized these were only thoughts floating through her mind. An interpretation of something she didn't have the answer to. Something that went into the same box labeled "is Eli as connected to Anna as she is to him?" That box was starting to get a little too full for comfort.

As Eli talked about some of the things he was interested in, he mentioned that Rachel and both of their kids had attended the class on death and dying. This was the same one that Anna had canceled in order to be with her mom at the end of her mother's life. She mentally rejoined the conversation.

"Why did you go to that class?" she asked. It seemed like an odd choice.

Rachel glanced at Anna, registering the flyaway brown hair, neat but uninspired blouse and jeans, and self-conscious tension.

Rachel immediately began to feel better about Eli's work with Anna.

She replied before Eli could speak. "Well, my husband asked us to, and he asks for so little that the kids and I thought that we should. None of us are particularly interested in the same things Eli is, but we knew it was important to him." She smiled at Eli, who looked oddly pleased. Anna, on the other hand, felt a tug of loyalty to Eli and was irrationally irritated at Rachel's tone of voice.

Dan asked the question that Anna had wanted to ask. "Why that class, Eli?" He seemed genuinely curious.

"The long or the short answer?" Eli responded, smiling.

"Oh, let's go with the long answer. We have time!" Dan laughed.

"Okay, I'll try to go fast enough to keep this from getting boring. The moment of death is one of the most important moments for the mystic, or spiritual seeker. Just like Anna had her Reiki initiation, death is a key initiation. If done 'right,'" Eli said, making quote marks with his fingers, "a person can bypass the wheel of karma, quit coming back to earth, and join directly with God."

He continued. "That class explains how death works and how to be successful at the time of death."

Turning to smile at Rachel, Eli said, "I wanted both her and the kids to know how to do that when their time came, and how to be of help to me when my time came."

Dan looked at Eli as he if had dropped to Earth from another planet. "Well, now you've piqued my curiosity," he said. "What does one do to grab that moment?"

Eli looked across the table at him as if he wanted to know whether Dan meant it or not, but something in Dan's face told him to continue.

"The class explains death from two perspectives. One is what is happening inside the person, how and when the soul leaves the body. The second is how to prepare the external environment to allow the dying person peace and quiet so he or she can focus enough to make use of the moment." Eli looked at Anna's husband for confirmation to continue, and he read Dan's faint nod as a yes.

"The soul leaving the body is a big deal because at the time of death, there is an opportunity to join God directly, to stop incarnating and arrive 'home'—reunited with God. Being one with God isn't something our human brains can grasp, but the mystic catches glimpses of it during meditation. Meditation is like 'practicing' for this moment at death instead of letting it slip away."

Eli turned his attention away from the others for a moment and focused on Anna. "Remember when we talked about vibration and frequency the other day?" She nodded, and he continued. "We use this lifetime to practice connecting with higher frequencies, to gain different states of consciousness, and to connect with the divine the best we can through meditation, prayers, rituals, and so on. We do this to learn our life's lessons and to seek to merge with the light at death. In any case, we live the best life of service that we possibly can. We're building our home, and we want it to be beautiful."

Eli tilted his head slightly as he looked at Anna. "So when I'm on my deathbed, make sure you tell me to follow the light!" He smiled for a second and then seemed to freeze.

Rachel was staring at him with her mouth slightly open. Dan looked from Eli to Anna, expressionless. Anna looked as if she wanted to merge with the light that minute.

Eli had the grace not to backpedal. He acted as if nothing out of the ordinary had been said; he just turned toward Dan and explained more. "It is best if the person can die at home surrounded by loved ones. Try not to use medicine that renders the dying person unconscious. The room should be quiet except for the sound of murmured prayers or mantras that are in keeping with the dying person's faith belief. You are trying not to distract the person. They need to stay conscious and focus on merging with the light, while simultaneously going through the confusion of leaving the earth."

Dan thanked him, and everyone agreed it was time to get home at that point. Dan and Eli shook hands, as did Anna and Rachel. Eli and Anna waved good-bye.

Eli expected Rachel to erupt in the car on the way home. She was driving. He turned toward her and said quietly, "I'm sorry."

"For what?" she replied.

Eli looked at her. Rachel continued. "Dan seems like a nice guy, asking all those questions about something he obviously has no interest in. Anna seemed quiet. Is she always that quiet?"

"She seemed quieter than usual. Maybe she was nervous," Eli said.

"Maybe," Rachel murmured.

Eli knew better than to relax. This wasn't over yet with Rachel. Not to mention dealing with his own guilt.

Dan and Anna arrived home about the same time. Anna decided to handle it head on and asked, "What did you think of Eli and Rachel?"

"Rachel is nice. A little too perfect for my taste, but nice. Eli looks like a totally normal guy until he opens his mouth."

"Just because he has different beliefs doesn't mean he's not normal, Dan!" Anna replied defensively.

"I didn't mean it as an insult. I thought he was pretty cool, actually. He explained that stuff pretty well. I bet he's a good teacher. What did you think of them?" Dan asked.

"Oh. Okay. Sorry," Anna apologized, and then she said carefully, "I really like Eli. I've learned an amazing amount already. Rachel seems nice, too. I was feeling very dowdy sitting near her, but she seems…nice."

Dan added, "It's got to be rough on Eli."

"What?"

"Having a woman student. Wanting to work with her and juggling things with a wife who doesn't look too keen about it. It's obvious he is very earnest about the spiritual stuff." Anna blushed at his words.

"I think our Eli might be struggling a little," Dan concluded.

"What do you mean?" she managed to get the words out.

"You know. Sitting there with his hand on his wife's knee, but with his eyes on you the whole time." Dan looked at her with a serious expression. "It's okay; I'm cool with it. I trust you."

Anna stood, mouth open. He pulled her into his arms. "Let's take a shower, Anna. I think tonight's a good night for that rain check."

Dan turned out the lights in the living room as he guided Anna toward the back of the house.

CHAPTER 24

THE NEXT AFTERNOON ANNA WALKED up to the booth where Eli was seated, leaned over, gave him a quick hug, and then sat down across from him.

"It was nice meeting Rachel. Thank you for setting that up," she said.

"Dan is a really nice guy, too. He was very good natured to let me go on about theories of death and dying," Eli said, a little chagrined.

"Are you kidding? He never listens to things he isn't interested in, and he definitely doesn't keep asking questions. I think he actually liked it, which is strange because normally he's not that interested in my spiritual life," Anna said.

"Really?"

Eli brightened a little. Anna noticed with surprise that he was less self-assured than she had originally thought. It surprised her even more when she realized his uncertainty made her feel a little better about her own esteem problems. She shook her head.

"What?" Eli asked.

"Nothing. Just a fleeting moment of insanity."

Smiling, Eli watched her but said nothing more.

She felt better instantly and began to relax.

Eli leaned back in the booth, strong hands resting on the table, and seemed to relax also. "What's our topic of conversation today?"

"Recapitulation work," Anna said in nearly a whisper.

"Before we get started, do you know why you're going through this hard replay of your life, this thing we call recapitulation?" Eli asked. "The reason I ask is because pain without learning anything from it is just pain. I don't want you to go through pain for pain's sake. We need to make sure you use the lesson for healing, which you definitely did with your first marriage."

Anna said, "I think the recapitulation work is a way of going through the past and removing the 'charge' from it, the 'ouch.' If I can move past that, it seems like I can better move beyond the ego and beyond illusion."

"Exactly right," Eli said. "Let's have some lunch and talk more."

Despite her nervousness about the upcoming conversation, Anna found the soup and tuna salad to be delicious and enjoyed every bite. Eli looked as if he was relishing his meal, too. Shortly after they had finished, the waitress walked briskly to their table. She looked to be in her forties and had brown hair and a solicitous manner.

"Can I get you some dessert?" she asked with a smile on her face. "We have great pie here," she added temptingly.

"We're going to sit and talk for a while," Eli said. "No pie for me, but I would like a cup of hot tea." He glanced inquiringly at Anna.

"Same for me," she replied. "English Breakfast, if you have it."

Once the tea arrived, Anna stood and moved to the other side of the booth, next to Eli.

He slid over to give her more room.

"These booths are huge, and I don't want to yell this across the table," Anna said apologetically.

"About a month ago, I was cleaning out the attic and found letters from my uncle. My mother's brother. He was a gifted artist and musician, but he was also disturbed.

"I was going to say he was a pedophile, but it was more than that. No one was safe from him, and nothing was out of bounds for him sexually. Men, women, children, animals, his daughter. He was sick. On top of that, he combined his sexuality with his Christian religion. The damnation part was fascinating to him; it added a thrill to what he was doing," Anna said.

She took a sip of tea as she collected her thoughts, and then she glanced at her teacher.

Eli sat quietly in the booth. His body language and facial expression signaled intense concentration and focus on Anna's story. Even now that the topic was clearly a difficult one, Eli looked relaxed but intent.

"My uncle sent me these letters from the time I was fourteen until I left home to get married at age eighteen. I was shocked when I found that I had kept them. For want of better words, they were artistically written, subtle pornography.

"Before I get into the letters, I need to explain something. My uncle was nine years older than my mom. He used to babysit her. I think that he probably molested her, although she said she didn't remember that happening. She did remember a time when she was six years old that frightened her so badly, she lost the ability to speak. It was temporary, but it affected her strongly." Anna sighed.

"His bad behavior was so common in the family that when I told my mom he had touched me"—Anne looked at Eli meaningfully—"she said to steer clear of him and not to be alone with him. 'He's like that' was how she phrased it. I grew up thinking that his behavior was normal."

Anna couldn't bring herself to go into more detail yet.

She took another sip of tea and then added more sugar. As she stirred, the tinkling of the spoon against the ceramic cup and the murmur of background voices seemed so normal. Normal and comforting.

"What I didn't realize was how much I internalized the shame of what happened."

Anna looked down at her hands, which she couldn't seem to stop rubbing together. She rested them on the table, embarrassed about her anxiousness.

As Eli sat and listened, she told him what her uncle had done, had said, had written. She told him about her father's funeral. Before today, only Anna knew all that had occurred. Now Eli knew. She was not alone with the memory.

From across the room, the waitress watched Anna and Eli. They were seated on the same side of the booth but angled toward one another.

"Bet you there's a story there," she said to herself.

As she stared at the man, the waitress wondered if a guy had ever listened to her that intently and what that would feel like. Her gaze turned toward Anna, speaking so quietly, her eyes downcast. Although the lady seemed cloaked in sadness, the waitress imagined she had a core of steel.

A survivor, like her.

The couple was in a world of their own, separate from the bustle and noise of the restaurant. An invisible boundary seemed to envelop them.

Lovers? the waitress wondered. Maybe, but if she had to guess, she would have guessed they had known each other from childhood.

When she saw the conversation had ended, she approached their table.

"Are you ready for the check now?" she asked gently.

Two sets of eyes gazed up at her, orienting themselves.

"I'll take it," the man said.

As the waitress moved away from the table, she was thinking, "That one's a keeper."

Eli followed Anna to her house for the second Reiki initiation. Cheryl was out of town, and they wanted to keep to the schedule as much as possible.

As he entered the front door of her cottage, he enjoyed the peacefulness of the living room. A large fireplace took up most of the south wall. Bookcases and stained-glass windows stood on either side of the fireplace. Bouquets of silk flowers in a palate of color added warmth.

"This is beautiful, Anna, really beautiful."

"Thanks," she replied, looking pleased. "My nest is important to me, especially since I both live and work here."

They set up the room to symbolize the elements of fire, air, water, and earth. Eli called it "creating sacred space." He completed a brief ritual to protect the space from lower energies.

"The second initiation," Eli explained, "focuses on the emotional and mental healing of Reiki. This initiation will help you personally with your own issues from the past, and it will allow you to be of service to others, too. Do you feel ready to begin?"

Anna said she was. As Eli called in the divine presence and began the initiation, Anna had the sense that the ritual was similar to the first one. The images that came to her were different, however. She did not see any past lives with Eli or others but experienced the downpouring of energy into the crown of her head. She felt every cell of her body glowing with an internal light.

As the initiation ended, Anna sat still and experienced that same sense of the Reiki settling into her being that she had felt the first time. She opened her eyes, and Eli smiled at her.

They began to chat briefly about the attunement. Anna was surprised that their experiences were so similar, but Eli merely smiled. After a few minutes, Anna said she wanted to show Eli something.

He waited in the living room. When she returned, Anna was holding the greeting cards and letters from her uncle, opened but still in the envelopes. They were yellowed. It had been over thirty years since they had reached their intended target. There was a pile of perhaps twenty envelopes. Despite being light in weight, they felt heavy in Anna's hands.

"I'm trying to figure out what to do with the letters," Anna said, her face shuttered. "It feels like I should do a ritual of some sort, a cleansing, but I don't know what kind of ritual to do. What do you think?"

"Anna, you could go many ways with this. Using fire and burning them is cathartic. Water is very cleansing if you have a stream or river nearby." Eli paused for a moment and thought. "I have a few more hours until I should get home. Would you want to perform a ritual now? On one hand, it might feel too close to your Reiki initiation, but on the other hand, the two rituals might work together for a strong emotional and mental healing. What feels right to you?"

"I think I would like you to be here and guide the ritual," Anna said, tearing up. She had prayed that he would participate. She didn't know if she could do it alone.

"Let's do something very simple. We have already created a sacred protected space, but for some reason I am being guided to close down this space and 're-create a protected space' for the next ritual. That makes sense to me." Anna nodded. It seemed right to her also, and he proceeded to do that.

"I think a simple burning of each card and letter in your fireplace would be a good ritual. What do you think of that?" Eli asked.

"Eli…" Anna hesitated a long time. "Would you be disgusted to read these cards before we burn them? It was real. It happened, but no one else knew. Could you bear sitting next to me? I feel like, like…I want acknowledgment that it happened. I'm sorry to ask…" Anna looked miserable.

"Of course, Anna. Let's sit on the couch together in front of your fireplace while we read them. First, can you light the fire in the fireplace?"

"Yes," she said and proceeded to do that. In a few minutes, the fire was crackling merrily, in contrast to the task in front of them. Warmth poured out to them as the logs occasionally exploded in a shower of sparks.

Anna set up a small table in front of the couch. When they had settled onto the couch, neither consciously noticed that Anna was pressed to Eli's side like a child to her parent after a terrifying nightmare.

The envelopes were stacked on the table in front of them, in order by date, with the oldest one on top. She pulled out the first card from the envelope. It was a sweet and simple drawing of a kitten playing with yarn. She opened the card so they could both read it silently together. In his highly artistic handwriting, her uncle had written, "Your precious visit to my home the other evening kept me awake throughout the night, dreaming of you. I marked the sacred spot on my rug where you sat and have touched it a hundred times. Dream of me as I dream of you."

"I was fourteen years old when he wrote this. My parents and I were visiting him and my aunt—his wife. My aunt, mom, and dad were sitting twelve feet away in the next room while he talked to me about having sex with a neighbor girl who was my age. I was sitting on the rug across from him so I wouldn't have to be next to him on the couch." Anna spoke in a flat voice, sitting motionless.

"I don't know why I didn't walk out of the room and go to my parents. I guess I thought it would be impolite," she said in the same monotone. Eli sat quietly, also motionless. As Anna reached for the next card, he returned the first card to its envelope and started a new pile.

They continued in this manner for a few minutes. Sometimes Anna commented about the message; sometimes not. Eli said nothing. At one point, she stared into the fire and addressed Eli. "Can you stand this? I hate to bring you into this ugliness." Her voice sounded hollow. She seemed removed from her body.

Eli said nothing but leaned his head against hers and nuzzled it comfortingly. As he sat straight again, Anna went on. They sat in this way for the next hour, until all of the envelopes were in Eli's pile and all of the cards had been read.

He carefully moved the table aside, picked up the pile of envelopes, and handed them to Anna. She knelt by the fireplace and fed each one to the fire. Eli knelt beside her as they silently watched the envelopes turn black and curled and then turn to ash. When it was complete, he held out his hand to assist her as she stood.

As they stood side by side, not touching, Eli murmured quietly, "What did the fifty-year-old woman learn from the letters that the child didn't know?"

Anna was still for a moment, and then she said quietly but without the flatness of voice, "The man cast a net over the child."

"Yes. What is a net, and what did it mean?" Eli asked.

"He created an illusion for the child, who believed it throughout her whole life. He wrote the cards as if she were a part of what happened, and she believed it. She thought she was bad and didn't deserve magic. And she created a life to validate that belief," she said, and then she turned to look at Eli.

Then, with certainty, Anna said, "That's what the illusion is, isn't it? It's not about whether there is really a table here or a wall there. It's about the belief systems we hold…"

Anna stopped, but Eli continued. "That hold us in place. For good or bad. Old belief systems," Eli murmured. "Your light was strong, even as a child. It brought the good and the bad flocking to you, but you had no one to protect you. Your poor mom was so caught in the web of denying what happened to her that she couldn't acknowledge it enough to protect you."

Anna was quiet for a moment, and then she responded. "She had to preserve the illusion that nothing had happened to her. If she saw it, she feared it would kill her. It had already made her mute, if only for a while. In keeping herself in the dark, she put me in danger, and put me in the dark, too.

"Eli, the more we fool ourselves, the greater the havoc we wreak in the world. It makes me wonder what my uncle was hiding from himself," Anna said.

"We can't know all of the stories, Anna, but we can know our own story. You are of the light. Find the way to let yourself be free. In our belief system, you chose to incarnate into a family with your mom and your uncle. Perhaps to learn about illusion. Thank God that you are here now, as your fifty-year-old self, learning about illusion. Free of the net. You can choose what you believe now."

Anna took a deep cleansing sigh. "Time for you to get home, Eli," she said, smiling. "Thank God for you."

As Eli drove, he thought about what had happened with Anna. He had tried to be the Magician's wand with her, letting the current flow through him, not taking on the pain. He felt the hot tears well up in his eyes, and his throat closed from suppressing the agony. He pulled to the side of the road.

There were adults on earth who believed their sexual or other needs were greater than a child's need to grow up whole. The pain that Eli felt in his heart overwhelmed him as the tears coursed down his face. He wanted to feel compassion for the screwed-up man who had lived his life making the world a worse place. And he would, eventually.

But all he could choke out at this moment was "God damn him; God damn him."

And his heart knew what his mind refused to see: it wasn't only Anna's uncle he cursed.

That night, after Dan had long gone to bed, Anna wrote her note to Eli. It had taken a while to get it exactly right. She wrote as if in a trance and then hit the Send button. She went to bed.

The next morning, Anna sat at her computer and reread what she had written the night before. She looked at the last paragraph. She reread it twenty times. She stared out of her dining room window. Looked back at the computer screen and slowly said, "Oh. My. God. What have I done?"

CHAPTER 25

Rachel woke up earlier than her usual hour and decided to clean out the garage. Eli had gone for a walk, and she figured he would help her when he got back. He wasn't much of a handyman, but he was in charge of the yard. She decided to save the yard tools for him and began going through boxes that had been stored in the garage for years. Kids' toys, books, old household items.

It made her tired to look at it, but she had given in to ignoring it for years. Today was the day. She had on her torn jeans, paint-stained T-shirt, and sneakers with the hole in them. It was a nice change to look a mess and not care about it. She laughed out loud. It felt good to work on a project she had put off and was finally completing.

"There you go. That's my self-help book on raising your self-esteem. Do something difficult and get it out of the way. Not to be confused with do something you hate every day. That creates the opposite of self-esteem," Rachel said out loud to herself. For some reason she was giddy, and it felt good.

"That sounds like a pretty good philosophy." Eli's voice came from the door to the house. She could hear him making hot tea in the microwave.

"Eli?" Rachel was surprised. "Are you back already?"

"Yeah," he replied. "I feel restless, but I don't know what I feel like doing," he said, poking his head into the garage.

"Hey, look at you, sexy!" Eli grinned.

"You think this is sexy?" she said back to him. "It has been too long if this outfit looks good!"

Rachel laughed, blushing a little. He often told her how nice she looked, but she liked the spontaneity of what he had said.

"How about you get your own sexy self out here and help me clean this garage?" she said.

Eli stared at her for a minute and then replied, "You know, that actually sounds like a good idea. Let me drink this tea, and I'll be right there."

After a while Eli stepped into the garage, shutting the door behind him. They went through boxes together, deciding what to keep, what to give away, and what to toss. They were both shocked to discover three hours had passed by the time they were finished.

Eli draped his sweaty arm over Rachel's shoulders. "I really miss working side by side with you. We're good, working together," he said, leaning over to kiss her cheek.

"Oh God, Eli. My cheek must taste like twenty years of dust!" she said, laughing. "You're going to have to brush your teeth."

"Come here, you," he said, holding her tighter against him. "When did I ever care about dust?" And he proceeded to kiss her more vigorously.

"I think we might need to take a shower." She looked at him longingly.

Eli stilled, searching her face to see if she was saying what he hoped she was saying. Whatever he saw caused his own face to brighten considerably.

"All right, Blue Eyes. Let me get you in the shower. I've got twenty years of dust to scrub off you, and it might take me a while," he said happily, directing them both toward the shower. He gave a deep sigh, but this time it was of contentment.

Two showers and one hour later, Rachel was clean for the second time that day and heading out the door. Eli was whistling on the patio, fixing the lawn mower. It was cold but sunny, and he was enjoying the outdoors while he could.

Every time they did make love, Rachel wondered why so much time passed before they did it again. This time she vowed that six months wouldn't go by. No way. She was thinking that another time tonight might set a good precedent.

With that happy thought in mind, she got into her car and slowly backed out of their very orderly garage. She decided to treat herself to a new outfit as a reward for tackling the early-morning project.

As she drove to the mall, she wondered why her grubby outfit this morning had been a turn-on for Eli. She worked very hard to make sure her hair, skin, nails—everything!—was perfect for her husband, but he barely seemed to notice. True, she'd get the perfunctory "You look nice" from him, but not the enthusiasm she had seen this morning.

She decided to call her best friend and ask her what she thought. Better yet, she'd ask her to come along shopping. Rachel made her call, her friend Ellen readily agreed, and they met at the galleria.

"Let's start off shopping and then sit and chat for a while," Rachel suggested.

"Fine by me," Ellen replied. She was not the shopping maven that Rachel was, but she did enjoy getting out every now and then.

After an hour of searching for the perfect outfit, Ellen had bought a new blouse for $30, and Rachel had spent $730 on a variety of clothes.

They headed to the restaurant and dropped into a booth, exhausted.

"I think I can treat myself to a blueberry muffin," Rachel announced.

Ellen looked at her suspiciously. "You know, Rachel, you have that look of a woman who got laid last night," Ellen said thoughtfully.

Rachel looked at her, startled. "Well, you are completely wrong. I most certainly did not get laid last night." Her eyes sparkled.

Ellen looked at her, waiting for the punch line.

"I got laid this morning!" she said with a big happy grin on her face.

"That's disgusting—still having sex with your husband after twenty-five years," Ellen said.

"Who said it was my husband?" Rachel teased back.

"Oh God, don't tell me you found somebody more perfect than Mr. Perfect himself!" Ellen said, knowing full well that Rachel would never cheat on Eli.

"Of course not!" she admitted. "I'd like to ask you something, though…"

Rachel explained the mystery of Eli's passion this morning. "Ellen, I was wearing a torn, paint-stained outfit that he thought looked great. I was disgustingly dirty after we cleaned the garage, and all Eli could say was that he had missed working alongside me like we did in the old days," Rachel said vigorously. "I'm confused. What was going on?"

Ellen looked at Rachel carefully for a few seconds. "When you say that you really want to know, do you mean you *really* want to know?"

"Didn't I just say that?" Rachel asked, more confused than ever.

"Yes, but many people think they want to know something but can't handle the answer. The answer to this one isn't simple, Rachel. So I'm going to ask again. Do you really want to know?"

"I don't know. If you put it like that, it sounds like something bad. So maybe I don't want to know." Rachel wrinkled her brow as she considered what Ellen was saying. "Okay, tell me."

"All right." Ellen thought for a minute. "Rachel, do you like me?"

"Of course. You're my best friend. Why would you ask that?"

"Okay," Ellen said, ignoring Rachel's question. "Why do you like me?"

Rachel sighed, not following where this was going but trying to be a good sport. "I like you because I've known you since high school. We know everything about each other, you don't judge me, and because…promise this won't hurt your feelings?" Rachel said hesitantly.

"Promise. It's okay. Keep going."

"Because you are so *you*! And you are so damn human!" Rachel finished with a flourish.

"Exactly." Ellen waited for the light to dawn. She sighed when darkness remained, then tried a new tactic. "Why did you spend seven hundred and thirty dollars today?"

"Because I needed a new outfit. We're going out next weekend," Rachel replied.

"You don't have any other clothes?" Ellen asked, knowing full well Rachel had two walk-in closets full of clothes.

"I wanted to look nice for Eli, since we're going out."

Ellen replied, "Torn jeans and paint stains seem to get you further."

Rachel glared at her oldest and best friend and then sighed. "Look, you remember how we grew up. We were the kids who kids laughed at. Do you remember that old-fashioned, ugly thing that kids used to say about having cooties?"

The light in Ellen's eyes dimmed briefly.

"Remember how they got 'cootie shots' if they had to touch us? Why? We were despised, Ellen. Not because we had it all, but because we had nothing." She tried to say the words lightly, but hurt tinged her voice, and her stomach churned from saying what had been left unsaid for forty years.

Rachel went on. "Eli had brains, and he made that company. He could have built that company without me, but I could've never built it without him. He's smarter than me, going to heaven sooner than me." She grinned at that one. Both she and Ellen joked good-naturedly about Eli's interest in metaphysics. "He's better looking than me, nicer than me, and people like him better than me." She paused. "All I have are looks and expensive outfits. I have to fake it every fucking day of my life."

Ellen reached across the table and took Rachel's hand. "All I'm saying, sweetheart, is that you got it backward. Eli loves you, and looking perfect doesn't bring a guy like him closer. It pushes him further away. You like me because I'm *real*. What you see is what you get. When you and Eli built that business, you were real. You got sweaty together. Your hair was messed up from pulling it out when the books wouldn't come out right. You were grubby from loving on little kids. You get my drift."

Ellen continued, softening her words. "You are real with me, Rachel. I love that about you. But I wonder how real you are with Eli. Because I would bet any money that he loved making love to your sweaty, dusty body this morning. And looking at your knee through the rip in your jeans. That's who Eli is. And you know it. So I'm going to tell you one more thing that might sting a little." Ellen stopped, as if asking for permission.

Rachel gave a quick nod.

Ellen continued. "You're not dressing up for your husband. You're dressing up for all those kids in school who made fun of you. You're locked into one big fuck you! to the world. And somewhere inside of Eli, he knows those people matter more to you than he does. But guess what? He loves you anyway, because he knows what's inside of you better than you do. And he waits around for it to come out every six months. I think he's as lonely as you are," Ellen finished.

Rachel's face seemed to crumple, just before the tears poured from her eyes. Ellen quickly gathered her friend's packages and hustled her to the car. She petted her hair and rocked her in her arms.

"It's okay, sweetheart. I'm so sorry, so sorry," Ellen murmured.

"I feel so embarrassed. I'm such a fool," Rachel hiccupped into Ellen's shoulder.

"No, love, you aren't. You still have that little abused kid inside you, and you think you have to dress her up. You're all grown up now, Rachel. They can't hurt you anymore, unless you let them. If you're spending seven hundred dollars for them, they're not worth it. Not even Eli is worth giving away your power. Worth comes because we decide to award it to ourselves. It's time for you, Rachel. Time to see that you survived them, and now you have to survive what you did to cope. You have to see there's a bright candle inside you. Look inside and you'll see it. Everyone else does when you take enough of a chance to show up as your naked self."

And with that, Ellen held her friend until Rachel could stand on her own again.

CHAPTER 26

RACHEL HAD HEADED OUT TO the mall, and Eli sat down contentedly at his computer after fixing the lawnmower. He stretched his arms high above his head and gave a prayer of thanks. What an amazing couple of days! He and Rachel had connected this morning on all levels, the way they used to. Anna had received emotional healing for old wounds. He had been able to sit with her in the high-frequency place he wanted to be, without lower-level thinking or desires. He wondered if crying in the car had provided a cathartic cleansing for him as well.

"Thank you, God," he said from his heart as he opened his e-mail.

He smiled. An e-mail from Anna that she had written late last night. He began to read:

Subject: A Loving Presence
I don't know what words to type after what happened today. I want to say something like "Thank you for my life." That, and "Thank you for being a loving presence on my soul's journey."

To be a Teacher is a sacred responsibility, you do it so well, Eli. You were right to listen to your Guides when they said, "It's time to teach." I'm glad I listened when They said, "It's time to find a Teacher."

Space had to be created on both sides, which was done ahead of time in preparation and in faith.

My job is to learn, grow, and give, so that the lessons are passed on and not lost. As others move through their own personal obstacles, they grow and give, too. It's beautiful to look at generations of Teachers across time.

I thought of one reason I'm glad about what happened with my uncle. I have lived a long time with a sense of shame, feeling deep within that I am a bad person. I don't feel a lot of guilt which is feeling bad about something one *does*, but I do feel shame, which is feeling bad about who one *is*.

Guilt can keep people out of trouble, so it has some usefulness. Shame only has one upside, as far as I can see—to connect on a fundamental level with others who live in shame. And to help them heal. You are the Loving Presence. I pray to be that someday, too.

I want to tell you something. It's about how much I love you—big, like the luminous sea. I always have, and I always will. I asked, and They said that you needed to hear it. And to tell you that They do too. Big time.

Eli read and reread Anna's e-mail. A loving presence to keep us grounded through the painful parts. That was a beautiful way to describe yesterday. His Teacher had been that for him, too. *We need a loving presence on our journey,* he thought. *It's essentially a journey we take alone. The companionship helps us to remember what the journey is about.*

He sighed at Anna's last paragraph. What frequency was it written at? He couldn't tell.

He sat quietly with his eyes closed for a moment, connecting with his Guides and Teachers. He prayed for understanding, and the answer settled into his mind very quickly. She had looked across time and space and had seen him. She had received a message at a very high vibration, and she had flowed him that message.

Not Anna. Anna's higher self. And not to Eli, but to the best of him also.

He opened his eyes. It had been a very wonderful couple of days.

CHAPTER 27

OCCASIONALLY ELI LIKED TO DELVE into the company books, check on customer satisfaction reports, analyze sales reports, and in general do the things he used to do when he ran their company full-time. So, bright and early on Friday morning, he decided to run a stat check on the business.

He left Rachel in bed asleep and headed into the office. Eli was surprised at how excited he was to dip back into things. The company had been his life for a long time, and when he handed over the reins, it was absolutely the right thing to do. He had been ready to let go of 24-7 performance pressure.

It was six o'clock, and Tim and Chris were usually at the office by seven. Eli knew he should tell the kids before he started mucking about in the business, but he had been feeling flat lately, marginalized. So while retirement was great, he needed to engage his brain in order to feel useful again.

Rachel rarely needed him for anything other than the odd job around the house. She was a very self-sufficient woman, and even though they could be spending a lot of time together in this semiretired state, they actually saw less of each other. Work had brought them together throughout the years, and the lack of that glue left them both circling around somewhat aimlessly. The other morning had been a good start to renewed closeness.

My mind might be fuzzy about remembering the Rachel I knew, but my body remembered immediately.

Eli no longer believed the man from the food pantry was Rachel's lover. He felt he could tell if she had been intimate with someone else. *Something's going on. I just don't know what it is. And I'm not sure I want to know.*

He turned his thoughts back to the business and his life.

The kids were competent to run things and didn't need him anymore, and his wife spent more time with her friends than with him. He didn't get to see many of his friends who were still in the work world.

Before he and Rachel had worked and played together the other morning, he had been feeling lost, except for one thing. Working with Anna had been a total joy. He could see the progress she was making, and although he tried to keep his own ego out of it, he felt pride not only in Anna but in himself. He was doing something good for another person. It felt exhilarating to be useful.

No wonder Rachel goes to the food pantry every week.

Eli also found satisfaction in his own spiritual work. He loved going to Awakenings, chatting with Hannah and the other people there. But what he missed was the piece that Anna was working on—integrating new learning with one's regular life.

When he had run the company with its fifty employees and many clients, something was always going on. Problems erupted and were solved. Clients got irritated and needed attention, employees and teams were developed, power struggles ensued.

Eli himself did a lot of work with mentors and within himself to be the best leader he could be. It was challenging and fun. It was great to take the spiritual lessons and apply them to the real world and to himself. That was true integration.

But these days Eli wasn't hitched to the wagon of his business. There was nothing that he *had* to take care of. No people problems, no technological challenges, no processes and procedures to figure out, no strategies to develop, no marketing plans to review. No wife to work late with as they shared a common goal. And no need to make love on the conference room floor because they couldn't wait to get home after those late nights together.

Which led to a different thought path. Eli was so grateful for the passion he and Rachel had shared the other day. It had given him hope. In fact, their lovemaking had fueled this renewed interest in the company. Creative energy. The energy of procreation. He hoped it could and would re-create their interest in each other.

But something had happened when Rachel had gone to the mall after their lovemaking. She came home quiet and withdrawn. When they kissed that night in bed, she melded her body against his, and they held each other tight. But instead of taking it to the next step, Rachel had gotten up and gone to the bathroom.

He thought he heard her crying, but when he knocked on the door and asked if she was okay, she said everything was fine. She had been a little distant since that morning. The contrast of the intimacy of the morning and the days following had reopened the well of loneliness. He felt emptier than he had before.

Sometimes it's better not to hope than to have hope crushed. He sighed while tapping his pen on the desktop.

He knew that a big part of him missed Rachel. And it hurt when he realized a part of him didn't.

This was who they had become. Flat, uninvolved. She read books; he read books. Just different books. She helped people; he helped people. Just different kinds of helping and different kinds of people. They both adored their kids. The basics were there, but neither put the time nor the attention into the friendship or the passion of their relationship. Almost by unspoken consent, they had gone on automatic pilot regarding "them." And put their passion, the best of themselves, into other parts of their lives.

Wednesday morning had been different, exciting, like a swelling wave. Which had again receded.

This was the inexorably sad swirl of his world now. Not even a swirl. Swirl implied energy and motion. Eli's life with Rachel and his business was at a standstill, like a longer-than-usual winter. The winter of the soul. That drop of spring had awakened him. He wanted spring to stay.

As he followed the trajectory of his thoughts, it scared him to realize that his mind was occupied more with Anna than with his wife. Anna's excitement, her discoveries, and his role in that. She was living in his mind. A lot. More than she should. Once he went through his paper work, he needed to figure out how to get her out of his brain. That wasn't the person he was or had ever been. He was not a man who thought of other women, and certainly not every waking hour.

As that last thought went through his mind, the revenue report he had been idly gazing at came into focus. Something wasn't right. These sales figures weren't the numbers Tim had reported at their last meeting.

There was a huge discrepancy for some reason. Eli felt his stomach lurch and his heart rate accelerate.

He quickly stood and closed his office door. Locked it. Returning to his brown leather chair, Eli sat almost gingerly. His eyes did not want to see what was on the paper in front of him; his brain did not want to understand. His breath quickened as he anxiously scanned the data, checking and rechecking dates and dollars.

What the hell had he done?

On the other side of town, Anna sat at her desk and worked on the new book. She was trying to keep her mind engaged on the job at hand when her heart began beating erratically. A thin layer of perspiration covered her brow and face. There was an empty space in her gut, and fear kicked in at full throttle.

Without thinking twice, Anna put her fingers to the keyboard and typed quickly and furiously.

Subject: What's wrong?
E
Are you all right? Something's not right.
A

She stabbed the Send button and sat staring intently at the inbox of her e-mail for sixty seconds. She didn't know why, but she felt he would see this e-mail and respond immediately.

There. A new message.

She clicked on it as Eli's name appeared.

Re: What's wrong?
Please send Reiki as soon as possible. Can't make class tomorrow. I'm sorry.
I am already missing our discussion.
More later…
E

CHAPTER 28

EARLY SATURDAY MORNING FOUND ANNA sitting with Nancy at McDonald's, chatting.
Finally Nancy huffed and said, "Tell me what's going on. You've checked that e-mail on your phone six times in six minutes, and your mind is a million miles away. What's going on? And no bullshit," Nancy said.
"Something's wrong with Eli, and I don't know what it is," Anna finally admitted.
Anna explained that she had had her second Reiki initiation on Tuesday and that she and Eli had done some healing work together. She didn't go into the healing ritual. It felt too personal. Anna did tell her what had happened early yesterday.
She continued. "The weird part is that I could tell something was wrong with him. I went into a panic attack, and I don't get panic attacks. I think I was experiencing his panic attack at the same time he was!"
"How did you know it was him?" Nancy asked, her curiosity piqued.
"I don't know how to explain this, because you won't believe me, but I feel like Eli inhabits my thoughts. I can feel the emotions he is feeling even when we're not together. I can feel when

he's thinking about me. What I don't know is whether he can feel me in his being. I mean, is it reciprocated, or am I only feeling him? Or am I making the whole thing up?" Anna looked miserable.

"Have you ever encountered something like this before?" Nancy asked.

"I know some people are empaths. They feel stuff from other people, like their emotions. Maybe their thoughts; I don't know. In the past I could pick up when my loved ones were very sick, like knowing that my aunt and my mom were dying. Same thing happened when my dad died. But never to this extent. It's weird. I really want to ask him if the same thing is happening to him, but I don't want to put it out there that much," Anna said, almost thinking aloud. "I don't want to connect at the wrong frequency."

Nancy looked confused. She didn't pursue it, but she summarized. "So you felt freaked out, wrote to him, and he actually *was* freaked out? That is so strange. You have an interesting connection to Eli. I keep coming back to the question, what is that about? Do you think the two of you got connected when he did that Reiki initiation and couldn't get unconnected?" Nancy mused.

"And when is the next initiation?" she asked suddenly.

"The third one is supposed to take place in three weeks. But I don't know what's happening on his end, so I don't know if he'll be able to get together," Anna said.

"The other thing that bothers me is this." Anna hesitated. "When I started at Awakenings, I wanted to learn the information, maybe meet some people who liked that kind of stuff, but mainly I wanted to learn."

She continued. "Then I met Eli, did the Reiki, and started working with him. He's not going to be at class today, and…I think it's going to feel lonely without him there. I...I really like learning with him. Hearing the same stuff in the class, and then talking about it and applying it—it's fun," Anna confessed. "But that sounds like such a codependent, wanting him to be there with me. And I already have that label by virtue of Dan being an alcoholic, even if he is in recovery. That makes me feel yucky." She exhaled a disgusted sigh.

"You know, Anna, I think you have a very high need to feel connected with other beings, human *and* animal. Actually *all* of nature. You like connection. You're a very loving person, and you need someplace to pour that love. It's kind of who you are. I don't think you should label it 'codependent' or anything else," Nancy said.

"And, I hate to say it, but you don't always get that sense of connection at home, even though Dan is doing better in that department," Nancy murmured.

Anna sighed. "I wonder what is happening to Eli."

"Do your woo-woo senses give you any indication of that?" Nancy asked, really curious.

"No, I feel his anxiety. But what I've been feeling since this morning is 'empty.' I think it means he's not thinking about me. His focus is elsewhere. But if that's what it really means, then it also means he thinks about me *a lot* otherwise. And that doesn't make sense. So I don't know if I can trust what I'm feeling. Or, to be more precise, I trust that I feel *something*, but I don't know if I can trust my *interpretation* of what I'm feeling. It would be a lot simpler if I could ask him," Anna said, looking into Nancy's eyes.

"Well, you'll figure it out one of these days."

And with that, they got caught up on Nancy's news about John's job offer, her daughter's soccer game, and her son's job prospects.

An hour later, they wrapped it up and walked to the parking lot.

"Be careful, Anna. Don't get so lost in Eli that you lose yourself." Nancy hugged her and then watched as Anna walked to her car.

What the hell was going on?

⁓

Anna stepped slowly into Awakenings, savoring the subtle aroma of incense. When Hannah rang the bell and everyone settled into their metal folding chairs, one chair stood empty beside Anna. Surprised at how empty she felt as well, she turned her attention to the class. Anna told herself to stay in the present moment and to *be here*.

The first class of the Tree of Life had been an overview. The tree was not actually a tree; it looked more like a hopscotch game. In fact, some people believed the game of hopscotch, which is very old, was really a method for remembering spiritual lessons.

The tree was made of three vertical columns. Ten spheres or circles were arranged along the columns, four on the middle column—the trunk of the tree—flanked by three other spheres on each side. Each sphere was connected by a pathway, all revealing important esoteric information.

Today Hannah talked about the middle sphere along the "trunk" of the tree, called Tiphareth. Tiphareth held a special place because it was located in the very center. It was the sacred heart of the "roadmap," where the divinity of the upper five spheres met the worldliness of the lower four spheres.

"The sphere of Tiphareth represents our highest and best self, our soul, our higher self. This is where the personality self 'rises' to meet the divine and where the divine reaches down yet remains uncorrupted by the physical world. Tiphareth is the Saturday morning of activities, the closest place where all is one. It is akin to being 'the best self that we are becoming.'"

As the class ended, Anna waved good-bye to Hannah and headed out the door. She wished Eli could have heard this beautiful concept, and then she remembered it was his second time to take the class. She found herself thinking about the personality self, which felt so separate. Much as Anna did now. And the higher self, which was the soul they were building, adding to it with each lifetime of learning. The higher self was closer to divine love, where nothing was separate.

Anna stopped suddenly as a thought occurred to her. The woman who was walking behind Anna had to veer suddenly to avoid a collision. Anna thought her name was Janet. In any case, the woman looked back and smiled.

"Use those brake lights, girl!" She laughed and continued on to her car.

Anna waved but continued to stand at the edge of the parking lot. Her thoughts were whirling. *The earthly ego, who I am this lifetime, is about being separate, each person within his or her own body, within his or her own skin. This is how we show up on this earthly plane.*

But it's not all bad. We first have to learn how to be separate so we can then learn how to be one. Like a child growing up, we must learn to leave the parents before we can learn how to rejoin. We have to come to earth to learn this. And to learn how to be the best person we can be.

And then to go on to learn how to be the best nonperson we can be— the higher self, the development of the soul. That's when we learn that being separate is an illusion.

What else is an illusion?

Suddenly, her mother's voice. *That's right, sweetheart. What else?*

Anna's mind paused for a moment, considered those words, and then went back to what she had been thinking.

Overlaid with the idea of the separate self, Anna thought about the connection she had with Eli. It felt as if she had a little glimpse into the divine—what life would be like if she and others weren't separate from everyone else.

An idea, more like a dream, softly entered Anna's mind. It came in gingerly, on kitten paws, and rubbed against her leg, asking for her attention.

What if Anna's higher self knew Eli's higher self? What if they weren't only friends or spiritual coworkers on earth, but what if their work was also being done on other planes? Other realities? Other lives? What was the nature of this connection further up the Tree of Life?

Anna had asked Eli to be her spiritual teacher. What if, unbeknownst to him, he was really teaching her about the divine connection by letting her feel it for herself? Really feel where they were all one and not just talk about it? Could he be teaching her on many, many levels—even levels he didn't consciously know about? Could both of their learnings, their lessons, be guided by the higher intelligence, by God? Were they both the student and teacher for each other?

Without realizing it, she had gotten into her car and was driving home. Her thoughts continued.

At the earth level on the Tree of Life, love showed up as infatuation, lust, desire to fill the empty spaces of one's own being with the validation of another person's love. Further up the tree, it was a sexual and energetic union beyond lust, and unconditional love. Beyond that, at the higher spheres, love was being of service to others, love of all mankind, lack of ego, connection to all.

Somehow Anna managed to stop at the red lights and go at the green lights as she drove home.

How far up the Tree of Life, how far along the mystical path, would this learning go? If she were honest with herself, she did wish for an earthbound man-and-woman relationship with Eli. And sex, and the union beyond sex. And the unconditional love, and being of service for their highest good. She felt all of those things with Eli.

And that was the crux of the problem about feeling connected to and so damned confused about this guy, this Teacher. How much would she learn, and how far up the Tree of Life, and how far into her self—her Self—would she eventually go?

Anna sighed. The only person who might know that answer was the very person she was swimming with in this stewpot. How could she possibly ask him? How could she not?

And beyond Eli—when we ask God for a Teacher, do we have any idea what we are really asking? Every person, everything around us, is a Teacher. The deer that leaps in front of our car. The man who breaks our heart. The mother who criticizes her child. All Teachers.

Do we even consciously know when we have asked to learn something? In what mysterious way does that occur?

She stopped and looked around. She had driven home and was now standing in her living room, gazing about and blinking. Adjusting to the mundane world.

She walked quickly to the computer, her connection to Eli, and sat. She didn't know what he was going through, but she did know she needed to get with him and figure out what was going on. Before she could send him an e-mail, she saw one from him in her inbox. He had written it while she was in class.

Subject: Little Time Off
Anna,
For reasons I won't go into right now, I feel I need to do some solitary inner work for a little bit. This is not a permanent retreat; I need some time alone to get perspective and insight on something. Keep going to class, learning, and doing good work.

It brings me great happiness knowing things are going so well for you. The blend of spirit and form is so evident in your life right now, and that is very beautiful! The work is paying off. What I'm doing will be a great topic of discussion for us, but I'm not yet ready for that right now. I need to do more on my own first.
Eli

Anna read and reread the words. Oh God. She needed him right now. She needed to bounce this off of someone who would get it.

She didn't understand the timing. Was he disgusted with her because of her uncle and all he had heard? Did he wish he weren't this involved in her life? The shame washed through her full force until she seemed to vibrate with it.

Eli was the loving presence, the rock of stability beside her when she had read the ugly words from her uncle. He was the loving parent who saw her as good and pure. But what if she had *forced* him to be that person? What if he resented the role? If he could not see her as good, did it mean she was truly bad? She was thinking like a child, but in this particular story, she was still a child, captured and held prisoner to the past.

Or was it that last paragraph she had written? Did he think it was a declaration of love, and he was offended? Her mind rushed from one reason to another. She stayed in that space of panic, confusion, and shame for hours. The punch in the gut had her doubling over as if it had been a physical blow.

Gradually, a perspective emerged.

Deep breaths. *Integrate the new consciousness*, Anna told herself. *If you vibrate at a higher level, if your frequency were more at Tiphareth rather than here on earth, what would be your response to this e-mail?*

Integrate what you are learning, and bring it into this world, especially in the areas where you feel sudden depression, sadness, anger, fear. Those are the areas crying out for healing. Anna said these words to herself, and they felt right.

Don't respond to the stories in your head when you answer this e-mail, Anna told herself. *Craft your response to the words he is telling you, not the illusion behind the words. Separate the event from the hurtful meaning that you keep attaching to the event.* She breathed, trying to release the old patterns.

And sat and began to type.

Re: Little Time Off
Eli,
Thank you for explaining your need for inner work and solitude.

I know we should be happy for the special learning that each of us must go through. After all, it is the work that leads us to a better understanding and a better place.

Nevertheless, on a human level, it is hard to watch someone who occupies a space in one's heart go through the pain of the learning. And so it is hard to feel you going through things but not being part of that journey with you. So I need to say this. If you feel alone, you aren't. Sometimes we must be the loving presence from a distance.

When you're ready, I'm here. Until then, I'm praying for your peace of mind and comfort. I'm backing off on e-mails and such because it sounds as if it would be easier for you right now. Even so, please feel yourself wrapped in a divine love hug.

Anna

Anna walked away from the computer. She found herself in the kitchen preparing dinner, which was usually Dan's job. Anna felt like being creative in a different way. Dan would be happy to have the night off. She decided to make him his favorite meal of homemade meatballs and spaghetti. For the next few hours, Anna focused on making it a good night for herself and Dan.

Later that night, after a wonderful meal, snuggling on the couch watching TV, and washing the dishes while Dan took his shower, Anna sat back down at the computer.

One e-mail in the inbox. Eli.

Re: Re: Little Time Off
Thank you for being so understanding, and thank you for the message.

One image that came to me at the start of this. A while back, Hannah did a private session with me where she saw me sitting in a cave, watching with equanimity a sandstorm that raged outside.

I realize now that the sandstorm is a metaphor for the emotions of my mind. My mind is the area outside the cave. The cave is the state of peace, the place from

which the true nature of all things can be seen. I'm looking to establish myself in that place once and for all.
Eli

Anna logged off of the computer. It was time to rest beside her husband and call it a night.

CHAPTER 29

Sunday morning dawned cold and overcast. Anna was awakened by the phone. Caller ID told her it was Nancy; it was odd for her to call this time of day. She grabbed the phone.

"Nancy?" Anna asked before her friend could even speak.

"Anna," she replied before bursting into tears.

"What's wrong? Is it John?" Nancy's husband had been out of work for a while, but he'd had a promising interview the week before. Anna felt that Nancy's tears were connected to John somehow.

"It's Cody, our dog. You know he's old, sixteen, and he's been sick for a long time. We're going to put him to sleep tomorrow. John's devastated. They have a special connection. He has gone through a lot of his life with Cody. And John's been so down about the job situation. Now this. I can't stand the pain he's going through. I'm sad, too, but not like he is," Nancy explained through her tears.

"Nancy, uh, would you like me to do some Reiki on Cody?" Anna had babysat the dog many times when her friends were on vacation, so she knew Cody well, and it made her sad to hear the news.

"Let me ask John. Hold on." Nancy was gone for a couple minutes. She returned and said, "Can you come over now?"

"I'm on my way." Anna quickly gathered some amethyst crystals, which were helpful for grieving and the dying, and headed out the door.

She got to Nancy and John's home fifteen minutes later. Nancy met her at the door and took her into the couple's bedroom, where Cody restlessly lay on folded blankets piled on the floor. John was sitting beside his dog, trying to soothe him. John's eyes were red, and it was clear he was trying to hold back his tears. Nancy sat on the rug with her husband and looked helpless.

Anna lowered herself quietly to the floor and sat facing Cody. She placed the deep-purple amethyst crystals on the windowsill near the dog.

"John, I'm leaving these crystals here with you and Nancy. They're for comfort during times like this." John nodded. Anna put her hand on John's hand and asked, "Do you know what Reiki is?"

"Nancy said it was an energy healing thing," John answered. While he didn't word it eloquently, he also didn't sound scornful or upset by it.

"Yes, it's energy work. This will be for Cody's comfort, so he can rest. Has he been able to eat at all?"

"He hasn't eaten for days, and he's very restless. It's killing me to watch him."

Nancy nodded her agreement.

Anna took a deep breath and mentally called in her Guides and Teachers, as well as God's healing current, the Reiki. Anna consciously imagined herself 'stepping aside,' being the Magician's wand, so the divine current would flow unaltered. She held her hands over Cody's body as she felt the Reiki begin to flow through her.

Briefly he became more agitated, and then he settled deeply into his blankets. Anna received guidance to create a peaceful image for the dog to keep with him during this period of impending death, his transition. Anna held an image in her mind of Cody being carried in John's strong and comforting arms and surrounded him with that image. She sent the intent to keep that image with Cody until the end came. Cody's breathing calmed, and he laid his head on John's hand, resting peacefully.

After a period of time, Anna stood. John gently laid his old friend's head on the blanket so he could hug Anna good-bye. John and Nancy walked her to the door, and they stood and chatted for a minute. They decided to wait and see how Cody was doing the next day to determine if he should be euthanized.

John folded Anna in his arms and murmured his thanks. There was a knock on the door, and Nancy opened it to find their neighbor on the doorstep. She was bringing food for John and Nancy. She had heard about Cody, and she was a dog lover herself.

"Anna, this is our friend Nina. Nina, this is Anna, Cody's babysitter and doctor." John smiled as Nancy gave Anna one last hug.

Anna had a moment of gratitude as she got into her car. It was amazing how fast prayers were answered. She had been the loving presence for Cody and John and Nancy. She mentally thanked Eli one more time for the gift of Reiki and headed home.

CHAPTER 30

∽

DAN SPENT A LOT OF time thinking about Lu. He liked that she trusted him enough to talk about the year her mom had died. She was fifteen. Her mom had kept the cancer a secret until she knew she had to share it. A month later she had died, and Lu's world turned upside down. Her dad was lost in his own grief and didn't know how to handle a grieving teenage girl.

She didn't blame her dad, but Lu began sneaking out of the house to be with friends. She drank with them and then alone in her room after she got home. It was the only relief she could find from the pain of losing her mom, who had also been her best friend. And she couldn't understand why her mom had kept the cancer a secret.

As Dan drove to the Marstons', he realized he had never looked so forward to going to work as he did with this job. Finding a friend and being himself with her was a gift. Making good money was a bonus.

He had started carrying on conversations with her in his head. Processing things out loud with her. Why rehab had never worked for him, how his stepdad's drinking had affected his life, why he felt shame about who he had become. He cared about her story, too. Loved listening to the threads of her life that had brought her here to him.

This morning he was thinking about Lu's question from the other week, "What frequency do we vibrate at?" He hadn't known the answer that day, but it kept coming back to him. His initial thought had been "at the frequency of shame," but that did them a disservice. He didn't think they were bound by their addiction and self-disgust, although sadly they both experienced it. Then it became "at the frequency of pain." That wasn't right either, but it was closer. It didn't set well that they were joined as victims.

Finally the answer came to him. They were bound at the frequency of love. Not romantic or idealized love, but love that occurs from seeing the light and the shadow of another and accepting the whole package—because the other person is worth it whether he or she knows it or not. Lu knew the good and the bad of him; she saw him. And she accepted him. And he felt the same about her. *The frequency of love.*

An idea took root. It had first come to him as a wish when he and Lu had discussed their friendship. A tiny, hopeful vine unfurling from the barren soil of their respective childhoods. *What if we could mutually support the dream of being sober?* Their own little AA group. What if he could hold the mirror for Lu to see how beautiful she was inside and out? What if she did the same and Dan could drop his self-loathing as easily as removing a stained jacket?

Acknowledge the shadow and strive for more. A chance for both of them to see who they could be without the steel cage of addiction.

As he parked the car in front of the Marstons' beautiful home, he skipped the sip of vodka and eagerly gathered his supplies. He couldn't wait to talk to Lu and see what she thought of the idea.

He pressed the doorbell, anticipating the sight of her mischievous grin.

The door opened slowly. Rich Marston stood there, one hand on the knob, the other on the doorframe. His face was drawn, his casual clothes sloppy. It wasn't his usual look, although Dan had seen him only a few times. Marston was a businessman, and he was normally gone before Dan's 8:00 a.m. arrival time.

"Dan," Marston said flatly, "come in. I need to talk with you."

Dan felt fear deep in his gut. A curious picture emerged in his mind as he crossed the threshold to the beautiful foyer. An image of his stepfather's large, worn work boot systematically grinding a tiny vine back into the dry, cracked soil from whence it had cautiously sprung.

And then the words. *There is a sun that shines, but not for you.*

CHAPTER 31

Rachel thought back to Wednesday morning when she had showered with Eli and lain in bed with him after their lovemaking. The soft sunlight had filtered through the blinds, creating a play of light and shadows across her belly and Eli's back. She had felt so connected to him and deliciously naughty for the stolen time together.

Ellen's talk had ravaged Rachel, but in more ways than Ellen had known.

Rachel had a secret. She realized now how angry she must have grown toward Eli to have allowed this thing to happen. Disconnection. Separation. An underground source spring of pure, cold anger.

She replayed Friday's call from her son Tim that had heralded disaster.

"Mom, Dad's in his office going over the books. I knocked on the door, and he didn't answer. I tried to go in, but the door was locked. What should we do?" Tim sounded desperate.

In that instant, Rachel had flashed to Eli kneeling before her in the shower, eyes gazing up at her, seeking her reaction to the pleasure he was providing. The water had flowed across his joyous face and down his broad shoulders. For a moment, she thought he had been crying, but she wasn't sure.

She was sure on Friday. He came home a beaten man. Before he had left the office, he had gone to Tim and Chris and told them to cancel the day's appointments and come to the house. He called Rachel and told her he needed to meet with her. Rachel recalled the pain the words "meet with you" generated. The pain. The coldness. And the fear.

The four of them met. Eli didn't yell, didn't rage. He asked them quietly yet distantly what they had done and who had done what. Who had known and what part each one had played. He told them not to sugarcoat it or lie about it. He just needed to know the truth.

It had been Tim's idea, a desperate one. He had taken a gamble on some expensive equipment and overextended the company. And, the worst of luck, they had lost several small to medium-sized business customers within a week. The individual companies were small enough that the revenue could be hidden. But added together, it was a sizeable amount. Nearly a million dollars. The good news was it looked as if they could replace that revenue with new customers who were almost under contract. But those accounts weren't closing as quickly as they should.

He had gone to his mother and asked her what to do. He didn't want to look as if he was driving the company into the ground after only one year, nor did he want to disappoint his dad. Rachel understood how hard it was to operate in the shadow of Eli's perfection. They decided to keep this a short-term secret until the new business came through. Then everything had begun to take longer than expected. Bills mounted; revenue lagged.

Tim could no longer keep it a secret from Chris, since she was involved with the day-to-day work. When he confided what was going on, Chris was horrified. She absolutely thought they should tell their father what had transpired.

It went from bad to worse. Tim and Rachel had kept the secret too long. They stayed committed to their original bad decision and hoped things would work out soon. If not, they would need to let employees go and inform Eli. Rachel wasn't sure their marriage could handle the additional stress, especially if Eli saw it as a betrayal.

Chris gave Tim and her mom an ultimatum. Either fix it within the next two weeks, or she was going to tell Eli. The three of them were sick with worry.

Rachel thought back to that horrific, fact-based, cold meeting on Friday afternoon at their home. Eli told Tim what reports he wanted run and that Tim was no longer at the helm. He told Chris what he needed from her. Rachel was no longer in charge of the books. Every decision, no matter how insignificant, was going through Eli for the foreseeable future.

Before the kids left to go to their own homes, Eli reassured them that he loved them. His love for them was not in question. Rachel realized he had not included her in that blanket statement, and she felt chilled.

He told them their judgment, however, was in question. And that his trust had been broken. Those two things meant he needed to return to running the company for now. He would have more information for them as he analyzed the situation over the next few weeks.

When Tim and Chris left, silently walking to their cars parked out front, Eli closed the front door and turned to look at Rachel. Tears ran down her face, but she made no sound, no excuse. She sat in the chair at their dining room table, numb, her stomach in a knot. She knew she couldn't stand, didn't think her quivering legs would hold her up.

Eli looked at Rachel as if he couldn't remember who she was. Or where he was. His expression was lost, indifferent, but the keen intelligence that had built their business was still trying to process this latest problem. He stared at her for a full minute before putting on his coat and closing the door softly behind him.

The click of the shutting door released Rachel from her state of numbness. Her gestures were harsh and exaggerated as she laid her forehead on the dining room table. The guttural cry that tore from her chest and throat barely sounded human. In this moment, in her most primitive mind, she knew her life would end as it had begun. Alone. What more could she expect? She didn't deserve more. She never had.

Two days had passed since Eli had found out that nothing was as it seemed. He knew there was a solid block of ice inside of him, but he had no clue how to melt it. He had spent those days completing tasks. Running reports, looking at bank accounts, staring at credit-card bills. Tasks about numbers. Numbers that would help him figure out what to do, understand if it could be saved. If they could be saved.

Sunday morning found him once again sitting in the woods near his house, wearing his warmest coat and watching birds flit from tree to tree. He didn't want this marriage anymore, or this business. He thought about selling the house and the leftover crumbs of the company.

Mostly he felt ashamed that he had been blindsided. Why hadn't he seen it coming? *What was the lesson?* He laughed, berating himself that he could have been arrogant enough to believe he could Teach. In one day his life was in shambles, but the shambles reflected the mirage of a life he had been living. That hadn't happened in one day. He had built that mirage over the course of years. Integrating spiritual lessons? *Not hardly.*

He thought about Anna. He had abandoned her right after the issues with her uncle. He knew about her shame. She very likely thought he was avoiding her. Yet she must have found her way through that, through the illusion of what had caused him to back away.

Her first thought would be that he had left in reaction to her or their work. Her tendency to feel shame would dictate that. Her second thought might be that it wasn't about her. Unless she got stuck in the first thought and couldn't move beyond it.

What was the illusion in the issue Eli was dealing with? And if he were looking beyond illusion, how would he think about it? What would he do? He had focused on the task of saving the business. Was it time to focus on the task of saving his family? Or had the contract run out on that, and it was time to move on?

He wondered what he would tell Anna if this was her problem. He might ask her at what frequency she wanted to vibrate. He contemplated that for a while.

Let himself miss Anna—feel her inside him, thinking about him at this very moment. He breathed in her essence, sent her his love. He stilled as he felt her reaching out to him. He didn't resist.

Wrapping his arms around himself, Eli pretended everything was okay. He sent Anna one last loving thought and hoped she received it. Then he turned his attention away.

Eli raised himself from the hard, uncomfortable rock where he had sat for the last forty-five minutes and stretched. He knew he had to talk to Rachel soon. *Can't live with a heart of ice forever,* he thought. He began the slow walk home.

"Rachel?" Eli called as he carefully closed the front door. Silence in the house. Seemed as if there had been silence in the house since that joyful Wednesday morning of connection.

"I'm in the kitchen," Rachel called out hollowly.

He hung his coat in the closet and moved in her direction. God, he felt old. He stood watching her from the doorway. She was cooking, and he noticed the beaten slump of her shoulders. When she looked over her shoulder at him, her blue eyes were dull. She turned back to the stove. She had aged.

Good. I've aged, too. And for once, he felt no guilt.

But aloud he said, "We need to talk." His voice echoed too loudly in the lifeless house. Keeping her back to him, she braced herself as if she thought he would strike her. Eli walked to Rachel and put his hands on her shoulders. They were tight. He turned her to face him. She looked so afraid, her eyes huge and blue. Her chest was shielded by her arms, hands near her throat. Protecting herself from words that were guaranteed to cut her.

Eli took her into his arms and pressed his cheek against the top of her head. Murmured soft words to her. Slowly rubbed his hands up and down her back.

"Eli." Rachel pressed herself into him. "I hurt you," she whispered.

He pulled her close to his chest. Tears rolled down his cheeks, first without sound, then deeply and uncontrollably as he broke. They stood wrapped in each other's arms as one, his body shaking. Rachel held him as she had her children when they were small.

She tucked him close to her without crying. He kept repeating something she couldn't understand through the cauldron of his tears and emotion until she held her breath to catch his words and the emptiness in his voice.

"I'm so lonely...I'm so damn lonely..."

And then she broke too.

CHAPTER 32

Subject: Things are better
Hi Anna,
I'm sorry I had to take a break so abruptly. A few things happened with work that needed my attention. It was more than a small thing, but I should have explained that to you. I don't want you to think I don't value our work together.
　　Thank you for the Reiki. I felt it, and it helped a great deal.
　　I believe I can get together for lunch on Tuesday. Would that work for you?
　　Miss you.
Eli

ANNA SAW ELI'S E-MAIL EARLY Monday morning. Dan was getting ready for work and noticed her at the computer.
　"Working this early, Anna? That's awfully ambitious," Dan said, staring at her a little too long. She felt herself blushing, and it made her mad. He had been distant since the dinner with Eli and Rachel. Anna had felt a little distant herself. Things had been better between them, and it felt off again. Was he jealous

of Eli, or drinking, or was Anna herself the one who was creating discomfort? She didn't know. Too bad she could tap into Eli's feelings instantly but couldn't begin to decipher those of her husband.

"Dan, want to go out to dinner tonight? We didn't get to see each other much over the weekend," Anna asked. "I'm finally going for the past-life reading with the woman from my Awakenings class this afternoon, and it would be fun to relax after that."

"I'll try, Anna. I might have to work late tonight, but I'll give you call later," he replied, giving her a wave as he headed out the door. He stopped and poked his head back in the doorway. "Have fun with the reading. I'm betting on your being a trained assassin. Which means you might be the only person in the world who doesn't get to be Cleopatra!" He chuckled as he closed the door behind him.

Anna smiled, glad he was making an attempt to be more convivial, and put her attention back to Eli's e-mail. It was nice of him to explain a little more. He was in her thoughts a lot, and maybe she could begin to ask him what he thought it all meant. Frankly, the past-life reading was an attempt to understand why her heart and soul felt so connected to Eli. Anna sent off her e-mail of acceptance and started work on an editing project that required every drop of her attention.

~

"I'm leaving, Rachel," Eli told his wife quietly.

"Okay. Tell Dave I said hi."

He nodded and walked toward the door. An odd thought crossed his mind. What if he really said those words, 'I'm leaving,' and meant it permanently? What would his life look like?

The stale feeling of a life left unlived—would that feeling leave him? Or would the despair overwhelm him until he lay down and never got up?

What the fuck does it matter? There is no good answer. And no sense thinking about it.

He closed the door softly behind him.

⁂

"Man, I don't mean to be cruel, but you look like crap! What the hell's going on?"

Eli slanted an irritated look at his brother's poignant observation before he sighed. "Well, to be honest, Dave, things are really screwed up, so it's not shocking that you noticed."

"What is it, Eli? You got me scared here. You're the one who has everything under control. When your life's spinning out… well, then I know the rest of the world isn't far behind." Dave realized he actually was worried about his brother. "Seriously, man, I haven't seen you looking this bad since our mom died." He waited.

"Bro, it might not look like it, but hearing your voice has cheered me considerably." Eli cupped long fingers behind his brother's neck and pulled him in for a bear hug. "It's so good to see you, man," Eli said, looking as if he really meant it.

"Shit, if I'd have known you were having a rough time, I'd have been here sooner," Dave said, voice muffled by the hug and faced pressed into Eli's coat.

"I know. Guess I'm not so good at reaching out," Eli confessed as if it were a secret.

"Tell me about it. Family trait. And not our best one, I might add," Dave replied.

They had been standing awkwardly in front of the restaurant where they'd agreed to meet. Stepping back from the hug, Eli gestured for Dave to go inside.

Although the day was cold, the sky was bright and it took a few minutes to adjust to the low light inside. Dave could barely make out the young woman who approached them. But he held up two fingers, and she directed them to a booth in the corner. *Perfect place to find out what the hell's going on. But I'll let my big brother bring it up himself. I'd better let him start it, or he'll clam up and I won't get a damn thing out of him.*

"Let's order first," Eli said.

"Uh huh. Give me a minute. It's been so long since I've been here, they went and changed the menu on me," Dave muttered, smiling to himself. *Do I know my brother or what?*

"Before I get into my stuff, what's been going on with you?" Eli asked, genuinely concerned as well as buying time for himself.

Dave let him get away with it and went through the litany of telling Eli about his new girlfriend, how sales were going in the pharmaceutical industry, what colleges his son had visited, and everything else he could think of. *By the time I'm done with this, Eli's going to be begging to tell me what's going on in his life, just to shut me up.* He smiled to himself, but a trickle of worry still ran through his mind. *Is he sick? Rachel? The kids? What the fuck is it?*

〜〜

"Your girlfriend sounds nice. Woman friend. Girlfriend sounds like an idiot at our age." Eli laughed.

"What about you, bro? You got a girlfriend?" Dave inserted casually.

"Jesus, Dave. What makes you ask a question like that? You know better than anyone I wouldn't cheat on Rachel. What made you ask that?"

"Because we've been dancing around what's wrong for an hour, and even though I have all day, I'd like to get to it before we're both dead and buried." Eli always could outlast Dave when it came to who would give in first.

Eli stared at his brother. "When'd you get so full of yourself?" he asked half seriously.

"When my net worth exceeded a mil." Dave grinned, but the smile slowly left his face. "Come on, Eli. What's wrong?"

The long story about Rachel, the kids, and the business came out. He even included the man Eli had seen with Rachel at the food pantry. Dave, as always, was a good listener and let the tale unfold at Eli's pace.

"Pretty tough stuff," Dave said at the end. His concerned eyes stared into Eli's and reflected back a sense of loss.

"Where's it stand now?"

"We closed the new deals. It's getting better," Eli said.

"Does 'we' mean 'I'?" Dave asked, his voice low and unthreatening on purpose.

Eli shrugged noncommittally.

"I'm not attacking, just asking…do you think Tim can do it? Run it?"

"I want to leap to his defense—it's what a dad does—but I honestly don't know," Eli admitted. "Dave, I'm going to tell you what I can't tell anyone else. I feel like a fucking fool. My son and my wife had this big secret for quite a while. My daughter at least had the sense to want to tell me. I live with Rachel, and I didn't see it coming. God, Rachel might be cheating on me, too. What did I do wrong? I think of myself as a somewhat perceptive person, but I couldn't see what was right in front of my face. I mean, really…what is that about?"

"Is that a rhetorical or an actual question?" Dave asked, and he held his breath for a moment.

"What? You look like you have something on your mind." Eli's expression was odd, almost fearful.

"I do have something on my mind, but I don't want to make things worse for you. Do you feel up to talking about something?"

"Recapitulation." Eli groaned.

"Is that a fancy way of saying 'Fuck you'?" Dave raised an eyebrow.

"It should be, but what it really means is a long, hard look at a person's life with an eye toward resolving the past. I'm being tortured for working with Anna and encouraging her recapitulation work."

"Who's Anna? The girlfriend?"

"Dave, if you say that one more time, I'm going to get seriously pissed. I don't have a girlfriend, woman friend, or intimate friend. I'm the most trustworthy guy on the planet, and you know it," Eli stated with great deliberation.

"Which brings us to what I was going to talk about—"

"Are you about to tell me I'm not trustworthy?" Eli asked in amazement.

"I'm about to tell you that any man who lies to himself, by definition, cannot be trustworthy," Dave said quietly, all humor drained from his voice.

"You've got my attention, but what are you talking about?"

"Let's change the subject for a minute. How would you describe our family growing up?" Dave asked neutrally.

"I guess I'd call us the Cleavers. Dad went off to work and did well as VP of sales at the company. Mom stayed home and took care of us, came to see our plays at school, volunteered as a room mother. I did well in school. You tried to do well in school." The last part was said playfully. "We were normal. Boring, in a way. Totally not like Rachel's family or Anna's."

"Eventually you're going to tell me about Anna. But back to the subject. You really don't remember anything about our life, do you?"

"I told you about our life. What don't I remember?"

"Do you remember how much Dad drank? Or the arguments he had with Mom?" Dave asked, watching Eli's face carefully. *Here we go...*

Eli was silent. Dave couldn't tell whether Eli was remembering or numbing out. Or both.

Eli sighed. "I remember that he liked his Scotch when he got home from work."

"Remember how much he liked it?"

"Are you implying he had a problem with alcohol?"

"No, I'm stating it as a fact."

More silence.

"Do you remember it?"

"No," Eli said so quietly that Dave heard it more as a whisper. "There is more, Eli. Do you still want to know?"

CHAPTER 33

It didn't take Anna long to get to one of her past lives. Julie was very good at this type of hypnosis.

She stared in wonder at the stone hearth, blackened from years of cooking with the massive dark kettle that hung in the center of it. She slowly turned and gazed behind her at the Great Hall. "It must seat over a hundred people," she thought, counting the long rows of wooden tables and benches. Exposed wooden beams gave a cozy Germanic feel to the largest dining room Anna had ever seen.

But even with the dried herbs and plants hanging from the ceiling, the room was a black hole of loneliness without people. She knew instinctively it was built for laughter and conversation, drinking and feasting. The contrast of what it was now and what it was meant to be made Anna feel as empty as the room.

She peered down at her dress to get a sense of the time period—1700s or 1800s, and not necessarily in America. Her feet were bare, so no clue there of when or where she was. Or why she felt so damned lonely. "It's the contrast of now and then, separation and connection" echoed in her mind.

Shock coursed through her body as the hearth suddenly glowed with light and a roaring fire. The huge iron kettle radiated heat, and stew bubbled within it; overflowing drops caused the fire to spit in reaction. What had been lifeless suddenly was filled with hot, radiating energy. And as she stared into the fire, Anna was again transported to another time and place, a much older time and a much older place.

A fire remained, but this was an outside, life-giving bonfire. A tribe of people huddled around it for warmth. The dark of the night was impenetrable except for the brightness of the stars and the twin spikes of a crescent moon.

In this new world, Anna was a three year-old girl standing on the lap of a woman who she instinctively knew was her mother. The woman was seated on a rock, black hair curling wildly about her face, the firelight reflected in her dark eyes. Her clothes were vivid, and everything about her felt alive.

"Daughter, one day you will be the leader of our tribe. A strong and wise leader," the woman told her, gazing first into the face of her child and then to the men, women, and children gathered around the fire. Love shone in her eyes.

"The time is coming when our people will need to leave this land and travel far to find new grounds. You will take them on this journey. There will be pain and heartache, but your job as the leader is to bring our people, all of them, to the new land. It will take time to rebuild, but it will be the right move."

"No, Mama. You're the leader," the little girl whispered.

"When I'm gone, you will become the leader of our people."

"Where will you go?" the child asked, her face puckered in concentration and confusion.

"I will leave the tribe. If I stay, you cannot come into your own power, to be your own kind of leader."

"Nooo…" the child wailed, and the force of exploding grief in her heart ripped her from a past that seemed more real than this moment and shoved her to the present.

"Oh God, oh God, she's going," Anna cried. "I don't want the power; I want her to stay!" Her tears flowed unchecked.

Julie, Anna's guide to past lives, handed her a tissue. "What happened, Anna?"

Anna explained about the Great Hall, the hearth, the fire, and the sudden entrance into a starry night with her mother and their tribe gathered about the warmth and flames of the fire. She felt a groan of grief and struggled to hold it within. Her logical mind wondered how she could so deeply miss a woman she'd met in a vision. She remembered what Julie had said before they began this session to return to past lives. "Who knows if there are past lives or not? So don't put pressure on yourself to remember anything. Or to worry if it's real or made up. Whatever you see is meant to be, regardless of why or how the images come to you."

Anna shook herself in order to focus. "I have some questions," she said, staring into Julie's blue eyes. Julie was a tall, willowy woman with long blond hair. Ethereal. If fairies were human, Julie was one. When Anna met her at the Tree of Life class, she felt instantly at ease. When she found out Julie worked at Awakenings and did past-life regressions and readings, she was drawn to know more. And it seemed that her mom, her real mom, had pushed her in this direction also.

They were seated in a small room in the back of Awakenings; this and a few other rooms were used for psychic and astrological readings. Reiki and massage were offered, too.

Julie smiled. "I'd be surprised if you didn't have questions!"

Anna returned the smile and asked, "How did I get from the Great Hall to the tribe? Was the hearth like a doorway?"

"Exactly right. There are places in the other world that function as portals. Doorways of sorts. The fire in the hearth jogged another lifetime, and you traveled 'through the fire,' or through the hearth, to the other world. It is likely we have doorways in this world, too, that take us to other places. Or perhaps in dreams."

Anna nodded, her brow wrinkled. *The dream as a doorway.* A wisp of a memory captured her mind for a fraction of a second and was gone.

Julie responded with a question of her own. "Where were you in the second past life? The first one seemed several hundred years old, but European, maybe Germanic..."

"Yeah, that sounds right. But the second one felt really, really old. I think it was a nomadic tribe. And my mother was the leader, so it might have been a matriarchal society. I wouldn't be surprised if it took place before Christ. But my mom was wearing a woven cloth outfit. We weren't wearing animal skins or anything. I remember looking down at my feet, like you told me before we started, to see what kind of shoes I was wearing in order to get a sense of the culture and the time period."

"What did you see?"

"My feet were bare. Little, brown, dirty feet. Fat and cute." Anna smiled fondly.

They chuckled together.

"What's next, Julie?"

"Anna, I think there is more about this particular past life than meets the eye. You said it was extremely vivid. It felt more real than this current life. I think there is something important to learn from it. Tonight, or when you feel ready, ask for a dream to tell you what you need to know."

Anna said she would, paid Julie, and left the shop. She wanted to browse, but she and Dan were going out to dinner tonight and it was time to get home. As she unlocked the door of the car, she heard her mother's voice strongly in her mind.

Yes, sweetheart, ask what you need to know. It's time to remember. Quickly.

They decided to head downtown for dinner, but it had been tense between them for some reason. Anna tried to carry the conversation for a while. Dan answered in monosyllables until she finally gave up. On the way home, he tried to be more conversational and asked how the past-life regression had gone. Anna began to explain what had happened until Dan abruptly stated, "It sounds kind of silly to me."

"Dan, are you doing that thing again where you check to see what frequency I'm vibrating at?" Anna asked, trying to decide whether to be playful or pissed.

"No, it sounds silly. What does it mean? Why do you care what you were in a past life? Does it change anything about your life today?" Dan was in a bad mood, and Anna knew better than to trust her tender thoughts and feelings with him when he was like this.

She changed the topic. "How'd the job go today?"

Dan increased the volume of his voice. "Seriously. There's no reason to change the subject. You're not asking about my day because you care about it. You don't want to have a fight or stand up for what you believe in," Dan replied. "I hate when you try to avoid something because it's uncomfortable. I mean it. Why does your past life matter?"

Anna looked at her husband and knew her expression was ugly. She couldn't do it anymore or take it anymore. Her marriage was finished. Dan's behavior the last few months, and especially the last week, suddenly made sense. She couldn't believe she had allowed the illusion to go on this long. It was obvious in a way she wouldn't see before that he was drinking again. After the last relapse, she had promised herself to never be fooled again, either by Dan or by her own mind, desperate to believe all was well. Rage consumed her.

〜

The voices in Dan's head screamed louder than Anna's irritatingly strident voice. She was berating him about something, but it was lost in the clamor of the scene at the Marstons' house the other day.

Marston saying quietly, lethally, "You were drinking with my wife. She was trying to quit, and you drank with her."

Dan tried to look around his client to find Lu. "Where is she, Marston?" he demanded with raised voice. "Did you hurt her?" Chaos in his brain.

"It's none of your damn business."

"Please…tell me," Dan whispered, his eyes pleading.

Something in Dan's expression spoke to Lu's husband. "I made arrangements for inpatient rehab. Her sister is flying with her to the facility. She's gone, and if you care about her, you'll let her go. Let her heal. And keep your stinking alcohol away from her."

Marston reached in his pocket. "I'm going to treat you better than you treated me and my family. I'm going to pay you for the work you completed. And then get the hell out. You could have killed her. She's an alcoholic, Dan, for Christ's sake. What kind of an animal takes advantage of a beautiful, sweet woman like Lu?" Rich Marston's eyes filled with unshed tears.

"I love her. She's my friend." Dan stared at Marston, as if daring him to respond.

Dan turned his eyes from their inward focus to the highway in front of him a second before he slammed on the brakes with both feet. The sound of metal hitting metal, followed by the punch of Dan's airbag inflating, was deafening. It was only when he heard the long scream beside him that he remembered Anna was in the car.

CHAPTER 34

ELI LISTENED WITH HALF ATTENTION as Rachel murmured a greeting, just long enough to make sure the phone call wasn't for him before he headed out the door.

"Eli, wait!" Rachel called out. She knew he was going to meet Anna. That was one of the things they had talked about yesterday and into last night. Rachel talked about the clothes, the money, and what Ellen had figured out. Eli was astounded when she told him. It made perfect sense to him. He had even gotten up the nerve to ask about the man from the food pantry. He was a lawyer and an accountant who also volunteered with Rachel. She had turned to him for advice about how to resolve the business problem.

"Is it for me?" Eli asked, feeling irritated. He had been trying to get out of the house a little early to meet Anna when the phone rang. He heard Rachel answer it and hoped it wasn't for him. He had felt anxious and distracted since last night when he had awakened in a sweat. While it was true he had plenty to be anxious about himself, it felt as if this was coming from Anna. And that created a pressure to see her that went beyond logical.

He wanted to get going and find out what was wrong.

"It's Hannah from Awakenings," Rachel told him, sounding curious.

That was odd. He picked up the extension and juggled the phone at his ear while he put on his coat.

"Eli," Hannah said, "I got a phone call from a friend of Anna's today. She wanted to reach you but didn't know how, but she knew you and Anna both attend classes here."

He felt a sense of shock and dread.

"Anna was in a car accident last night with her husband. He was injured less seriously than she was, but they are both in the hospital. Anna is pretty badly hurt, but she is expected to live. Same with her husband. I'm sorry to call and tell you this, but I know you are friends."

The words stuck in his throat. "Where is she? Which hospital?"

Hannah told him. Eli's thoughts were scattered; he couldn't seem to concentrate on what to ask. "Hannah, did her friend say what happened? Where were they?"

"From what the police can tell, they had gone out to dinner and were going back home on forty," she said, referring to the interstate. "Her husband must have been drinking at dinner, because his blood alcohol level was high. He crossed the highway and ran into a pickup truck. The driver of that vehicle is okay, thank God. I've put Anna and her husband in our prayer book here at the store."

Eli didn't remember saying good-bye to Hannah, but somehow he'd gotten off the phone. It was back in the cradle.

He turned to Rachel in a trance. This couldn't be happening. It was too much to bear in too short a time.

"Eli, what happened? Who's in the hospital?" Rachel asked, concern in her voice.

"Anna." Eli said the one word, his voice anguished. "I have to see her. I'm going now."

Rachel moved to intercept him as he headed to the door. "Wait, Eli. I don't think you should go. You're too upset. You'll have an accident too. There's nothing you can do at the hospital. If she's in serious condition, they probably won't let you in to see her. Wait here until you know more."

"I'm going. I'm not letting her lie there alone. Her parents are both gone. That bastard of a husband is also in the hospital. She needs me," Eli said firmly, trying to clear his head and think logically.

"Don't go, Eli." Rachel stared at him. "Not if you really want this marriage to work. You know you shouldn't go."

"Are you kidding me, Rachel? Do you seriously think you have a leg to stand on telling me what makes this marriage work? After this week?"

Eli wasn't being nice about how he said the words. They dripped with sarcasm, which was not his style unless he was pushed to the limit. Which he had been.

Rachel stared at him—whether in fear or in anger, Eli couldn't tell. This time he didn't care.

"Right now there isn't one word you can say that will make me not see her when she needs a friend. Not one word. So don't try. I've been here for you through thick and thin. Through one of the worst betrayals I can imagine. No, Rachel. I'm not the betrayer. I'm coming home to you. But I am going to that hospital now."

Eli grabbed his cell phone and pulled the door shut behind him. He was shaking when he got into his car. He paused for a minute and took deep breaths. He couldn't believe what he had said to Rachel. *Jesus*. Taking one last deep breath, he turned the key in the ignition and backed out of the garage. And tuned into Anna.

Anna lay on her bed in total despair. Another relapse, another betrayal. Following his usual pattern, Dan had been secretly drinking for several months, maybe a year. It had gotten progressively worse until he couldn't hide it anymore. Spent several days detoxing in a motel, and Anna had no idea where he was. She thought he was dead. No, he just wanted to be.

She was telling Eli the story. She knew he wasn't there with her, but she told him anyway.

"I once had an experience with an angel, like we see angels pictured with the feathery white wings. Even as I was having the experience, I knew the angel was presenting in a familiar form to be comforting and not scary, and what could be better than the angels of our childhood?

"I was lying on my bed in the afternoon, which was unheard of for me, drifting into the sleep of depression. I had the realization I wasn't on the bed, but on the angel. I could feel the feathery thickness of its wings. I was on my stomach with my head to the side, ear pressed to the angel's heart. I don't know if they have hearts, but anyway, that's what happened.

"Suddenly there was this download of code. A streaming line of code. The angel was translating to me through its heart, and even though I didn't recognize the language, I heard it and it made perfect sense. The language was a language of love and comfort. When I lifted my head, I could not remember one thing the angel had said, except I still felt very peaceful. I could feel its wings under me.

"I asked him his name, and he said something I couldn't understand."

———

No, wait, Anna thought. *That was a long time ago.* She couldn't seem to open her eyes. She struggled to make sense of what was happening. It came to Anna suddenly that she was in a hospital. *Don't think about it.* She snuggled into the angel and slept.

Time passed, and Anna woke and repeated the process of figuring out where she was. The angel felt warm, and she felt safe for the first time.

"Ask the angel his name," Eli said to her from a long way off. So she did.

She heard the name through the angel's heart.

"What is it?" Anna asked again.

"Elijah."

Oh, I know you. You've been with me forever. Anna smiled, fell back to sleep, then dreamed again.

———

Her mother died when Anna of the nomadic tribe was eight. And her mother was correct. The tribe needed to move to another area. The temperature had shifted, and they couldn't handle the cold and remain a wandering tribe. Wandering was in their blood; they weren't built for living in caves or man-made structures. Their leader was a child of eight, yet she was the chosen one. They respected the child's mother too much to second-guess her decision, and it was obvious the Little One would grow quickly into her leadership. But right now the child needed help, or they would perish.

"Sisters and brothers, tonight we will gather in ceremony. We have much to decide," the Little One announced to the eleven trusted advisors of her mother, which included her two brothers. They spent the day in preparation for the ceremony. Food was cooked over the fire, plants were gathered to mix into a paste for application to their bodies. Sacred objects were removed from the woven materials that cushioned them and were cared for and prepared in the ancient tradition. Important matters such as these were passed along orally as stories, memorized by even little children so the knowledge would not be lost.

As the time drew near, the moon was fat and spilling over. The familiar sharp crackle of the flames comforted the twelve who sat companionably around the fire. They rested a small distance away from the much larger fire where their people huddled for warmth. They performed a ritual of protection and purification.

Then the Little One spoke. "We know we cannot stay here any longer. I don't know enough of this land to determine where we must seek. Do any of you know from your travels in this world where we must go?"

While they knew the area of perhaps a hundred miles in circumference, no one knew of a specific safe destination. They did know they should head west, and there would be mountains to cross. The little leader chose three of them to scout and lead the way.

"I know we will need food and water for our journey, and a way to protect ourselves."

In a systematic manner, the Little One covered topics that needed to be addressed to make a multihundred-mile journey with nearly sixty women, men, children, and their animals. Teams to solve problems were formed based on areas of expertise. The teams were small enough to be flexible and large enough to include the proper talent to solve the problem. By herself, the child could solve nothing; her experience with the world was too limited. She didn't know the answers, only the questions.

As they neared the end of the ceremony and planning session, Little One had a final thought to communicate to her trusted advisors. "We twelve have been given a sacred mission. Our people have wandered this land for centuries, and in this moment of our long history, we must move to a different land. We have our journey and a sacred trust. It will not be enough to find the new land. Each of the precious souls entrusted to our care must also arrive safely to our destination. If we are going to accomplish that, the twelve of us must function as one being, so close that there is no space, no room for dissent between us."

Everyone nodded their grave understanding of the enormity of the promise and their acknowledgment of how united they must be.

"Jinah and Ishla," she said, turning to her brothers, who were eighteen and sixteen years old. In a matriarchal society such as this one, men were rarely consulted on important matters. They were protectors only. But Little One's mother had set a precedent by including men in the tribal leadership if they possessed the necessary strategic and planning skill. Little One had learned from an early age that all beings had gifts and talents, and they were not dependent on age or sex but the individual.

The two brothers smiled at their little sister with love and respect in their eyes. She returned the same loving gaze. "What must we do to seal the bond between the twelve of us?" she asked, placing her total trust in their answer.

They explained what must be done, and the others agreed to their plan. At the end, Little One stood and spoke the final words of their bond. "We will be of service to one another throughout time. This contract to help one another grow and be successful reaches further than our earthly success and this land; it binds us at the level of the soul. We are bound together beyond the grave, time, and space. Are you in agreement?"

As the twelve clasped hands as one and spoke their agreement, the intention and passion in their cry resonated far across the desert. They stood as one, gazing into the moon, which on that sacred night stared back as unblinking as the eye of God.

It had begun.

Anna awoke and knew where she was. Without paper, pen, or the means to use her hands to write, she lay bandaged in the hospital and reviewed the dream over and over so she wouldn't forget.

Dream, vision, or memory? She wasn't sure.

She *was* sure it mattered to remember what had happened.

Oh yeah. Don't forget to tell Eli.

CHAPTER 35

ANNA WAS GOING TO LIVE. And walk, breathe, think, and do all the things she had done before the accident. Everything hurt. Parts that weren't necessary for life—some of those were taken out by the doctors. But it didn't matter. Anna was going to be okay. What didn't survive the car accident was her marriage.

Eli visited her two days in a row. He and Nancy traded off their visiting times so Anna would have someone with her most of the day. Eli held her water cup so she could drink from the straw. He petted her hair, but her hair was getting pretty dirty. Sometimes she felt self-conscious, other times not. He told her stories. Eli was going to write a book called *The Wild Side of Mysticism*. She thought he was kidding, but who knew? He was funny.

Anna had plenty of time to tell Eli about her past-life regression in the nomadic tribe and the council of twelve people. Eli looked at her strangely.

"What?" she asked.

He stared into space. "I'm not sure…it feels like I dreamed that same dream one time." He kept thinking about it, but the memory stayed cloudy. He could feel Anna looking at him, but no matter what he did, he couldn't bring it into focus.

On the third day, he walked into Anna's room to find her sitting up in bed.

"Hey, you! You're healing by leaps and bounds!" Eli said with a big, happy smile on his face.

"I think it's the nonstop Reiki and prayers you've been sending me," Anna said with an equally big smile.

He glanced down at Anna's lap. She was writing and drawing something. Nodding toward the paper, Eli asked, "Whatcha doing?"

Anna took a deep breath. "I was looking at the beating of my heart on the heart monitor, and I started thinking about frequencies."

He nodded as if to say "Go on…"

"If there were a monitor that looked at all aspects of a person's physical body, we could see their physical strengths up here…" Anna pointed to the frequency peaks on her drawing. "And their physical weaknesses down here." She pointed once again to her drawing, but to the low points or troughs.

"Before the accident I had stamina, a good immune system, a good heart, and so on. Since the accident, the frequency of my physical body has changed. My peaks are less high and the troughs are lower as I'm healing. Hopefully I'll be back to my former physical body, or maybe even higher if I eat well, exercise, drink more water—you know, all the stuff they tell you to do to be healthy."

Eli replied, "That's interesting." But Anna could tell he didn't know where she was going with this yet.

She smiled and continued. "Let's say we had similar monitors that looked at our emotional self, our mental self, and our spiritual self. They would all be pulsing and measuring those aspects of ourselves, right?"

"Give me an example," Eli said, beginning to understand but needing to hear more.

"Okay. One area where I have a low point in my emotional makeup is the shame I go to from the stuff with my uncle. One of my emotional high points, or peaks, is my natural optimism.

"Let me give you another example from the mental self," Anna said. "My mom was in denial about her brother, which ended up causing trouble for her and for me. She wouldn't let herself clearly see what was happening because her mind didn't think she could handle it. That blind spot was a low point, or trough, for her mental self.

"On the other hand, if I have a belief system that I can accomplish something and figure out how to make that happen, I have a peak in the mental self."

Eli said, "In the spiritual self, if you spend time praying, meditating, saying affirmations or mantras, that adds peaks to your spiritual self, right?"

"That's right," Anna said thoughtfully. "A person could map his or her physical frequencies on one page—like on a transparency, so you could see through it—and do the same for the emotional, mental, and spiritual parts. One on each page of the transparency. Then take those four pages of transparencies and put them on top of each other so you could see all of them at the same time. You could measure your lowest and highest points for the person as a whole," Anna explained, getting more excited.

She continued. "Now think of the saying that a chain is only as strong as its weakest link. And look at the troughs of the four frequencies. A person is only as strong as the lowest point in those four parts of the self. I might be incredibly smart, but if I have a blind spot emotionally, it will drag me down as a person."

Eli took her thoughts to the next level. "And if I am trying to be the best person I can be in this lifetime, then I want to work on those low points of each part of myself. That is what helps to evolve my soul. I become better in this life, and I become better at the soul level!"

"Exactly," Anna said. "And the cool part is that it doesn't matter if you are Christian, Jewish, Muslim, Buddhist, or whatever. Or whether you believe in heaven, one lifetime, or reincarnation. By focusing on your frequency, shoring up your weak spots, and building on the strong spots, you can accomplish an important human and spiritual goal.

"And that is why recapitulation is important. Or having a mentor, therapist, priest, minister, coach, or teacher. To overcome the blind spots that hold you back!" Anna concluded.

Eli looked at Anna's drawing of the frequencies. He mused, "The lowest points are our greatest obstacles. And our greatest obstacles are our greatest teachers. Once we really know that in our heart of hearts, really integrate that into our being, then there are no good or bad people in our lives. There are only chances to learn, chances to burn off karma, and chances to grow."

"And like the saying 'The rising tide raises all ships,' working on the low points of each aspect of ourselves raises our whole being higher. And the higher we vibrate, the greater our ability to see through illusion."

Eli looked at Anna sitting up in bed for the first time since the accident. He thought of the heart monitor and the story it had revealed to her. Looked down at her drawing. Then, in a very un-Eli way, he said, "Damn, girl. You're good!"

Anna beamed. And Eli suddenly knew what he had to do.

"When are you coming out here next?" Dave heard as soon as he picked up the phone.

"Soon, Eli," Dave said carefully. "Why?"

"I'm ready to hear the rest of it."

"I'm supposed to come back at the end of this week. Would that work for you?" Dave ventured.

"I can't believe I haven't seen you in six months and you're back in town twice within two weeks. Kind of feels like divine intervention." Eli sighed.

"Maybe there is a god," Dave joked.

They made arrangements and hung up the phone. A minute later, Dave was on the phone with his manager. "Bill, I got a favor to ask. I have to head back to Saint Louis on some personal business for a few days at the end of this week. You okay if I take a couple days of vacation?"

Eli told Anna what happened with the business. He hadn't thought he would, but they had to pass those long hospital hours somehow, so out it came. He didn't cry. He was getting past that part.

His son Tim couldn't get past the guilt, however. Anna told Eli that guilt can become shame if it hangs around too long. Eli didn't want that to happen, so he resolved to begin working closely with Tim so he would understand what had gone wrong. It was a great learning opportunity. A good way to raise those frequencies.

On the fourth day, as Eli was getting ready to go home from the hospital, Dan came into Anna's room.

"Oh, sorry," Dan said, as if Eli were the husband and Dan interrupting. Eli decided to stay awhile longer. Dan caught himself and asked Eli if he would mind giving him and Anna some privacy. He needed to talk to her about something.

"Anna, would you like me to stay?" Eli asked, ignoring Dan.

Anna was in a no-win situation. "Uh, Eli, do you mind waiting outside the door, in case I need you?" She looked and felt very awkward. Anna hated conflict.

"No problem. I'm right here." He smiled and stepped outside. Eli wasn't above being very quiet and standing very close to the open door.

"Anna, I'm sorry. What I mean is, I don't even know how to say those words when it's something this serious." Dan looked shamefaced.

"I know, Dan. It's hard. But this was my last relapse," she said. "I don't have any more inside me." Anna said the words gently, but Dan knew she meant it. "I've spent this time in the hospital thinking about unconditional love. And where it fits into a marriage where there's an addiction."

"What did you come up with?" Dan asked. He didn't know the answer to that question either.

"I decided that I love you unconditionally, whether you drink or not," Anna said, and Dan brightened visibly. Eli heard and tried not to groan.

"But that doesn't mean I want to stay married. I don't want to live my life that way, wondering if I'm going to get the two percent of poop in the bowl of chocolate pudding," Anna said, too tired to explain more.

"I'm not sure what the poop part means, but I understand what you're saying." Dan decided he'd better get going before he had another meltdown, this one in public.

"Can I visit you here in the hospital?" he asked.

"You know," Anna said, trying to be gentle, "for right now I have to pay attention to what I need to get better. I don't do that much, but I need to do it now. I think it would be better if you didn't. I'll call you when I feel better. I would like you to move out of the house. I'm being released from the hospital in about a week, and I think it would be best if you aren't there when I get home. I'm sorry."

Anna owned the house. She had bought it before she and Dan married.

"Okay." Dan leaned over and kissed Anna's cheek. "I fucked up. I'm sorry." He walked past Eli without looking at him. The click of Dan's boots on the shiny hospital floor made Eli think of a movie. One with a sad ending. He wondered what would become of Dan.

Eli poked his head in the door to Anna's room before he left. "Everything okay?" he asked.

"Yep," she said. "Working on my frequencies. Had to put my focus on the right things to raise the bar. I know that being of service resonates at a very high frequency. I thought I would accord it to myself for a change." Anna grinned crookedly. "I'm determined this is my last lifetime on earth."

Eli saluted her and left the hospital. In the car, he called Rachel from his cell phone.

"I'm on my way home," Eli reported.

"How's she doing today?" Rachel asked.

"A lot better than she was. I think she's out of the woods," Eli said, smiling.

CHAPTER 36

"WHAT MADE YOU READY TO hear this now?" Dave asked with honest curiosity. They faced each other in a sun-drenched booth in the restaurant near Eli's house.

"Something Anna said. And before you ask, Anna is a woman who asked me to help her with some spiritual stuff. She thinks I'm her angel. She doesn't realize she's mine."

"You like her?"

"Not the way you're thinking. But yeah, I like her a lot."

Dave wisely chose not to say more about Anna.

"I need your help. I don't remember much about our life growing up, but you obviously do. I need you to fill in the blanks," Eli said. His brother thought it might be the first time Eli had ever asked for help.

How to proceed? Deep breath. Dave began. "You said before that our family was like the Cleavers. The Cleavers were a TV show, an illusion, not reality. Our life was an illusion, too. You know Dad was a successful executive. That part was true, and we have the inheritance to prove it. One good thing he did. He was also good at telling stories, which was probably why he did so well in sales. A bullshit artist. Everyone liked him. Unless, of course, they really knew him.

"Mom grew up in a family not unlike Rachel's. Poor, possibly abused."

While Eli's face had been carefully blank during the recitation about his dad, he flinched and looked down at the cup of tea in front of him when Dave talked about their mother.

"Like a lot of people in sales, including me, dad liked his Scotch too much. His mean side came out when he drank. He'd start at lunch and finish at bedtime, but he got results at work, and that tends to trump everything else.

"Mom tried to keep us as quiet as possible to avoid his notice. That's why you were so good at school. You stayed in your room and studied a lot. The reason I was so bad at school was because I wanted to stay near mom. I didn't like how dad would get by nine or ten at night. I saw what happened.

"Like in a lot of large suburban homes where everyone lives their separate lives, you couldn't hear Dad berate our mother or see him slap her or push her down. But I did, and it wrecked me. The last thing I wanted was to be like Dad, but it turned out I was pretty good at sales, and it turned out that alcohol is a good way of coping. That is, until it isn't. Like when the solution to the problem becomes the problem. That's why I go to AA. I'm not going to let a loser like our dad define my life."

Eli flinched again, but this time he kept his eyes on his brother. "Why didn't I see it, Dave? How were you able to see it? And what's wrong with me that I couldn't?" Shame was heavy in his voice.

"Actually, you did know."

Shock crossed Eli's face.

"Here's how I know...I overheard you talking to Mom one night. Apparently you had come downstairs and heard Dad screaming and cursing at Mom. You were about fourteen; I was eleven. Mom was crying, and Dad stalked out when he saw you. I think he got embarrassed when you saw him." A flicker of pain went through Dave at the memory.

"You walked up to Mom and put your arms around her. Even at that age, you were taller than her. She probably came to your chin. You were trying to comfort her. You told her how you coped with our family. You said you had little boxes in your head, and when something bad happened, you put it in the box. Then you would seal it up so you wouldn't have to see it, feel it, or remember it again.

"It chills me to remember what our mother told you to do. She said, 'Then put what happened tonight in one of those boxes, sweetheart, and never open that box again. Go upstairs and forget about this. Study hard, every night. Go away to college and grow up to become a good man, a good husband, and a wonderful father. I'm okay; don't worry anymore.'

"I remember you cried and said you couldn't leave her like that. She made you promise. And you kept it," Dave finished, his eyes haunted.

Eli felt his mind grow numb immediately after the searing pain in his heart. His voice was flat when he said, "I need the boxes, Dave, or I couldn't keep doing this."

"Do you understand why a man who lies to himself can never be truly trustworthy?"

Eli reached across the table and held his brother's hand. "You are so brave. Just like Anna. I don't know if I can do it..." his voice trailed off. "I don't know if I have it in me. It hurts too much. I can't." He lowered his eyes, then his head. "I'm sorry."

CHAPTER 37

IT WASN'T AN EASY RECOVERY, but Anna worked at it diligently. She couldn't believe how much it hurt to learn to walk again. Or how irritating her lack of patience with her energy level was. But between home health care, physical therapy, occupational therapy, doctors, nurses, insurance companies, and her friend Nancy, Anna regained her strength. Eventually she would need a knee replacement. Both knees had jammed into the dashboard despite her seat belt. Dan's car was too old for an air bag on the passenger side. There was one on the driver's side, which was why he had fared better in the accident than she had.

At night when she was exhausted, a memory haunted her. *Twelve united souls. Where are they now? The unblinking eye of God.* What was it supposed to mean?

Shortly after Anna returned home from the hospital, Eli came to visit.

"I need to ask you something," he said, looking uncomfortable.

"Sure. What?"

"Remember how you e-mailed me during the crisis with the business because you felt something was wrong?" Anna nodded.

"Can you tell me more about that?"

"I felt like I was having a panic attack, but I didn't have anything upsetting me. It felt like it was coming from you. If I had to call it something, I would say I recognized your energy signature," Anna said. She wondered if they were going to have the whole conversation about their connection, or a piece of it.

"I woke up around the time you had your car accident, in a panic. We were supposed to meet the next day, and I couldn't wait to get to the restaurant to see if you were okay. Something felt very wrong," Eli said.

They stared at each other. Anna decided to take a risk. "Do you think about me a lot? I mean, do you feel like I live inside you somehow?" she asked, really uncomfortable now.

"No," Eli said. "I mean, I do think of you, but not all of the time. Not like that." He felt a childish urge to cross his fingers behind his back. He decided not to pursue this line of discussion any more today. Too dangerous.

"We know we've had some past lives together. It's probably connected to that," Eli said, closing the topic.

Anna, never one to know when to stop, said, "Nancy asked me if I felt your panic because you did the Reiki initiation. Like we got stuck and couldn't get unglued," Anna said, embarrassed.

Eli chuckled at that thought. "It would be a good theory, but there is a symbol the master draws at the end of the initiation to separate the two 'beings' again. I drew that symbol, so it couldn't be that." He paused. "I was just curious about what you had felt," he said, and they moved on to other topics.

Near the end of his visit, Eli said, "Anna, would it be okay with you if I give you your third Reiki initiation in a few days and then take some time off from visiting?"

Anna's eyes darkened in shock. She realized in an instant she had become dependent on him since she had been in the hospital and since Dan was gone. She couldn't bring herself to ask what she had done wrong, done to make him want to leave. *I should have pretended that I felt nothing.* The ice of shame filled her. Her face flamed in embarrassment. Mindlessly she wondered how both things could happen at the same time.

Eli, of course, knew. He put his hands on her shoulders and pulled her close for a minute. He rested his chin on the top of her head.

"It's not you, Anna. You know that." He paused. "I need to get this business moving again before we lose it. I need to work with Tim and Chris, as you so thoughtfully pointed out to me. And I want to do some healing with Rachel. You needed me during this time, and I wanted to be here for you. You have your life back on track, Anna. I have to get mine on track, too."

She wished she were allowed to love this man.

She gave Eli a quick hug and then stepped back and flashed him a too-bright smile. "I know. I've been selfish." Eli shook his head no. It's okay. I'm doing fine now," she said. "Get home; you've got responsibilities. Can't be hanging out with me all the time shirking your duties," she joked.

Eli let it go.

She walked him to the car and gave him one more hug. He pulled her close, too close, and held her longer than usual. Then he pushed her back and went on as though nothing had happened. They made plans for Anna's Reiki III initiation and waved good-bye. Anna went back into the house, closing the door quietly behind her. Empty.

CHAPTER 38

"He nearly killed me, Nancy. Good Lord. To die because your husband has to sneak a drink. That's unbelievable. And on top of that, he's still drinking. The only difference is he quit hiding it!" Anna and her friend sat side by side on the couch at Anna's house. Recuperation took a long time.

"Anna, he's got to feel incredibly guilty. It's no excuse, but he's probably drinking to forget about the fact that he nearly killed the one person in the world he loves," Nancy said.

"You think he loves me?" Anna said, shocked.

"He absolutely loves you. He's got this monkey on his back. That's what addiction is, Anna."

"I know," Anna said, "but it's the worst illness. The person has some control over it. They know what they need to do to stay healthy and whole. But they take that one drink, and that's it. He perpetually fools himself that he can take the one drink.

"You know," Anna continued, "I have my screwed-up stuff, but I am grateful addiction isn't one of them." Nancy looked at Anna with a raised eyebrow. Oh, fine," Anna said. "Chocolate, but not alcohol or nicotine."

Nancy nodded meaningfully and then said, "And Eli."

"Oh that's a low blow, Nancy," Anna said, playfully swatting her friend's arm. She went on more seriously and thoughtfully. "Eli's a mystery to me. The strange connection we have, whether he wants to acknowledge it or not. Why is he in my life? I can't 'have him' without being so far out of integrity that I couldn't live with myself, and he couldn't either. Who is he to me? I mean spiritually."

"What about soul mates?" Nancy asked.

"Maybe, but I'm not sure if I even know what that is exactly. It certainly sounds very romantic." Anna paused. "What I do wonder is if we somehow vibrate at the same frequency, or close enough to connect on the emotional, mental, and spiritual levels."

"You missed physical."

"On purpose, so let's not go there," Anna said sternly, but smirking.

"Well, enough about your addiction. Let's get back to Dan. When are you going to talk to him?"

"Soon. And time is running out. I've got something I want to tell you," Anna said with a smile, and she pulled Nancy onto the couch beside her to share her news.

Dan knocked on the door. He was weak as a kitten. Detoxing alone in a motel room, after drinking vodka for days without eating much, had taken its toll.

Anna answered the door and let him in. "I don't want to be mean, but you look like shit, Dan. Are you okay?"

"Not really, but what else is new. You said you needed to see me. Did you want to talk about the divorce?" Dan asked. It was hard for him to concentrate. "Can I sit down? And do you have some water?"

Anna took his arm and led him toward the couch. "Sit. Can you eat anything?"

"I'd better not risk it," Dan murmured.

Anna walked to the kitchen to get him a glass of water, her heart heavy. He was in such bad shape. She wasn't sure how long he could keep up the cycle of drinking, not eating, detoxing. And starting it all over again.

"Anna, I hate to ask this," Dan called from the living room. "Do you mind if I stay here for one night? I'm at John's place tomorrow night, but I don't have anything for tonight." Dan couldn't work anymore. He couldn't stay sober long enough to complete a job.

Anna sighed. "It's okay for one night. You can stay on the couch."

"I have another favor to ask you." She looked at him with an expression of disgust and exasperation. "I can't do money, Dan."

"It isn't money. I was wondering if you would do the Reiki on me. You did a good job with the dog." His voice caught. "I can't do this by myself, Anna. I can't get better. I keep doing the same thing. I don't know how to be different. I've been to inpatient places, outpatient places, AA, therapy groups. I can't stop, and I can't keep going. Will you do the Reiki on me, please?"

Anna felt ashamed of her comment about the money.

"I will, Dan. You rest for a while. Take a shower. I'll make you something to eat, and then I'll do the Reiki. I don't know if it can make a person stop drinking, but it will make you feel calmer and maybe clear your mind. You need peace."

He closed his eyes and leaned back on the sofa. "Lord knows I need peace. That's right."

As he lay resting, Anna held her hands near his head. She felt the Reiki flow. He briefly opened his eyes and murmured, almost too quietly to hear.

"I'm so sorry, Anna."

Dan had fallen asleep on the couch, and Anna let him stay there. She removed his shoes, put a blanket over him, and hoped he could sleep peacefully.

Anna sat at the computer. She had news, and she wanted to let Eli know as soon as possible. They hadn't seen each other since she had had her third and final Reiki initiation a few weeks ago, but they did exchange e-mails.

Subject: Guess What!
Something amazing happened. I got a job offer in Arizona! Not just any old place in Arizona, but in Sedona. I know that's your favorite place on the planet. Mine, too.
One of my clients needs a full-time editor, and they asked me first since I do a lot of freelance work for them.
I'm pretty sure I'm going to take it. Is there any chance you can do lunch soon? I'd like to talk about it and get your opinion.
Anna

It was late in the evening, and Anna didn't expect Eli to get her e-mail before tomorrow morning. She closed down her computer and sat gazing at Dan sleeping on the couch. Why did he have to go through this terrible affliction? What was the purpose behind lifelong pain and struggle? If there was anything that embodied illusion, it was a soul-gripping addiction.

Dan was such a good guy. He was kind and generous, smart and funny. When he drank, he mostly hurt himself. And, by default, those who loved him. If she could wave that Magician's wand and make him whole, she'd do it in a second.

In the middle of her sadness about Dan, Anna was crushed by anguish. *God, it hurts, this pain.*

It rolled in waves, and it wasn't coming from her. *Eli.*

Words filled her mind while she doubled over, holding on to keep from flying to pieces. Words echoed in her mind. *I have to let her go. Dear God, how can I let her go?*

CHAPTER 39

THE NEXT MORNING RACHEL STROLLED to the kitchen in her bathrobe, yawning and searching for coffee. She saw Eli sitting at the kitchen table and asked, "Did you sleep in the spare bedroom last night? I didn't hear you come to bed or get up this morning."

"No, honey. I couldn't sleep last night. I sat and thought."

Rachel looked at him with concern. She felt afraid. Had he decided he couldn't forgive her about the business after all? She moved hesitantly to the table and pulled out a chair. Then lowered herself and sat facing him.

"What's wrong?" she asked, searching his face. He looked so tired and worn, so human. Her heart beat like the wings of a sparrow; her eyes were soft and compassionate. *We're in a new stage of life*. Her husband had begun to look his age. Compassion was quickly followed by guilt that swelled and tightened her throat. Her fault.

"Eli, what's the matter? You're scaring me."

"Honey, I have to tell you something." Eli stood at the precipice. One foot edged close to the emptiness.

"Come here." He reached out to Rachel and pulled her on to his lap. "I have to tell you something important. It's going to be hard to hear, but I'm here with you, and we'll go through it together. I am asking your permission for something."

Her eyes were huge, blue mirrors. He saw his fear reflected in her eyes. He held her like a child and told her everything, and what he must do.

"Please don't," she whispered. He stared into her face and knew he had taken something from her.

"You'll come back?" He nodded.

"I might hate you," she whispered.

He nodded again and waited.

"Do it."

Eli remembered one of Anna's e-mails. "Sometimes the highest love lets go for the sake and the soul of the beloved."

―――

Anna saw Eli's e-mail when she awoke. She had gotten up and fed Dan, and he got ready to go to his friend's house. She told him she would send Reiki to him every day for healing and sobriety. That made him smile, but she saw his eyes were still sad.

"Anna, all I can do is hope until hope is no longer needed," Dan said quietly.

"That's beautiful, Dan. We'll hope together."

They hugged good-bye. "I love you, Anna. Always have." And he turned and left.

―――

Eli was coming over for lunch. He had asked if he could come to her house rather than meet at a restaurant. Anna was excited and spent the morning straightening up the house and preparing lunch. Something felt different.

At his knock at the door, Anna's nerves kicked in. As soon as she saw Eli's face, her own face registered concern. He looked tired and worn. She took his hand and brought him into the house before quietly closing the door.

"What's wrong?" she asked, her throat tight.

The same thing that was wrong when Rachel asked earlier, Eli thought, but he didn't voice it aloud.

"I have to talk to you, Anna. First, that's incredible about the job. Living in Sedona will be a wonderful experience. Do you think you'll take it?" He looked into her eyes.

"I think so." Anna decided to be open with Eli. She would rather risk being rejected than never know if there could have been more between them. "Eli, is there any way…" she stopped. It was so hard to say it, ask it. "Any way you can come with me?" She continued to hold onto his hands.

Eli sighed and looked over her head, and then into her eyes. "I came over here to talk about this with you. The other week, I could tell you wanted to hear more, understand more about you and me. I couldn't have that talk then. I needed to talk to Rachel first." Anna's eyes widened at Eli's words.

"I need to explain something. Rachel's father cheated on her mom. Not just her mom, but on the whole family. He had another family for years they didn't know about. One day he left her mom and didn't give them a cent or an explanation. They searched up and down the streets for him and eventually found him with his other kids. It was horrible for her," Eli said.

"Rachel was married once before she married me. He cheated on her, and she found him in their bed with the other woman. She can barely trust, even with me. Anna, I have never cheated on Rachel. I made a vow to her, God, and myself that I never would be the reason for my wife to lose one more drop of trust in the human race." Anna nodded sympathetically.

"I have something I need to tell you to be in integrity with you. The problem is this. If I get in integrity with you, I'll be out of integrity with Rachel. This morning I told Rachel the same things I am telling you. I asked her permission to talk to you. And I told her what I needed to say.

"I love you, Anna. I always have and I always will, big as the luminous sea. You remember that?" Anna nodded slowly. You are in my heart every day as I work and every night as I sleep. You wondered if I was freaked out when you wrote that e-mail to me. Yes, of course I was. I felt the same. But I needed to know what frequency you were on when you told me that. I asked my Guides and Teachers. They showed me what they showed you: both of us rising above the crowd of humanity and recognizing each other across time and space. Our higher selves remembering each other. Yes, I was very afraid when I read that," Eli said.

"I lied to you the other day when I said you weren't with me all the time. You are."

"I know, Eli," Anna said, relieved to know she wasn't crazy. That this thing she felt had been reciprocated.

Eli looked at Anna with soft eyes. "Which is why I must ask you to help me do the right thing. You and I will always be there for each other. Rachel needs me now, in this lifetime. I need to honor the promise I made to her and to me. She could release me, but I can't release myself. I can't diminish her. I just can't."

Eli took Anna's hands. "I love her, but there's more. She's… she's in my care. I don't know how to say this. I can't express it… but she's my responsibility in this life. I can't abandon her."

He went on. "I don't understand any of this. It feels like you're my wife of the spirit. But we don't have a role here, on Earth, for the spiritual spouse, the spiritual partner, when someone already has an earthly spouse. I meant to teach you, Anna; I failed you in that. I should have stopped as soon as I had feelings for you. My own teacher was a man, and I didn't encounter this before." His eyes were moist from the sadness he felt.

"I knew last night you would let me go," Anna said sadly. "And I already miss you."

"I have to let you go because time will make this worse. It will lead to a temptation that I might not be able to resist. I won't resist. I can't be at that frequency with you. It would kill everyone I love. It feels like it will jeopardize my soul, like I made a promise to Rachel beyond the wedding vows. I know this doesn't make sense…"

Anna sighed. "Somehow, inside, I do understand. I don't know how I know, but somehow I do, and I agree." She paused, thinking, and then went on. "I'm going to take the job. It will help both of us, and it's a good place to heal. Lots of magic in Sedona." Eli nodded and smiled at the memory of their talks.

"I'm so grateful you told me," Anna whispered. "It had to be so hard for you to tell Rachel and for her to hear."

Eli nodded, brown eyes anguished.

Anna thought of something. "Do you think we'll stop feeling the emotions of each other when I move?"

"I don't know. But I have a thought. There is a ritual, a cord-cutting ceremony that severs the ties that pull people together. It is a way of separating our physical, emotional, and mental selves, a way of releasing one another back into ourselves. Do you think we should do it?" Eli asked.

"I think we'd better. We can't end up being 'half a person' without the other. We need to find wholeness in ourselves. You didn't mention spiritual cords. Should we keep those?" Anna asked.

"Please," he said quietly.

~

When Eli walked through his front door two hours later, he feared, and hoped, that Rachel would be gone. She stood waiting for him in the kitchen and met his eyes.

"I'm mad at you," she said.

"I know. I'm sorry."

"Don't hurt me again." Her lip trembled with the emotion she held within. He had forgiven her so much. She could meet him at that frequency.

He nodded and held out his arms for her.

CHAPTER 40

～

As ANNA DROVE ACROSS THE country toward Arizona, she thought about the never-ending to-do list of the last month. Preparing the house to sell, putting it on the market, the surprise of a quick sale. And the surprise of the grief she felt at leaving Saint Louis. Her home, her own personal illusion of what this life was going to be. Dan. Eli. The comfort of her McDonald's routine with Nancy. A closed chapter of a life only half lived to begin with.

I wish I were dead.
I wish I were alive.

～

Flanked by canyon walls, Anne drove the narrow road between Flagstaff and Sedona, Anna's thoughts went back to the last visit with Eli. He had backed away from her until the final day in the house, and then he came to visit. The house was empty and scrubbed, awaiting its new family. The closing would be the following day, and Anna would be on her new journey.

His knock at the door had echoed hollowly, she remembered. He came through the front door and reached for her.

His kiss was urgent, and his tongue explored the warm cavern of her mouth. She didn't pull away or pretend to not want him. She pulled him closer, and he was hard against her belly. He reached behind her, cupping her bottom in his strong hands. He pulled her up and tight against him. Her arms encircled his neck, and their kiss deepened and ended as he nipped her lower lip with his teeth. As he set her down and they stepped apart, Anna's hands trailed along his thighs, her fingernails lightly scratching on their downward journey. Eli tangled his hands in her hair and clutched her close one more time.

He finally spoke, and his words shocked her. "Stay away from me. Get the hell out of here before I ruin both of us." Her shock was not because the words were said harshly, but because they were spoken like a love poem. He cupped her face one more time, kissed her forehead, and left. Anna realized later she hadn't spoken a single word.

~

It was during the last mile to Sedona that Anna decided she had one regret. Not the betrayal of Eli's marriage vows, although she knew she should. She regretted she had not tasted the warm skin of his chest.

Then another thought. She had never felt safe. Not in her mother's womb, nor on her father's lap as a child. Not with her two husbands. In all the years of anticipating danger, the most dangerous place Anna had ever stood was in Eli's arms. Yet she had clung to him and never felt safer.

~

"How do I get started?" Eli asked his brother in measured tones after preliminary small talk about the weather.

"What do you want to accomplish?" Dave said, consciously relaxing his grip on the phone.

"Good question. I'm tempted to say peace of mind, but maybe that's why I made these boxes in my head in the first place. And before you ask, How's that working for you? don't, since we both know the answer."

"Yeah, well, what do you want to happen?" Dave asked again.

"I don't know what I want to happen. Look, I know I sound like an idiot, but why did you go to the therapist? What were you trying to achieve?" Eli asked, honestly at a loss.

"Look, Eli, you gotta remember I had two divorces in five years. I drank too much. I cheated on both of my wives. I spent too much money on things. Got in stupid lawsuits over custody, child support, or alimony. Other than being good at making money, I didn't have much going for me. I was lonely. My kids didn't even want to see me. I needed serious help. You talk about peace of mind—I was trying to find peace of mind and some semblance of a normal life."

Dave went on. "And I have to tell you that it got worse before it got better. You don't go digging around our childhood and come out unscathed. You remember how you had to come out here after Toni left me? I was suicidal, Eli. You got me hooked up with that divorce support group, which led me to my therapist. My drinking got worse before it got better. Then AA, then different friends, yada yada. You remember."

"I'm sorry, Dave. I wish I'd done more," Eli said, regret heavy in his voice. "Put like that…I hate what you've been through. I have to tell you the truth. It was Rachel who realized how bad things were with you. She's the one who sat me down and practically forced me to get on a plane. My blindness could have killed you, Dave."

"I'm grateful to both of you, however it happened. You got here, you got me help. I hit rock bottom and was ready to accept help. All of that needed to happen. And it wasn't your blindness. It was my blindness. Me fooling myself and hurting everyone, including myself."

Dave continued. "And now you're in pain. The difference is that you don't hurt others; you end up hurting yourself. On the surface, you look a lot better than I did. Yes, it's your second marriage, but you and Rachel have been together for a long time. Great kids. No alcohol problems, no drugs, no affairs. You look good, Eli. But I still know you're hurting. The boxes you talk about helped you get through the bad times. Now they're standing in the way of the good times. They were a refuge, and they turned into little prisons. So what do you think you want to accomplish?"

"I want to see."

"What's that mean?"

"I don't even know how to word this, Dave. I created a story of my life. Not a life, a story in my head of what my life was all about. A story about who I am—a hardworking business owner. A faithful husband. A caring father. A good friend. If it didn't fit in those boxes, I ignored it or maybe tried to justify it like I did the last day that Anna was here." Eli told Dave everything about Anna, even the things he was ashamed of.

"That's why I let Anna go. I couldn't find a way to fit her into the story of my life. And maybe she wouldn't have fit anyway, but I didn't even try. She pushed me to tear down the boxes, and I was relieved when she moved away. I slipped back into my dream world, my illusion. She tried to grow and tried to help me to grow. But I couldn't fit her...her words...anywhere. The most out-of-the-box thing I did was to go to the hospital when Rachel didn't want me to."

Dave heard the self-loathing in Eli's words.

"Eli, you *are* all of those good things—faithful, caring, a good person. But you are *more* than those things, too. More than a cut-out version of a good person, but a whole person. There are worse ways you could've coped than being too good, for crying out loud!"

Even Eli had to laugh at that. "Yeah."

Dave went on. "But Anna scared you. Without trying to, she showed you another world, another possible life. You're right. You freaked. Maybe with good reason; who knows? But let's go back to your original question—how do you get started?"

Eli was silent. Dave waited.

Eli took a deep breath. "I think I need to take each box and look inside. Maybe starting with the one called son, or good student. Something from our past, back when this all started. Tear off the packing tape and look inside. With a flashlight..."

"Maybe a spotlight," Dave added lightly.

"Yeah. But how?"

"What was that 'fuck-you word' about taking a good hard look at your life?"

"Recapitulation." This time he didn't growl the word; he whispered it. Smiled a little sadly and thought of Anna. "I'm going to try, Dave. I'll get a therapist, and maybe it's time to do some spiritual work with a teacher again. This time starting from a whole different place."

"Eli...what about the marriage box?"

"I think it's gonna be the last one. It's the one that holds the greatest possibility of hurting Rachel and the kids. I've got to practice before I get to that one. And I have to be really, really sure of who and what I am."

Dave nodded, even though Eli couldn't see him.

"There's one thing I'm keeping in the box for now."

"Anna. Right?"

"Yeah. Anna. For now, I'm going to let her go. There are a thousand worlds in her and in me, Dave, and a thousand boxes. I'm going to focus on my past and then my present. If she's meant to be in my future, she'll still be there. But I can't walk the worlds of maybe and yes at the same time. I have to start somewhere. I need to heal what's in front of me."

"You know I'm here, right?" Dave said quietly.

"Damn straight, brother. You're going to be the therapist!"

"I know you're kidding. You are kidding, right?"

Eli laughed. "Well, I could torture you a little longer, but even I'm not so delusional as to believe I don't need professional help. So you're off the hook. Unless, of course, it's three in the morning and I need someone…"

"That goes without saying."

Dave laughed quietly. "Eli, I'm imagining the visual you're going to create with some amazing software that illustrates each box and a timeline for solving it. You'll design it, sell it, and make a gazillion more dollars!"

"Yep. Trust me to put the process of tearing down the boxes in a box called Healing."

"You're gonna be okay. Call me at three a.m. anytime you want. Except tonight. I gotta get up at four to catch a flight to Boston tomorrow morning."

"You therapists! So inaccessible!"

Anna loved her job, and she loved the red rocks and energy of Sedona. It didn't stop the daily torrent of tears she experienced the first six months away from Saint Louis. Grief, hot and potent.

She learned that severed cords of connection could still shoot forth new growth and seek the beloved like tangled vines seeking sunlight. She still felt his presence and his thoughts.

Months later she learned the only thing worse than feeling the thoughts of a loved one was feeling the absence of that person's thoughts. He was forgetting her, Anna realized. How was it possible when he never seemed to leave her heart?

In month eight, she hadn't cried in two weeks. She knew she should celebrate, but she cried instead. In another year or two, Eli might become a fond memory. She would have given up on him, just as she could feel him giving up now. She wanted to be whole. With him or without him, she had to reach a place of peace and balance.

She chopped the vines that reached again and again for him. One of these days she would be free.

CHAPTER 41

"Dan, my God! It's been years! How are you?" Anna's friend Nancy had received his call this morning. It had been at least four years since Anna divorced Dan and moved away. Nancy hadn't heard a word from or about him since that time.

"I'm good, Nancy. Really good. I've been sober for the past three and a half years. I'm in a relationship with a great woman. She has a child, a son, and I find I love being a father. And I finished college!" Dan said, and then he continued. "Nancy, I don't have too much time right now, but I'm trying to track down Anna. I'm in Phoenix on business and wondered if she was still in this area. Do you have her phone number? I lost touch with her after the divorce, and then she moved."

"I have it right here, Dan. I miss her, but we're still on the phone with each other every week. In fact, you should call her soon. She's going into the hospital in Phoenix for a knee replacement." Nancy paused, and there was an awkward silence.

"Was it because of the accident?" Dan asked, praying that it wasn't.

"I'm sorry, Dan," Nancy said. "Yeah. Her knees were never the same. Dan, I have to tell you this. Anna forgave you a long time ago. Don't hold on to it and let it make you sick."

"Thanks, Nancy. That means a lot to me. Do you think she'll mind me contacting her?"

"I think she'll be so happy to hear your news. And one more thing. She's been sending you Reiki every day since you broke up."

Tears threatened to overflow. "I think it worked, Nancy. Thanks for telling me."

"Dan!" Anna cried, pulling him into a tight hug. "I can't believe it! You look wonderful!"

"It's a lot easier to look wonderful when you don't drink or have secrets," he said, hugging her again. He buried his face in her soft hair and breathed in the essence of his once-upon-a-time wife. "God, I missed you."

"Sit down. Tell me everything." Anna directed him to the couch in her little home in Sedona.

He told her the whole story about Lu Marston. The drinking, losing her and Rich Marston's trust, and finally about how they had reconnected after he'd achieved a year of sobriety. They now had their own AA group and continued to keep each other sober.

Then about the woman he lived with, loved, and planned to marry. About her amazing fifteen-year-old son. They were a package deal, and he was grateful every day for both of them.

He finally got to the part of the story he dreaded exploring. "Anna, you must hate me for what I did. And you're still living with it because of your knees. Nancy said you're getting an operation." Dan ached with guilt.

"I have to tell you a story, Dan." Anna paused. "Just listen." She smiled to let him know it was a good story.

"I was filled with anger for a long time. Too long. When we were married, I loved you, and I thought we could have a pretty good marriage. I had an idea in my mind of what that would look like, and I thought if only you would change, we could have that marriage, that life. I blamed you," Anna said.

Dan interrupted. "Rightfully so."

"Sshh. My story; hush." She smiled and went on. "I had a lot to learn about life and people, and myself. Anyway, I realized about two years after our divorce, I had forgiven you. And I forgave myself for getting fooled." Anna sighed.

"Thank you, Anna," Dan said softly.

"There's more." A long pause. "One day I was cooking in my kitchen. This was maybe another year after I forgave you. You came into my mind, clear as day. And something miraculous happened. I realized there was nothing to forgive. I had brought you into my life to learn about love and illusion. My own, and yours. That was the moment I loved you for who you really were, and I loved myself—something I still had not managed to do up to that point in time."

Dan looked down, sudden emotion choking him, and then said, "Anna, I learned as I got sober that the first forgiveness is with the self. But the story you told me gave meaning to this thing I've carried forever. That is a gift that only you could have given me. Thank you."

"Likewise," she murmured. Her eyes were bright with unshed tears as she gazed at the face of her friend.

CHAPTER 42

"I HAVE TO SAY, WHEN you decide to do something, you don't stop until you've turned over every rock," Eli's brother said as they walked together through the woods near Eli's home.

"Or have opened every box," Eli added, his eyes crinkled with laughter. He took a deep breath. "I'm glad you're here, Dave. Thanks for coming."

"Nothing could keep me away. You've been pretty closed-mouthed about things. I wanted to give you space. But you've been on my mind a lot, and I jumped at the chance to come here."

"Thanks, brother. I told you I was going to start working on the past and work my way up to the present with therapy. Last year, Rachel and I started couples counseling, so there's been more and more clarity in a lot of areas."

Dave nodded encouragingly as he looked at Eli's face. *Less burdened, softer, and happier.*

"It's been an amazing experience. She and I are closer than we've ever been in our lives, including the early years. I've learned so much about myself and about her. So glad we did this. Part of why I was hoping you'd come here was to thank you for urging me down this path."

"Thanks for saying that, Eli, but you're the brave one for opening the boxes."

Their mutual soft laughter was closely followed by equally soft sighs of compassion.

Dave glanced at his brother, and while he wanted to be happy for where this was going, a flicker of...disappointment... went through him. He loved Rachel as a person and as a sister-in-law, but deep inside, he had never thought that Eli and Rachel brought out the best in each other as a couple. But it wasn't his business, and both Rachel and Eli looked happier than he had seen them look in years.

"I love Rachel now more than I ever have before, which is why what I'm going to tell you might not make sense. Rachel and I have decided to end our marriage." Eli stopped and turned to Dave, watching the look of shock, and something else, on his face. "What is it, Dave? What are you thinking?"

"My God! Is it mutual?" Dave's initial surprise and touch of relief had turned to concern for Rachel. He'd always felt there was a fragile child beneath her placid exterior, and a rush of protectiveness overwhelmed him. "How's she holding up? She seemed okay when I saw her at the house...but is she all right with this?"

Eli nodded and gestured toward a large boulder with two carved depressions. He gave a wan smile as he said, "Let's sit here in my 'office,' and I'll tell you what happened."

As the two brothers settled side by side on the rock, Dave continued to regard Eli with concern. "What happened?"

"Well, keep in mind that we've been seeing the counselor for over a year. During that time, a ton of things have happened—the normal ups and downs of life, plus Chris got married. Then Tim and Sarah had a baby, so we became grandparents, not to mention that Rachel was offered the job of director at the food pantry where she volunteered. I hate to say it, but while they'd been growing, I'd been feeling stuck—I felt like I lost my true north over the last couple of years. I still take classes, do a little mentoring with young entrepreneurs—that kind of stuff, but I felt stale. I felt like I was going through the motions of life. I don't mean that about the kids and our grandson—that's been incredible!—but I personally felt lost."

Eli took a deep breath and stared into the woods. Dave waited for him to continue.

"I'm going to give you the gist of it, but suffice it to say that a lot happened in our family, and a lot of growing was occurring with Rachel, too. It took me a while, but between the therapist, Rachel, and my own thick skull, I realized I was depressed. It shocked me, Dave."

Eli went on. "Turned out there was a lot of shit in those boxes. A heck of a lot of stories in my head about what I should and shouldn't be or do as a person. You were right about our mom and dad. I suppressed a lot. One of the things I suppressed was the guilt I felt about not saving our mom from our dad." Eli felt Dave's startled reaction beside him, but he kept his eyes on a sparrow that had drawn near to them, curiously unafraid.

"I ended up remembering what you heard mom tell me all those years ago. The whole thing about 'go off and be successful, and don't look back.' I did it, and I blanked it out of my conscious mind. But I paid a price, brother," Eli said, finally turning his head to look into Dave's dark eyes. "I paid by trying to be perfect. The guilt of leaving her like that killed me. And, weirdly, I transferred my guilt for not saving mom into thinking I was saving Rachel."

Dave stayed silent, nodding his head slightly in subtle agreement. Something about that made sense to him.

Eli continued. "The bad part about thinking I was saving her was that I put Rachel in the one-down position. It wasn't conscious, but the implication was that she *needed* saving. This dynamic was part of what pulled us to each other, and she was particularly vulnerable coming off her bad first marriage. And vulnerable from her childhood, which left her feeling alone and lost."

Dave mused aloud. "Are you saying that our childhood set you up to want to save someone, and her childhood set her up for feeling fragile and thinking she needed to be saved? That she wasn't strong enough to do it on her own?"

"That's exactly what I'm saying. And this underlying story playing in both our heads made me look like the 'healthy one' and her like the 'sick one.' And in having to be the healthy one, I never looked beneath the surface of my own press to really understand who I was. And in having to be the sick one, Rachel didn't get a chance to grow 'from the inside out.' If she became strong, I might 'lose my purpose' and go away. If she stayed weak, she got to keep her life but could never really grow and develop into the incredibly capable woman that she is. She coped by dressing up her exterior self with lots of expensive clothes and jewelry. She couldn't fix the inside without losing everything, so she focused on the outside."

"My God, Eli. That's unbelievable."

"You started the ball rolling, Dave. And Rachel and I are both incredibly grateful. Once we started working at this level and looking at 'the stories in our heads'—that's what we're calling what happened—well, the depression resolved pretty quickly. I had been suppressing a lot of anger because I was playing a role instead of being an honest-to-God person. Rachel was suppressing a lot of anger, too, for the same reason. That anger played into the secrets she and Tim had a few years ago that almost brought the company down."

"But, Eli, why break up? You said you guys feel closer than ever."

"I know. We're two humans talking to each other now instead of two characters from a story, although it's so easy to fall back into playing a role. We keep each other honest now. I'm so grateful to her, and I wouldn't trade what happened for the world. We brought some amazing kids into the world, we created a great business, and even with the stories—the illusion—there was a lot of genuine love and caring. Neither of us would trade it for anything." Eli sighed before he continued.

"Remember four years ago when I told you that my goal was 'to see'? I didn't even know what I meant by that. I had no clue what I would see or where it would lead. I knew enough to be scared, but not enough to know what could really happen. Rachel and I talked about this. We could stay together and keep achieving more and more clarity. We love each other; we know we get along. It might be easier on the kids. But Rachel mentioned it first, and then I came to the same conclusion. We want to give ourselves a chance to 'be', out there in that bigger world. Rachel wants to spend time learning who she is, this fifty-something version of herself. And I have something I want to find out, too."

Dave stared at his brother, gently nodding. Finally he said quietly, "Anna."

"Dave, sometimes you're so perceptive, it's scary. I haven't mentioned her name to you in four years. Why would you think it was about Anna?"

"Because when she moved, you lost your light. That's the only way I know how to describe it. What are you going to do?"

Eli straightened, almost as if he expected an argument. "I'm getting on a plane in a few weeks and going to see her."

"I didn't know you guys were still in touch," Dave murmured.

"We're not, but there's no way I'm going to call or e-mail all of this to her. I know where she lives. I don't think she's remarried, but I have no idea if she has a boyfriend, or anything."

"Man friend," Dave said, straight faced.

"Hearing those words upsets me, which is ridiculous."

"Isn't it risky, flying out there without asking her ahead of time? What if she isn't home?" Dave felt he had to say it.

"I'll wait."

CHAPTER 43

THE OPERATION HAD GONE FINE, but a severe infection had set in overnight. Very unusual. Voracious, fast, deadly.

A nurse called Nancy on the phone and read the note that Anna had written. *I'm really sick and I have a bad feeling about this. They had to transfer me to the hospital in Phoenix. Dan's in Phoenix on business again. Can you call and ask him to come here? I'm scared.*

Nancy called Dan immediately and told him what was happening.

He explained to his boss that he was taking some time off. He called his girlfriend and her son and explained everything. She told him she loved him and to take as much time as he needed.

Anna looked so tiny and pale lying in the hospital bed with tubes and monitors. She held on to his hand and cried. It was hard to let go.

"Anna, do you want me to call Eli?" He wasn't sure why he asked, but he felt he needed to.

She nodded slightly as the tears and her breathing got worse.

Dan could barely stand the pain. He promised her and then decided to take it a step further. He'd bring Eli out here to be with her, just in case. Dan shot off an e-mail.

Subject: Need Your Help
Eli, I don't know if you remember me. It's Dan Woodland, Anna's ex-husband. Through a series of coincidences that would take too long to explain, I am with Anna at a hospital in Phoenix. It doesn't look good. I remembered our dinner conversation that one time when we talked about death and dying. I think she would like you to be here with her. Can you? I will pay for you to come out, but I think there is very little time. Can you let me know?
Dan

~

Eli was sitting in the living room, staring out his window at the crows and listening to their magnificent caws. He was thinking about Anna and feeling tense. He focused on the silhouette of one of the birds. It stood tall on the largest tree of their property, a contrast against the winter sky. As the sky was pierced with its cry, Eli's heart began to race. Something terrible was happening.

He looked at Rachel, who was on the computer. She stared back at him oddly. "What?" she asked, as if from a long distance.

"Something's wrong," he whispered.

Rachel looked down at the computer, reread the e-mail from Dan she'd seen yesterday, and stared again at the man who would soon be her ex-husband. Taking separate paths was for the best; she knew that and felt it within her being.

Nevertheless, her hand hovered over the keyboard, finger on the delete button. Without fully knowing why but with trancelike deliberation, she slowly pressed it.

Dan sat with Anna and held her hand. He hadn't heard back from Eli. Not a word. *Didn't think he was that kind of guy. The e-mail address must not be good.* He couldn't leave Anna's side to search out Eli, but he would find him later. He would keep his promise to Anna.

Nancy was on her way. He prayed she would make it in time. He searched his memory for everything that Eli had told him about death at dinner that night. It had been years ago. Dan had still been drinking then. In the past he had used every drop of alcohol to erase the memories of his childhood and to forget the pain he had caused others. For once in his life, he prayed he would remember.

Anna was resting on the angel. The wings were thick. Elijah was his name. Nothing hurt anymore. She felt distracted by the monitors. Something about the frequency, something she was supposed to remember. Something important.

"Please remember, sweetheart, please..." her mother whispered insistently.

Then another voice, the voice of someone dear. Dan? "Go to the light, Anna," he whispered. "Lean into the light."

"I have to work here, sir. You need to let me check on her," a different voice said from the dream.

"Get the hell out of here. Leave us alone!" Dan's voice again. Strident.

A door closed sharply, startling Anna.

Dan laid his head on her heart, gently.

"Listen to me, love. Go to the light." His voice was insistent. Suddenly she remembered everything, understood it all. Laughed in amazement at it all.

Dan lifted his head in shock. Anna opened her eyes, locked her gaze on Dan.

"Thank you for my life," she whispered.

Dan didn't know where his words came from; certainly not from him. "Go home. It's your turn. Follow the light. I promise—I'll find the others."

She opened her hands and reached up for something he couldn't see. He prayed and gently positioned her head so the light could pour into her.

The pulse of her monitor went flat, its shriek piercing the room. Footsteps pounded, running to the door. Pandemonium.

He held inside the deep keening as he covered her ears with his large hands, trying to block the chaos. No distractions, he remembered. He murmured softly until he was sure. Then kissed her good-bye.

The peace of the moment was shattered by the abrupt, frantic voices of the medical team.

"Move him aside!" a voice barked urgently.

Dan was shoved from Anna's body as they struggled to save her. But he knew it was too late as he leaned against the wall for support. She was gone.

CHAPTER 44

"I WANTED TO LET YOU know," Dan said to Eli over the phone.

"I knew." Eli listened to the sounds of Rachel packing.

"Did you get my e-mail?" Dan asked, sudden rage gripping him on Anna's behalf.

Eli stared at Rachel.

"I was told about it, but I already knew. I went into the woods near my house and prayed." He paused. "I couldn't reach her...I wanted to be there." Eli's voice was faint, his mouth too far from the receiver as he stared without seeing. "Dan, what happened?" he asked softly.

"I'd like to talk to you in person. Do you mind if we get together? I'm here in Saint Louis. I also have something I'd like to ask you." Dan waited.

"What is it?" Eli asked, although somewhere inside he already knew.

"I don't know how to word this. Anna showed me something at the end. Something she was seeing."

Dan heard Eli's soft intake of breath just before he asked the question that had been on his mind since that moment in the hospital.

"What did Anna show you?" Eli asked, a little more abruptly than he had intended.

Dan had come over to Eli's house that night, and they were sitting together in the study. Dan looked good, younger and more vigorous than Eli remembered.

It still bothered Eli that he hadn't been there when Anna had needed him. And he was glad that Dan had been, except for a small, all-too-human part that resented him. In the past he would have put that uncharitable thought in a box and told himself he was above such a petty feeling. But he'd done a lot of work on himself, checking those boxes with ruthless clarity. And he really didn't like it, but he knew he had to integrate and come to terms with the thoughts and feelings that seemed beneath him but which he still experienced. He was done lying, especially to himself.

"Please, Dan. Tell me everything."

Dan gazed into Eli's eyes. Something was definitely different. He didn't seem as self-assured as he had at dinner all those years ago. Right now he looked haggard, his hair shaggy, and the tension rolled from him in waves. *Vulnerable...that describes it. He looks worse for wear, but he feels more real. Interesting.*

Dan began by explaining how he had ended up at Anna's house before her operation and their conversation. Eli nodded as he listened. A host of feelings played across his face. It was clear that he cared deeply about Anna. As Dan talked, he could hear Rachel packing in the living room and wondered again what was going on in their household.

"So that's how I came to be at the hospital when Anna contracted pneumonia. Thank God she was with it enough to get a message to Nancy, who in turn called me. The timing of this was amazing. I hadn't seen Anna since the divorce, except for my one visit to her home a week before this happened. Anna got worse the next day," Dan said, his voice uneven.

"I remembered some things you said about what to do when someone was dying. We had talked about it at dinner that one night you and Rachel and Anna and I got together."

Eli interrupted. "I can't believe you remembered any of that. Thinking back, I can't believe, as we sat there talking, that one day you would use that information for Anna." His voice caught. The two men sat quietly for a moment, remembering that night and Eli's slip about Anna at his deathbed. Eli closed his eyes briefly and then asked Dan to tell him the rest.

"I was with her, and her heart stopped beating. She was attached to a lot of monitors and stuff, and the monitors went crazy. It was so loud, Eli, and all I could remember was that it should be quiet so she wouldn't be distracted. So she would see the light and go to it. I reached over to cover her ears to block the sound, and I laid my head on her chest, at her heart. There was no heartbeat, Eli. It was the loudest silence I had ever heard. I was trying not to lose it. I needed to give her time to find the light. I think I might have kicked the doctor away from her, because they were all rushing into the room at that point," he said, half ashamed and half proud.

"Good for you, Dan. You were incredible." Eli nodded his strong agreement.

"Well, maybe not too good because, thank God, they were able to revive her, and I might have stopped that from happening. But very good in this way: while my head was on her heart, Anna somehow poured what she was seeing into my mind. I found out later that she was already in the light." He had to stop before he broke down, and he took a moment to regroup.

Dan continued. "She was in the light and merging with it. That's how she explained it."

"What did you actually see, Dan?"

"Pictures, like a quick movie, but I somehow knew the meaning behind the pictures. It was 'inserted' into my mind. I just knew…" His voice trailed off, partially in exasperation that he could not describe the indescribable. "I saw in the light, but I also saw other images. Anna doesn't remember the other part, only the light. It was as if she passed me the baton of these images for safekeeping and then lost them from her mind."

"My God, Dan. I can't imagine what you were going through. Trying to remember what I'd said, trying to help Anna at that key moment, and then seeing what she saw. My God," Eli whispered, his expression dazed.

Dan nodded. "It's easier to tell you the meaning of the story rather than the rapid-fire images that I saw. So let me tell that, and then I'll try to fill in the experience of it."

"Okay."

Dan continued. "Do you remember when Anna had her past-life regression at Awakenings with the woman there?"

Eli nodded and looked startled. "She was the leader of a group of nomadic people. Her mom died, and she became the leader when she was about eight years old, just a kid. She described a group of twelve wise men and women. They were preparing to move the whole group to a new location. That's it, right?"

Now Dan looked startled. "She did that regression four years ago. How did you remember it?"

"It was weird, but when she told me about it, I felt a sense of déjà vu. I felt like I had been there too, which is why it really stuck in my mind." He didn't add that he remembered nearly every word he and Anna had shared. It had been a precious time.

"Yeah, you and me both. I felt the same thing, except I was such a hardhead back then that I thought it was all bullshit. I rationalized it away, but if the truth be told, I felt like I was sitting at that fire, taking the vow to act as one and to help one another throughout time. And I felt like an idiot for even feeling it."

"It is understandable," Eli murmured, and then he asked, "What does it mean?"

"It means that you and Anna and I were actually there. It really happened. There are twelve of us. Some of us are on earth now, and some of us will be born soon. We took a vow to help one another," Dan said, and then he hesitated. "Apparently souls like to travel in groups of twelve."

Dan cocked his eyebrow, as if daring Eli to refute what he was saying.

Silence.

"Who knew," Dan finally said, shrugging.

They both burst out laughing.

Rachel poked her head into the study. "Are you guys all right?"

"It's okay, honey. I'll tell you about it later." Eli sent an affectionate glance, which Rachel returned. She left and returned to packing.

Eli noticed Dan's confusion as he stared at the spot where Rachel had been standing. Companionably, Eli caught Dan's glance as well, and he repeated, "I'll tell you about it later, too."

Dan nodded, and a brief smile flickered across his face. *I think we've turned a corner.*

"Anyway, the twelve of us decided to help one another and apparently have been farting around for eleven or twelve hundred lifetimes trying to figure things out."

Eli replied, "You know, I've always wondered why people sound so proud when they call themselves 'an old soul.' We're old as dirt, and all it means is that we're the slowest learners on the planet!" Both guys sat quietly, shaking their heads in disbelief.

"Well, it seems we got a little smarter lately." Dan paused, and then he continued. "Oh, wait. I have to tell you about the White. The White is where we hang out between lifetimes and reflect on the meaning of what we went through in the last life and decide what we want to work on next. This is the dream that Anna kept having but couldn't remember. The one that was driving her crazy. A lot goes on in the White!

"It's kind of like the soul makes a contract about what it wants to learn in the next lifetime. Then it goes to earth, and the person totally forgets about the contract. Oh, and manages to get into a lot of trouble connected to that specific learning and does a lot of 'woe is me!' while forgetting that he or she invited that lesson into his or her life in the first place."

Dan reflected a moment and then said, "This system was either designed by a genius or is the most screwed-up thing in the universe."

Eli leaned closer to Dan. "I've read this stuff in books, but I've never experienced or even met someone who's experienced what you saw with Anna. It tracks with what I've studied. It's incredible. What does Anna say about it all?"

"Anna only remembers being in the light and then seeing her mom and dad. They told her to stop, that she needed to finish something before she could go further. It took her a while to reorient, what with being sick, her heart stopping twice, and having to leave the warmth and love from the light. She is exhausted. I hated leaving her, but her friend Nancy's with her in the hospital. I needed to get here right away to get your take on this. I haven't even told her what happened on my end," Dan said, and he sighed from his own exhaustion.

"Dan...did you tell her you were coming to see me?"

"I didn't. I was still pissed that you hadn't responded to the e-mail, and I wanted to find out where you were at on this...where you were with her...before I said anything. She's too sick to have to deal with..." Dan trailed off as he looked meaningfully at Eli.

"With my stuff. I know. You did the right thing. Do you think it will be okay if I go out there to be with her?"

"When are you thinking of going?" Dan asked.

"Tomorrow morning."

Dan looked at Eli oddly. "It's none of my business, Eli, except that I'm making it my business—are you free to do that? Go out there and be with her? I mean, really be with her?"

"I am," he stated without further explanation.

"I think it's an excellent idea. She's going to need a lot of healing, and you might be the right healer." Dan smiled gently.

Eli nodded, and his eyes looked more peaceful. "You mentioned before that we seem to be getting smarter. What did you mean?"

CHAPTER 45

Eli's plane landed in Phoenix the next afternoon, and he took a cab directly to the hospital.

He stood outside Anna's room, steadying himself. Too many years had passed. He had wondered why the torn place in his heart couldn't seem to heal, but he was beginning to understand.

He stepped into her room. She was sleeping, and still so very sick. Eli gazed at Anna, and the light reflected off the sheen of perspiration that covered her pale face. "Another hospital," he thought as he moved closer to her and settled into the big blue chair to the right of her bed. She was attached to the monitors that stood guard on the left side, near her head.

Eli reached for her hand. It was warmer than he had expected. Her skin was nearly translucent. She looked worn out, the lines around her mouth more firmly etched. He cupped her face with his free hand and ran the pad of his thumb along her cheek. He smoothed the lines that had appeared since he had last seen her, saddened that she had grown older without him by her side.

Eli waited for the gentle touches to awaken Anna, and they did. She stared at him without comprehension for a few seconds and then smiled tentatively.

"Am I dead?" Anna said, sounding drugged.

Eli felt his loss even more profoundly.

"No, thank God. I needed to see you for myself. So I got on a plane to make sure," Eli said quietly. "And you scared Dan half to death in the process."

Anna tried to keep her focus. She was exhausted from the last week. "Total blur. I've been trying to remember, but it's all bits and pieces."

Anna looked around the room, a little lost. "Where's Nancy?" she asked. "She's been staying here with me since…since it happened." Anna couldn't bring herself to say the words.

Eli smiled gently at Anna. "She went to the cafeteria to give me some time with you," he murmured.

"I can't believe you're here…so glad." She was tiring.

It wasn't the words alone but the happy spark he'd glimpsed in her eyes that lightened his heart. When she rested her head against his hand, Eli felt tension drain away. They were going to be okay.

He leaned closer and put his mouth close to her ear. His breath was warm and ticklish as he whispered, "Little One, when you're feeling better, I'm going to tell you a story. But it can wait until you're stronger. One more week won't make a difference."

―

"There are twelve of us. We don't know how many are in form—that is, how many are alive on Earth right now—and how many are waiting in the White for us to return."

She snuggled against him, tired again. "Can't wait until my energy comes back."

Eli nodded in sympathy. He let her sleep.

~

"Okay, let's try again; start from the beginning," Anna said, her voice stronger.

The two of them were curled together in Anna's hospital bed. Eli had laughed to himself thinking how much 'bed time' he and Anna had logged without anything more than hugging and talking. He was counting on more somewhere down the line, but right now Anna needed healing, and they both needed to process a lot of very wild stuff.

"Remember how the twelve members of the tribe took a vow to stick together and help one another throughout time?"

"I remember seeing it in my past-life regression, but I don't 'remember it' with my current brain."

"Good distinction, Anna. And you might never have remembered it...well, we might never have remembered it...except you saw it clearly as you were dying—look, I hate saying those words, but I need to get used to saying that because that's what happened, not once but twice before they brought you back for good—so I'm forcing myself to say it."

Anna nodded. She'd been having the same problem.

"You saw it clearly, and you somehow managed to pass the images to Dan. Here's what else you showed him. We twelve call the space between lifetimes the White. The best Dan could tell is that souls tend to travel in groups. Which might mean that Rachel and my kids are part of this, too. Or Nancy, or other meaningful people in our lives."

"My God, that's so amazing."

He smiled and nodded. "Incredibly amazing, and kind of cozy, too." Anna rested her head against Eli's. Cozy. She was ready for cozy.

"Just as we thought, earth is like a school. On earth we have physical bodies, emotions, thoughts—and it's a wonderful place full of life, drama, and stories. There are so many ways to learn. But"—Eli made air quotes—"the air is thick down here."

Anna looked puzzled.

"These physical bodies and emotions and stuff are amazing things, but everything that happens gets filtered through our bodies and our experiences. In other words, everything is an illusion—we can't see clearly. In the White, we decide what we want to work on in a particular lifetime. Then we get here and forget what we wanted to work on," he said wryly.

"That sucks," she said seriously.

"Yeah, Dan and I thought so too." He smiled, remembering their conversation.

"No wonder it takes so many lifetimes to get anywhere! You could spend a hundred of them on the same lesson, saying 'Huh?'"

"I know. I'm pretty sure I *did*!" Eli said, looking forlorn. "I always thought I was a quick learner. Well, in *this* lifetime! Of course, it turns out I wasn't so swift in this life, either."

Anna asked, "What do you mean? You've accomplished a lot."

"Long story for later, and part of why Rachel and I decided to end our marriage."

"I know you told me that your marriage was over, but I can't believe I haven't asked you what happened, Eli. I'm so sorry. My God, I'm lying in bed with you, and I haven't even found out what happened." She stiffened in his arms.

"First of all, Rachel is good with it, and I'm good with it. The kids are a little less good with it, but they're okay. So please don't pull away. It was all good and all amazing, but right now I want to lie here with you and figure this stuff out. Please?" He felt her body relax against him and pressed his head against hers. "There's been divine timing at work, sweetheart. All good, but I'm ready to be here with you."

"Okay, we'll save that for later. What's next in our story?"

"Where was I? Yeah…okay. This last time in the White, we apparently tried to find a way to remember what our goal was."

"What was our goal?"

"To understand that we were living in illusion and to get beyond it."

"We met our goal?" Anna asked excitedly.

"You, Dan, and I did, but now we have to find the others and help them to understand, too. Although let's not get too excited about believing we met the goal." He looked into the dark brown of Anna's eyes.

"Because we still live in a world of illusion, which means this is part of the illusion too. Right?"

Eli nodded. "While I want to believe we're at a different place than we were before, we don't want to swap one illusion for another."

"Constant vigilance."

"Exactly," Eli said, and then he continued with the story. "As best as Dan can tell, the twelve of us agreed that *two* of us had the best chance of somehow remembering why we were here and helping the others to remember."

"Was it you and me, Eli?" Anna asked hesitantly.

"No, sweetheart. It was you and Dan."

Her eyes widened in surprise, and then in understanding. "I learned about illusion from living with an alcoholic. Addiction is one form of illusion. Dan sacrificed this lifetime to be the Teacher by taking on the incredible pain of addiction."

Eli nodded and appeared for a moment to be lost in thought.

Anna was quiet a moment also. "Then he got sober, another hard job, and found me at the right time. I don't understand how the images got passed to him…wait a minute. Do you remember when I was in the car accident and the heart monitor gave me a lesson about frequencies?"

Eli nodded. It felt like a lifetime ago.

"This time, just before my heart stopped and I was so close to death," she said slowly, "the sound of the monitor beeping felt like it was trying to tell me something. Something important I needed to remember. It was like a flood. I suddenly knew—I mean, I knew in my whole being; I needed to go to the light. I went to it, Eli. I tried to align with the frequency of the light, and it poured into me. I saw my mom and dad. She held up her hand as if to say stop. And I did," Anna said slowly, and then she went on. "The monitor reminded me, and if Dan's accident hadn't put me in the hospital the first time, I wouldn't have had that experience or that memory!"

Eli kept trying to take it in. All the nuances of what had happened. The timing. The tiny parts that had to come together in this way. "Dan told me he laid his head on your chest, at your heart, and the images came into his mind like a story. The meaning of it flashed like a light in his mind. When you died and then came back, it was gone from your mind. But you had already passed the message to Dan. Without the two of you, we would still be starting over in the next lifetime."

The enormity of it was mirrored in their eyes.

"Anna, first we're going to get you better. And then you and Dan and I are going to find the others. I don't know how we'll know who they are or how we'll go about it, but we're going to use these big dumb brains for something important for a change. Do you agree?"

"Yes. Oh my God, we have to find them now!" She tried to get out of bed.

Eli held her tight. "First you get better. Then we look." There was no arguing with the firmness in his voice. As he nuzzled her face with his, he said more softly, "I'm not losing you. We're going to get them, but I'm not doing this part without you. We're also going to find out one more thing."

"What?" she asked earnestly.

"We're going to find out if you and I are meant to be together. It feels like the answer is yes, but we both need to run 'us' through the litmus test of our stories."

Anna looked bewildered. She said, "Not this minute, but sometime soon, please explain what that means."

"I will, but it has to do with not swapping one illusion for another." Then he smiled and held her tight. "I'm praying that you're her, Anna."

"Who?"

"My mate and my partner. And not just for traveling through lifetimes, but also to travel through *this* lifetime."

She smiled and nodded. There was no question in her mind.

~

Dan's phone rang insistently one afternoon. He felt as if he had been in a dream the last two months, since he and Eli had met. Terri, his fiancée, was worried about him. For whatever reason, he hadn't told her yet about what he had seen with Anna, although he wanted to. He reached into his pocket, grabbed the cell phone, and glanced at the caller ID before answering.

"Hey, how is she?"

~

That evening, Dan and Terri sat quietly reading together in their bedroom. Terri's son John was in the other room sprawled on his bed, also reading. Dan looked up and cleared his throat. "Honey, I have something I want to talk about with you, but first I want to ask you something."

"Okay," she said, closing her book so she could focus.

"I need to go to Sedona to spend some time with Anna and Eli, and I'll tell you why in a minute. But first I want to ask if you and John will come with me. School's out, and I know you have vacation time coming up. Would you mind? Coming with me, I mean."

"Of course not, sweetheart. I'd love to meet her, and I'd love to take our first trip as a family," she said warmly.

"I'm glad." He reached for her hand. "I have a feeling we've been a family for a long, long time. That's what I want to talk about."

John wandered into their room. "What's up?" He had an eerie ability to sense when something was going to happen.

Dan stood and pulled them both into his arms. Two sets of curious eyes were riveted on his face.

"We're going on a journey together. Or it might be more accurate to say we're *continuing* on a journey together."

"Where're we going, Dad?"

Dan smiled, filled with gratitude for this amazing boy he now called his son.

"We're going on a quest to find some people who have been waiting for us for a very long time. So we're gonna go where the path takes us."

Dan saw delight and expectation on the faces of these two souls he loved more than anyone in the world.

"Who are they?"

Dan looked down for a moment, embarrassed. "I don't know who they are right now. But I think we'll recognize them. We'll know who they are when we see them." He bit his lower lip self-consciously.

Terri and John both stepped quickly out of Dan's arms and he felt his heart sink. He'd lost so much already.

"Too weird?" he asked hesitantly.

Terri looked at him with soft brown eyes, subtly shaking her head no. "I'm going to pack for the journey, sweetheart."

John stepped back into Dan's arms and held him tight.

"Dad, there's nothing too weird to say between us. It's our path, too." Then he also stepped from Dan's embrace and headed to his room to pack.

The End of Book One of *The White* Trilogy

About the Author

Jo Anne Myers has always been intrigued by life's mysteries and the hidden truths that lie just beneath the surface. Her interest in the daily choices all of us make in our lives, as well as the belief that there is more to life than meets the eye, culminated in *When We Remembered*, the first book of a trilogy called *The White*.

Myers owns a management consulting business where she encourages others to grow professionally, but more importantly, to listen to the still voice within and choose a path for their higher well-being.

She currently resides in Northern Arizona with her dog Buddy, working full-time and writing when she gets a chance. Book Two of *The White*, as well as a business fable about how managers (mis)communicate with employees, are currently in the works.

Author photograph by Ken Reynolds